PLEASURE

DISCARD

PLEASURE PLANET

EVANGELINE ANDERSON

APHRODISIA

KENSINGTON BOOKS

http://www.kensingtonbooks.com

APHRODISIA BOOKS are published by

Kensington Publishing Corp.
850 Third Avenue
New York, NY 10022

ISBN-13: 978-0-7582-1649-6
ISBN-10: 0-7582-1649-1

First Kensington Trade Paperback Printing: March 2007

10   9   8   7   6   5   4   3   2   1

Contents

The Girl, the Geek, and the Time Machine   1

Mirror of the Heart   97

Wildmen and Wormholes   187

The Girl, the Geek, and the Time Machine

1

"Take a deep breath. Now let it all the way out. Another deep breath. Allow the herbal aroma to enter your lungs. Are you feeling relaxed? Very good. Now close your eyes. We are going to take a voyage of exploration through your psyche and try to determine the root of your fear of intimacy and commitment."

The therapist's voice droned on and Kara Wilson shifted impatiently in her hammock chair, watching as her fiancé of five years, Brad Dodgeson, had his psyche probed. The fumes from the purifying sage incense tickled her throat, making her want to sneeze, and the fruity tones of the therapist made her want to gag. She was beginning to think that the Holistic Healing Couples Clinic on Kennedy Avenue had been a poor choice on her part. But it had practically taken an act of Congress to get Brad there in the first place, and she was pretty sure if she tried to change therapists now, he'd quit therapy altogether.

She'd chosen the Holistic Clinic because it was just down the street from her job at Smythe Labs, enabling her to take her lunch hour for therapy sessions. Today, the hour was almost up. She glanced anxiously down at her watch, noting that she had less than ten minutes to get out of the clinic and rush down Kennedy before she was late. And if she was late just one more time her supervisor, Lilith Buchanan, would almost certainly fire her.

"Excuse me?" she whispered to the therapist, a tall, thin woman with thin, mouse-colored hair that was twisted into a bun and held in place by decorative black lacquered chopsticks.

The therapist stopped waving the herbal incense in Brad's face and gave her a disapproving glare. She raised one skinny eyebrow as though daring Kara to interrupt again.

"I'm sorry but I sort of have to go back to work," Kara said desperately. "If I'm late one more time—" She ran a hand though her flyaway, naturally curly red hair, hoping she didn't look as frantic as she felt.

"You may go if you do not wish to participate in the healing of your beloved's psyche," the therapist intoned. She had a surprisingly deep voice for a woman and if looks could kill, Kara knew she would've found herself flat on the all-natural fiber, oatmeal-colored carpet.

"Kara?" Brad cracked one pale blue eye and got into the conversation. "Are you leaving? It was *your* idea to come here in the first place."

"No, no." She settled herself more firmly in the ergonomically correct hammock-chair that was hung from hooks in the ceiling, like the rest of the furniture in the office. "I'll stay, honey. I'm sorry."

"Fine." He closed his eyes again and the therapist, with one last reproving glance, went back to fanning incense into his face. The smoke almost obscured his carefully gelled blond hair.

Kara watched her fiancé relax in the hammock couch which was swaying lazily in time with his breathing. It was a wonder it could hold him up, she thought uncharitably. Brad wasn't much taller than her own five-foot-seven, but he was one of those short men who makes up for lack of height by having huge muscles. He had surfer-boy good looks and was a personal trainer at the gym she attended, which was how Kara had met him in the first place five years before. Back then she'd thought his physical presence was attractive but lately she was wondering how any man could be so physically strong and so emotionally weak at the same time.

She glanced at her watch again. The small diamond ring that Brad had grudgingly given her two years before when they finally moved in together winked at her reproachfully, daring her to think more mean thoughts about the man she loved.

"I think it all started my sophomore year in high school," Brad's slightly nasal voice began. He hadn't liked the idea of therapy in the first place, but he was instantly into anything that made him the center of attention, Kara thought sourly, glancing at her watch a third time. That was it—she was officially going to be late. There was no way she could get to work on time now. She sighed and settled back in her hammock-chair, trying to pay attention.

Brad was relating a story of high school angst she'd heard him tell many, many times before. It was actually a pep talk he used to motivate his clients at the gym. ". . . so there I was—just me, a ninety-eight pound weakling facing off against the three biggest, meanest guys at my school . . ." he was saying.

Kara bit her lip in frustration. She was going to lose her job to hear *this* old story again? She'd heard it so many times already she could practically quote it word for word with him as he spoke. It was, according to Brad, the defining moment in his life, more so even than the day his mother choked to death on a pork chop or the day his father lost the family fortune on an ill-advised stock pick. It was the moment when had decided to turn his life around and start weight training.

After the three bullies held his head in the toilet and flushed repeatedly, he had gone straight to the nearest gym and started bulking up until he was the fine physical specimen that appeared before them today, he always told his clients. The next time he faced off against the bullies, *Brad* was the one doing the ass kicking and the toilet flushing. And his life had never been the same since. Blah, blah, blah . . .

Suddenly the therapist's voice cut into Kara's impatient thoughts.

"And you feel this caused you to build a wall around your emotions? This decision to never be weak again is what makes you feel unready to commit to marriage?"

Wow! Kara's head popped up and she stared at her fiancé. Could there really be a nugget of wisdom hidden in that old story? One she hadn't seen before because she'd been so bored with hearing it over and over again? She suddenly felt ashamed of her impatience. After all, if this was what it got to get Brad to say "I do," then losing her job would be worth it. She'd been waiting for him to pop the question for over five years now and, as her mother was constantly reminding her, she wasn't getting any younger.

Not that a girl couldn't have a perfectly happy and fulfilling life without a man but Kara had invested a lot in this relationship. Getting Brad to therapy was a last-ditch effort to convince him they were ready to become man and wife, not just roomies. Maybe her dream was finally about to come true.

". . . very good. I feel that we've made a real breakthrough here today, Bradley." The therapist sounded pleased. She blew out the incense and rose gracefully from her hammock chair. That was more than Kara could manage. The swinging chairs were obviously made for tall, graceful, model-type people rather than girls who were constantly watching their weight.

You would think with a personal trainer for a fiancé she would be in excellent shape, but that wasn't quite the case. As she struggled out of the deep, swinging fabric chair, Kara promised herself to lay off the midnight raids on the Hershey bars. It was just that she got so *tired* of protein shakes and plain chicken breasts for dinner all the time.

Brad and the therapist were already making arrangements for the next session but a glance at her watch told Kara that she had to go. If she ran like a crazy person, she might make it back to Smythe Labs only fifteen minutes late. And if Lilith, her supervisor, was taking a long lunch, she might manage to avoid the axe.

"Thank you very much," she babbled, pumping the therapist's skinny hand. "See you later, sweetie." She planted a hasty kiss on Brad's muscular cheek and dashed for the door.

2

Smythe Labs was an imposing black monolith of a building right at the corner of Kennedy and Westshore in South Tampa. It was down the street from the Starbucks where Kara usually got her lunchtime cappuccino. But there was no time for coffee now. Kara skidded to a halt. Or was there? Her mind ticking rapidly, she ran for the Starbucks.

Her boss, Lilith, was the only person she knew that had a bigger sweet tooth than Kara. If she came back from lunch late, but bearing a big glass of that fancy new hot chocolate they were serving, chantico, topped with whipped cream, Lilith just might overlook her tardiness. It might not be very honest to bribe her boss with chocolate, but at this point Kara was desperate.

Thanks to the friendly counterman, who she knew from her other lunchtime forays, she got the grande hot chocolate and was on her way in next to no time. She was now going on being twenty-five minutes late, but the hot drink in her hand was going to be her salvation—she just knew it.

Kara hit the front doors of the shiny glass building running, the cup held out in front of her like the Olympic torch. Sure enough, Lilith was sitting at Kara's usual seat behind the high marble reception desk, a scowl firmly plastered on her pinched features. She hated having to answer the phones when Kara was late, hated having to do anything other than the stacks of paperwork that seemed to fill her life with grim joy.

"Ms. Wilson," she snapped, coming out from behind the high sides of the rounded marble desk. "Do you have any idea what time it is?"

"I know and I'm so sorry," Kara said rapidly, continuing her headlong flight across the slick black marble floor. "But when I saw the Starbucks I thought you might like—" From the corner of her eye she saw a figure in a lab coat step into her path. It was the absentminded Dr. Robertson, his nose buried in a mass of technical data as usual. He was stepping right between Kara and Lilith, who was standing with her arms crossed over her pristine, and no doubt very expensive, white silk blouse, tapping her foot impatiently.

"Look out!" Kara yelled, unable to stop herself on the slippery floor. Dr. Robertson turned his head toward her. Behind his glasses she saw his large brown eyes widen, no doubt in shock, to see a crazy redhead with a large cup of very hot liquid bearing down on him like a runaway train.

He ducked, but not fast enough to get completely out of her way. As though in slow motion, Kara saw everything happen without being able to stop it. She stumbled over the crouching scientist, squeezing the hot cardboard cup reflexively as she fought for balance. The lid on the grande chantico popped off and a long waterfall of steaming hot chocolate and whipped cream flew through the air on a collision course with her boss's clean white blouse.

"Oh, no!" Kara wailed as chocolate and silk collided. She would have fallen herself if a pair of strong masculine hands hadn't caught her and set her back on her feet.

"Are you all right?" Dr. Robertson was peering into her face, looking worried. His research was in a white drift of paperwork scattered at his feet, but he seemed more concerned with Kara.

"No," Kara said, too upset to be polite. "I'm not okay. I think I just lost my job." She turned back toward Lilith, whose expression had gone from mild irritation to outraged fury in an instant.

"Ms. Wilson," she ground out between tightly clenched teeth. "Do you have any idea how much this blouse cost?"

"I'm so sorry!" Kara shook off the concerned hands of the scientist and ran to her supervisor. Grabbing a handful of tissues from the dispenser on the reception desk, she began blotting at the steaming dark brown stain that covered the front of Lilith's blouse. Underneath, Lilith's sallow skin was turning an alarming red. "Are you burned?" Kara asked anxiously. "Do you need to take it off?"

"Stop it!" Lilith slapped at her hands angrily, halting her progress. "Do you think I want to strip down to my unmentionables in front of the entire lobby?" She eyed Dr. Robertson, who happened to be the only other person in the large reception area, as though he was a known serial rapist on the loose.

Does she really think he wants to see her bony old carcass in her underwear? Kara thought, before she could stop herself. She turned her head toward the scientist as well and saw a slight smile twitch in the corner of his full mouth. Apparently it was a shared thought. She looked away quickly before she broke out in hysterical giggles. Spilling hot chocolate all over Lilith was bad enough, laughing about it would only make things that much worse.

"Doctor," she managed to say, avoiding his eyes, "if you could give us a little privacy I'll be happy to bring you your paperwork in a few minutes."

"Certainly, Kara," he said, surprising her by knowing her name. "I'll be in my lab. Thank you and I'm sorry I was in your way."

"Oh, no—I shouldn't have been running—" she began.

"You shouldn't have been late in the first place," Lilith snapped, cutting her off.

"I'm sorry," Kara began again as Dr. Robertson slipped away. "But I meant you should go to the ladies' room to take off the shirt—not strip right in the lobby."

"Oh, you'll be sorry all right," her supervisor said grimly. "And you'll be collecting unemployment as well."

"Honestly, I only wanted to bring you some hot chocolate," Kara protested weakly, but she felt her heart sink. This was the last straw and she knew it. Lilith had been itching to fire her almost as soon as she had been hired. Why her supervisor disliked her, she didn't know. Maybe it was because Kara had learned the names of everyone in the building in a matter of hours and exchanged friendly jokes and greetings with people Lilith had never given more than a frosty nod to in her years at Smythe Labs.

Kara knew she wasn't great at paperwork or being perfectly on time every single day, but she was friendly and outgoing and genuinely liked her job as a receptionist at Smythe Labs, whereas Lilith disliked anything that took her away from her beloved columns of figures. Kara had been hired for her people skills and, no matter what Lilith said about her tendency toward tardiness and the hot chocolate all over her white silk blouse, she was about to be fired for them, too. If only she'd had the money to finish her business degree she wouldn't be in this mess right now!

"You will stay and finish the day while I go get myself cleaned up," Lilith said, confirming her fears. "If you choose not to stay, I will personally see to it that you do not receive your two weeks severance pay. And as of five o'clock today you will turn in your key card and consider yourself terminated. Do I make myself perfectly clear?"

"Yes," Kara said miserably. She stooped and began gathering the white snowdrift of papers that Dr. Robertson had left behind, as she watched Lilith's ramrod straight back march to the ladies' room, no doubt to see if cold water would take out the stain.

3

"You don't look so good," Dr. Robertson observed as Kara lay the neatly stacked pile of paperwork on the table he was sitting at in the lab.

"I'm *not* so good," she confessed with a sigh, sitting back on one of the high lab stools for a moment to rest her back. Getting his paperwork back in order, especially when it was essentially all Greek to her, had been no easy task. It had taken her several hours and her termination was looming closer and closer.

"What happened?" His large brown eyes were genuinely concerned behind the glasses he wore. For the first time, Kara realized that he wasn't too much older than she—certainly he was the youngest scientist on staff at Smythe Labs. He had the reputation of being a brilliant researcher, having come straight from Harvard with a degree in some kind of physics.

"I got fired," she admitted, looking down at her hands. "I was afraid if I was late one more time . . . and of course spilling that all over . . ." She shook her head, unable to continue, tears stinging her eyes.

"I'm so sorry—this is all my fault." Dr. Robertson ran a hand through his thick black hair distractedly.

"N . . . no, it's not. It's all *my* fault," Kara said, trying unsuccessfully to hold back the tears. She usually hated to cry in front of people but this had been such a terrible afternoon she didn't seem to be able to help herself.

Robertson came around the lab table and patted her shoulder awkwardly. There was so much simple caring in his gesture that Kara suddenly found herself in his arms, spilling the whole sorry story in his lap—the crazy therapist, her commitment-phobic fiancé, her lost job . . . it all came out. If Dr. Robertson was surprised to find himself suddenly holding a double armful of sobbing redhead, he didn't show it. He just handed her tissues and let her cry, listening patiently as though he was as used to hearing personal problems as he was to solving quantum physics equations.

"I'm really sorry," Kara said, sniffling a little. She knew she ought to let go of him, but he smelled nice and felt so solid beneath the crisp white lab coat he wore. Not so crisp anymore, she thought unhappily when she pulled back and saw the wrinkled mess she'd made of his jacket. There were smears of mascara on the white fabric that she was afraid wouldn't come out. "This seems to be my day for ruining people's clothes," she said, nodding at his coat. "I'll pay to have that dry-cleaned but you might have to meet me outside with the bill once I turn in my key card. Lilith will probably call the cops on me if she catches me in the building again after tonight."

"That's not going to happen," Dr. Robertson replied firmly.

"Oh, but Dr. Robertson, I don't mind paying for it, really—"

"Call me Ethan," he interrupted her. "And I'm not talking about the dry cleaning. I'm talking about you losing your job. It's not going to happen."

"Oh," Kara said, beginning to see where he was going with this. "I really appreciate that, but if you overrule Lilith's decision and make her keep me, she'll be even worse to work with than she is now. I really think I'd be better off looking for another job."

"You're not going to look for another job because you're not going to lose this one." He had a strange light in his dark brown eyes that the thick glasses couldn't hide.

"Um . . . I'm not sure you understood me," Kara said carefully. "See, I already lost it."

"No you didn't," Ethan Robertson said. "Or you won't have, once we go back in time and fix this whole mess."

4

"Go back in time?" Kara stared at him uncertainly, an old quotation she had heard somewhere running through her mind. *"Too much learning hath made thee mad."* Of course, Ethan Robertson didn't look crazy, but looks didn't always count for everything.

"Come on, I'll show you." Ethan had her by the hand and was pulling her toward a smaller, private lab in the corner of the main work area. Kara followed him reluctantly, careful not to knock over any research equipment or paperwork. It was a good thing it was the end of the day and there was no one else in the lab to hear him talking like this, she thought.

"It's a private hobby of mine, and I just perfected it recently." His deep voice was full of excitement as he keyed a simple sequence into the keypad at the door of the smaller lab. "I've only tested it on myself and a few animal subjects so far but..." He broke off as he opened the door and gestured proudly to the equipment at the center of the room.

Kara stared blankly at the large glass structure that looked like an old-fashioned telephone booth without the telephone and with only three sides. There were wires with electrodes hanging from one of its clear walls and a bank of instruments that displayed several digital readouts on another. Surrounding the clear booth were several shelves filled with hairless white rats and mice—many of them banded with strange colors.

"What *is* this?" she asked blankly, staring at the equipment and the multicolored mice that crowded the small room.

"This, Kara, is the prototype of my temporal portal—my time machine." He looked so proud that Kara didn't have the heart to be nasty about the whole thing.

"It's very nice," she said politely. "Thank you for showing it to me."

Ethan Robertson frowned. "I can see you don't believe me— allow me to demonstrate." He walked rapidly to one of the cages, talking as he went. "Time travel has long been thought, by the best scientific minds of our time, to be a complete impossibility. Not because it isn't possible—theoretically it is. But because of the—"

"Huge power source you'd need to make it work?" Kara asked, cutting him off.

Ethan stopped in the middle of removing one of the hairless mice from its cage and turned to face her, a look of surprise on his naturally tan features. "Why, yes. But how—?"

"My little brother is a science fiction freak," Kara explained with a little grin. "I've taken him to I don't know how many conventions because my mother didn't want him going alone. He and his friends were always talking about time travel, UFOs, alternate universes, string theory—you name it." She shrugged. "It was like living in an *X-files* episode. I guess I picked up some of it. Wouldn't you need to be able to harness a black hole to make time travel possible in reality?" She raised an eyebrow at him, showing her skepticism.

Ethan looked at her as though she'd grown a second head for a moment, then nodded slowly. "Well, yes, in theory. But

I've found a way to create a controlled and very limited wormhole powered by organic, biomechanical energy enhanced and amplified by emotional extremes and the lattice structure of certain crystals."

"What?" Kara asked blankly.

"I use myself as a battery," Ethan explained patiently. "Look, the human body creates and expends much more energy than you'd think, and harnessed and amplified properly . . . Well, see for yourself." He took one of the hairless mice from its cage and placed it on the floor of the glass booth. "I'll set the arrival time for exactly one minute from now," he said, consulting his watch and setting the digital controls rapidly. "That's a small amount of time so it shouldn't drain me or require any emotional boost to achieve." He reached inside the booth and pulled out one of the electrodes hanging there. Opening his shirt, he pressed the electrode over his heart.

Kara had just enough time to notice that he had a very nice chest for a scientist, when he pressed a button and the mouse on the floor of the glass booth disappeared. She jumped, startled and Ethan nodded at her, smiling.

"Yes, it's quite a shock, isn't it?"

"But how—?" Kara wanted to lean her head into the booth, which appeared to be filled with shimmering air, like a mirage in the desert, and look for the mouse. Ethan put out a hand to hold her back.

"No—don't do that! Do you want your head to be a minute ahead of the rest of your body?"

Kara hadn't considered that possibility. "Of course not," she began, but just then the mouse reappeared, apparently no worse for its temporal journey. "Oh my," she said faintly.

"Isn't it wonderful?" Ethan grinned proudly, reminding her of her little brother when he got first place in the science fair. Abruptly, she decided that she liked Ethan Robertson—liked him a lot.

"It's great," she said, smiling at his boyish enthusiasm. "And thank you for showing it to me, but how is it going to help us save my job?"

"We'll simply go back in time and intercept that cup of coffee before it has a chance to drench old whatsername," he said, as though it was the simplest thing in the world.

"Uh, whatsername is Lilith," Kara said, trying to hide a smile. "And it was hot chocolate."

"Whatever." Ethan waved away the unimportant details. "Do you want to save your job or not?"

"Of course I do. Let's go." Kara started to step into the booth again but he held her back.

"Oh, no, you can't go like that." He was stripping off the mascara-stained lab coat and loosening his tie as he spoke.

"Like what?" Kara asked, wondering what he was doing.

"With your clothes on." He said it as though it was the most natural thing in the world, taking off his starched blue button-down shirt as he spoke.

"Okay, I see where this is going." Kara put her hands on her hips, deciding she didn't like him so much after all. "How stupid do you think I am, anyway?" she demanded, glaring at the half naked scientist.

She was surprised to see that he had a *really* nice chest—better than Brad's, in fact, which was really *too* muscular. She'd never liked men that had bigger breasts than she did and Brad was getting so over-pumped lately . . . *Stop looking at his chest and pay attention!* she commanded herself. This man was obviously trying to seduce her in a way that really insulted her intelligence.

"I mean, just because I don't have a PhD in quantum physics doesn't mean I'm an idiot," she said, clenching her fists.

"Actually my degree is in experimental condensed matter physics," he said mildly. "And I wouldn't ask you to take off your clothes if it wasn't completely necessary. Look." He reached into another of the cages and brought out one of the hairless rats. He sounded so sincere that Kara came closer even though she didn't like rodents very much.

The rat, which was wriggling in Ethan's large hand, had a band of green discoloration all around its mid section. It didn't look like anyone had used a marker or paint to color it either— it was as though that part of the rat's skin was naturally green.

"What is it?" she asked, unwillingly. "Some kind of genetic mutation?"

"Now it is," Ethan said seriously, turning the rat so she could see all of it, including the long, naked tail whipping back and forth. "In fact, it's now a dominant trait that this rat will pass on to its decendents, much as I might pass on my brown eyes or you might pass on your beautiful red hair." He smiled at her briefly and Kara blushed.

"But how—?" she began, trying to ignore the way he was looking at her.

"I tied a piece of green ribbon around this rat before I sent it thought the temporal portal," he explained. "And this is the result. It changed not only the rat's outward appearance, it also altered its DNA—permanently. That is, I haven't found a way to reverse the process. So while you look lovely in that black dress, I'm sure you wouldn't want to be wearing the outline of it on your skin permanently."

Kara shuddered, thinking what a mess that would be. Bikini season would be much scarier with a huge black dress tattoo on her body than the few extra pounds she'd picked up on her midnight Hershey raids. Not to mention the fact that she might pass it on to her children . . . if Brad every got around to marrying her and giving her children, that was.

"So you can't wear *anything*?" she asked, wondering if she could at least keep her bra and panties on.

"Nothing at all," Ethan said firmly. "I promise you that I wouldn't ask you to take off your clothes for no reason—I'm not trying to take advantage of you." The dark brown eyes ran over her body appreciatively. "No matter how, ah, appealing the prospect might be. I give you my word I'll be a perfect gentleman."

"Okay," she said, feeling self-conscious. "I guess I believe you. But . . . but what happens when we get there? We can't just appear naked in front of our past selves and . . ." She frowned. "If we're really going to do this, won't we have already done it? So then wouldn't I have seen the future me appear naked and catch the hot chocolate and—"

Ethan smiled approvingly. "I like the way your mind works, Kara. You're talking about creating a paradox, of course. It's a valid consideration but in fact, my research has led me to believe that there are so many parallel universes out there that everything that can possibly happen has already happened in at least one of them. So we can safely go back and change some small events of the recent past without disrupting the future too terribly."

"Okay, so we're just going to jump out there naked?" she asked again. He seemed to be missing the point which in her opinion wasn't a possible paradox, but embarrassing full-frontal nudity in the middle of the Smythe Labs black marble lobby. Another thought occurred to her. "You know, Lilith is going to see us too. And even if we *do* keep the hot chocolate from drenching her, she's still going to want to fire me for streaking in the middle of my shift. Not to mention that if she sees us both naked together she's going . . . well, she's going to assume the worst," she finished, blushing.

"That *would* be a problem if we were going in real time," Ethan answered. He was a little red himself, which made Kara like him better. "But we're not," he said. "We'll use the half-time mode and we'll be completely invisible to our past selves and to Lilith."

"Half time?" Kara asked. "What's tha—?"

"Ms. Wilson, are you up here?" A strident, shrewish voice suddenly interrupted their conversation. It sounded like her soon-to-be ex-supervisor was right outside in the main lab. "Ms. Wilson, it is five o'clock and I must insist that you return to my office with me and hand over your key card," Lilith's brittle voice continued. "Where are you?"

"Quick!" Ethan's big brown eyes were wide behind his glasses and he was stripping off his pants and socks and shoes all at once. Kara found herself stripping too, hauling the black dress over her head and struggling madly with her bra strap and panties. It was as though they were in a crazy race to see who could get naked the fastest. As a last thought, she took off her small diamond engagement ring. She loved Brad, but she didn't want to be branded by a symbol of his love forever.

"Hurry–*hurry!*" Ethan, already completely naked, was motioning her from inside the small glass booth, an electrode already pasted over his heart as he set the controls for several hours earlier.

The door handle to the small lab was turning as Kara crammed herself wildly inside the booth, facing Ethan's tall form, with no thought of modesty at all.

"Ms. Wilson!" The door opened and she had just enough time to see Lilith's shocked face as she took in the sight of the nude Kara smashed up against the large muscular, completely naked scientist. "So *this* is what you've been doing!" Lilith bugled, her pinched face going red and white at the same time.

"Here." Ethan slapped an electrode onto Kara's chest, directly over her left breast and put his arm around her. "Get ready," he said in her ear.

"Your glasses!" Kara said. She reached up and plucked them off his face, dropping them in a corner of the booth behind her and added, "This better work."

"It will. Here we go."

There was a slight humming and the small lab faded from

view. Then she felt a strange, tight, tingling sensation all over her body. It was as though she were inside a large tube of toothpaste and a giant hand was trying to squeeze her out. For a moment she couldn't breathe and then the sensation stopped almost as soon as it had started.

"Here we are," Ethan Robertson's deep voice said in her ear. "Kara, welcome to the past."

5

Kara suddenly became aware that she was still pressed up against the very naked Ethan and that their bodies were touching almost everywhere. It was very warm and close in the tiny booth and she was terribly embarrassed. In the rush to get away from Lilith, she'd been quick to disrobe but now she couldn't believe she'd actually done it.

She'd never been naked with any man but Brad and even then it was mostly in the dark. The few times she'd let her fiancé see her with her clothes off in the light, he always had a professional opinion on what she needed to do to be tighter, firmer, and in all-around better shape. It was not fun, Kara had found, to be told you ought to be doing a hundred ab crunches a day to lose the flab when you were trying to get in the mood to make love.

Ethan shifted against her and muttered, "Uh, excuse me. I can't really see much of anything without my glasses."

Kara felt a rush of relief. "Oh, good!" she blurted out, before she thought about it.

"Thank you for taking them off my face, though," Ethan

continued politely, as though they were talking at a social gathering instead of crammed naked into a small booth together. "Was that just quick thinking or because you didn't want me to see you?"

"Um . . ." Kara blushed hard, deciding not to answer that particular question. "Is it safe to get out of the booth?" she added, trying to change the subject.

"It should be." He squinted out the one open side of the glass enclosure. "We're in the lobby, right? That's the location I was aiming for."

"Yes, we are." Kara surveyed the vast black marble reception area with fascination. "I didn't know your, uh, temporal portal could move through space as well as time," she added, stepping carefully out onto the cold marble.

"Remember that the fourth dimension is actually not another plane of existence—it's what Einstein defined as space-time," Ethan said, smiling nearsightedly at her. "So it's just as easy to move in space as it is to move in time."

"That's good, especially if you have to show up every place you go naked." Kara wrapped her arms around herself and shivered. Knowing that he couldn't see her looking, she took the opportunity to check him out and see if the rest of him matched the gorgeous chest he'd revealed before everything went crazy. It did, she decided, taking in his long, muscular legs and thighs, his tight ass, and his naturally tan skin. As for what was between his thighs—she blushed and tried not to look. Hubba-hubba—Ethan Robertson might be a physics geek like her little brother, but he was also a hunk! In fact, without the glasses and the lab coat, he might have just stepped off the pages of *Playgirl*. She wondered if he had any idea how good looking he really was and decided he probably didn't.

"Are you okay?" he asked, sounding concerned and she realized she'd been standing there staring at him for almost a minute.

"I'm, uh, just cold," she said, shivering for effect.

"I'm sorry about that. I was actually going to grab some lab coats for us to wear until whatsername barged in." Ethan sounded apologetic. "You see, you can take things with you, like clothes, or in my case these." He felt around on the bottom of the booth until he found his glasses. "You just don't want to have direct contact with them when you time jump."

"What about us?" Kara asked, keeping her hands firmly in place, although covering her full breasts with one arm was nearly impossible. "I mean we had a lot of, er, contact. Is that going to change either one of our DNA structures?"

"Surprisingly, no." Ethan fit the glasses back on his face, looked at her, and looked quickly away. "Uh, the uh, structural integrity of living organisms remains uncompromised during a journey through the temporal portal. Even if they're in, uh, close proximity," he muttered, obviously still trying not to look.

Kara blushed. She'd felt much more comfortable talking to him when she knew her body was just a vague blurry outline to his unfocused eyes.

"So now what?" she asked, surveying the lobby of three hours ago. She saw that the past Lilith was sitting at the reception desk with a sour expression on her face and the past Ethan was just starting to make his way across the room. They didn't appear to be moving at first, but then she saw that they were actually going very slowly. As she watched, Lilith's frown deepened slightly and the past Ethan, his nose buried in paperwork, took a very slow step.

"Now we wait for you to get in the door," Ethan answered, stepping out of the booth to stand beside her.

Kara looked and saw her past self just outside the doorway but it was taking her forever to get in. In the meantime, she was standing around in the cool, gloomy lobby completely naked with a man she barely knew, even if he was amazingly cute. She wished the Kara of three hours ago would hurry the hell up and then she realized what a weird thought that was. "So . . . should we go take the cup out of my hand and put it on the counter?" she asked, starting forward to go and do it. It seemed like the only way to go and speed things up.

"No, wait." Ethan put a hand on her arm to stop her, then withdrew quickly. "I, um, wouldn't want to scare you," he said. "I mean, the past you. It's one thing to lose your grip on the cup and have it land on the counter. It's another thing to have it completely disappear from your hand and materialize fifteen feet ahead of you in a completely different location."

"Oh, I guess you're right." Kara smiled at his thoughtfulness. "I might think I'd suddenly had an out of body experience or gotten religion or something." She laughed and looked at him sideways only to see that he was sneaking a glance at her, too.

Ethan blushed and looked away when their eyes met. "I'm sorry," he said, clearing his throat nervously. "It's just that, well, you're very beautiful and it's hard not to look."

Wow. Kara looked at him again, blushing with pleasure. "Thanks," she said. "I was, uh, kind of thinking the same thing about you. Do you work out? Because your body is really . . . I mean, because my fiance's a personal trainer and I can always tell when somebody's, uh . . ." she trailed off, embarrassed. Why did she always put her foot in her mouth?

Ethan looked amused. "Well, I don't go to the gym but I do jog every morning and lift weights in my garage," he offered. "My grandfather on my mom's side is Navajo and I used to spend summers with him on the reservation. He always said, 'the body must be fit if the mind is to be sharp.'"

So he was part Navajo—that explained the black hair and his gorgeous tan, Kara thought She herself was much too pale because, being a natural redhead, she never tanned—only burned and freckled.

"So if your, uh, fiancé is a personal trainer, you must work out, too, huh?" Ethan asked, interrupting her train of thought.

"Oh, I don't work out nearly as much as Brad thinks I should," she said, nodding down at herself and blushing. "I mean, he's always telling me I need to do more crunches and lunges and leg lifts and that kind of thing."

"Really?" Ethan raised one black eyebrow and looked at her appraisingly. "You, uh, look fine to me."

"Thanks," she said again, smiling. She was thinking what a strange situation she was in—standing three hours in the past, about to try and change the future, flirting with a naked scientist while she was equally nude. On being hired at Smythe Labs, she and every other worker in the place had to go through a mandatory sexual harassment seminar, but of course, nothing about the sexual etiquette of nude temporal travel had been even remotely covered. She wondered if Ethan was going to go public with his time machine—they might just have to add a section to that seminar if he did.

Across the floor from her, her past self was still only halfway to the angry-looking Lilith and the past Ethan wasn't nearly in position yet.

"So, how did you get interested in time travel in the first place?" Kara asked, to make conversation.

"Oh, you know . . . I guess I've always been kind of a science fiction geek. I loved *Star Wars* and *Star Trek*, pretty much anything like that." He shrugged, looking sheepish. "And of course, I loved the old *Dr. Who* episodes. See, it's about this guy—"

"Oh, I know what it's about," Kara said excitedly. "I *love* that show."

"Really?" He grinned at her. "You're kidding—I've never met a girl that liked it. I thought you said your little brother was the one who was into all that."

"Oh, well." Kara shrugged. "I guess I kind of am, too. I remember when I was a kid I asked my mom to put my hair up in two rolls on the sides of my head for school picture day. You know, the Princess Leia cinnamon bun look?"

Ethan laughed. "Really? And she did it?"

"Yup," Kara admitted. "You should see the picture. I never heard the end of it from the other kids. And—oh, there I go!" The past Kara had finally reached the crisis point and was about to squeeze the lid off the grande chantico and spill hot chocolate all over the frowning past Lilith.

"Hurry!" Ethan said urgently. "Any one point in time can only be tampered with once."

Forgetting that she was naked and everything was jiggling, Kara ran forward and rescued the steaming cup from her past self's hand and set it carefully on the counter of the reception desk. Then she turned to see the result.

Her past self looked first horrified and then confused as the cup of hot chocolate disappeared out of her hand. Then she was caught in midfall by the past Ethan who was looking at her with concern, his papers all over the floor. Then they both seemed to notice at once that the hot chocolate had reappeared on the reception desk and her past self offered it to the scowling past Lilith who accepted it grudgingly.

"Here we go," Kara said breathlessly, watching as the scene played out in slow motion in front of them. "If she likes it, she'll let my lateness slide—I just know it."

The past Lilith raised the steaming cup to her lips and took what seemed like a long, long sip. When she lowered the cup, her scowl had almost become a smile. The power of chocolate was a wonderful thing, Kara thought, breaking out into a smile herself.

"That's it," she said, grinning at Ethan. "It's okay—we can go."

Ethan set the controls, muttering something about emotional amplification and they crowded back into the booth together. This time Kara was much more aware of the large male body jammed against her own. Ethan had to be at least six-two or six-three and her face was practically pressed against his broad, muscular chest. He had a spicy, masculine scent that was sexier than any aftershave she'd ever smelled and they seemed to fit together perfectly.

She'd been wondering if the mutual attraction she'd felt was a figment of her imagination but it became quickly apparent that it was very definitely real. Ethan shifted in the booth, muttering an apology as something large and hard brushed against her thigh. Kara tried not to look. She could feel her heart drumming in her chest and then there was the sensation of being squeezed all over and then they arrived back at exactly one second after they'd left.

Kara peered cautiously out of the booth but there was no angry, accusing face at the door of the small lab. Lilith, with no reason to come looking for her, had probably already gone home. She sighed with relief as she stepped out of the temporal portal. Turning her back to Ethan, she began quickly putting on her clothes again.

When she turned around, after slipping her diamond engagement ring back on her finger, she saw that Ethan was dressed too. The shapeless white lab coat hid his body and she knew that she never would have guessed he looked so good without his clothes on if she hadn't just seen him with them off. The thought made her blush—she *had* to stop thinking about him naked!

"Well," she said, suddenly at a loss for words.

"Well," Ethan echoed her. "I, uh, guess this is the end of the line."

"Yes." Kara took a step forward and held out her hand for him to shake. It seemed like a stupid, meaningless gesture after they'd been crammed naked in the time booth together, but she was at a loss for anything else to do.

"Thank you for helping me keep my job," she said quietly.

"You're more than welcome. I'm glad I could help." Ethan took her hand gravely and shook it. "And, well, I'm glad I got to know you a little better," he added, smiling. "I've wanted to talk to you for a long time but your always seemed so . . ." He shrugged.

"Busy?" Kara suggested.

"Beautiful," he corrected, and then frowned. "I'm sorry, that came out wrong. I, uh, know you're engaged and I just . . ."

"No, it's okay, really." Kara couldn't help the blush of pleasure she felt washing over her skin. How long had it been since Brad had called her beautiful? And now Ethan had said it twice in the space of an hour. *Stop thinking like that—Brad's your fiancé,* she told herself sternly. And if the therapist was right about him having a breakthrough, he might be ready to set the date for their wedding tonight. Holding on to that hopeful thought firmly, she said, "Um, I guess I should go. Will I see you tomorrow?"

"Absolutely." Ethan smiled at her and she couldn't help smiling back. Even with those glasses on, he was really cute. Then she made herself put a leash on her libido and went home to Brad.

6

"You want me to what?" Ethan raised black eyebrows almost to his hairline, staring at her in surprise.

"Use the time machine to take me back so I can cure my fiancé of his commitment phobia," Kara repeated in a rush. "Please, Ethan, I know it's a big favor and it's probably not what you invented the temporal portal for in the first place—"

"Well, it wasn't the application I had in mind, no," he said dryly. "And to be honest, it may not even be possible."

"Why not? Is it only good for going backward and forward a few hours?" Kara realized there were a lot of questions she should have asked yesterday while they were fixing what she had come to think of as 'the hot chocolate incident.'

"No, no." Ethan shook his head. "It can actually take the user as far backward or forward in time as their lifespan extends. For instance, I couldn't go back and kill Hitler and stop World War II because I wasn't alive in the thirties and forties. But I could go back and talk to my old kindergarten teacher if I wanted to. Which I don't."

"Well, Brad's only five years older than me and the thing I need to fix happened when he was a sophomore in high school." Kara sat beside him on one of the tall lab stools. "So that's doable, isn't it?"

Ethan ran a hand through his thick black hair, looking uncomfortable. "Well, technically speaking, yes. But the bigger the jump through time, the more energy is required."

"But I thought we could use our own bodies as energy—that's what we did yesterday, wasn't it?"

"Yes, but we were making a very short jump," Ethan reminded her. "But a longer one . . ." He shook his head. "Look, let me explain from the beginning."

"I'm sorry," Kara said humbly. "Here I am asking you to use your wonderful invention to help me without even asking about how it works. That's so rude of me." She was ashamed of her bad manners.

"Hey, no, that's all right." Ethan patted her shoulder, his large warm hand lingering on her skin where the sleeveless blouse she was wearing ended. Kara couldn't help herself from enjoying his touch.

"No, it's not," she argued. "After all, it's not like I'm asking to borrow your power drill or something like that. This is your creation—your baby."

"I guess so." He smiled. "I *have* been working on the idea since I was in high school. But let me explain my reservations on making a longer jump."

"Please." Kara gestured for him to go on, feeling a little like she ought to be taking notes.

Ethan sighed and rumpled his hair again. "Let's see . . . When I first built the machine, I was able to send the rats and mice I was using for control subjects pretty far into the future and past respectively, using my own body as a power source, as I explained. But over time I found that my distance into either the past or the future decreased and I wasn't able to send them nearly as far. I couldn't find any reason for that and I was beginning to think I had hit the proverbial brick wall."

Kara hid a small smile behind her hand, at his earnest figure of speech and nodded for him to continue.

"But one day, I came into the lab after having a huge disagreement with Dr. Sloan about the nature of dark matter and its possible effects on charged particles—we almost came to blows. You know Dr. Sloan?" he interrupted himself.

"Oh, yes." Kara nodded. Dr. Sloan was a sour-faced little gnome of a man who never returned her cheery morning greeting. He'd even complained once to Lilith that Kara was too perky. "I'd like to punch him myself," she added, remembering how much trouble his complaint had gotten her into.

"You and me both," Ethan said seriously. "But anyway, I went into the lab afterward while I was still so mad I couldn't see straight. I knew I shouldn't mess around with the portal in that state of mind but I didn't care. And to my surprise," he made a sweeping gesture with one hand, "I was suddenly able to send the mice much further than I had ever been able to before."

Kara remembered him muttering about 'emotional amplification' several times while setting the controls on the machine the day before. "Your anger boosted the power source," she exclaimed.

Ethan nodded, clearly pleased that she had drawn the conclusion herself without him having to explain in detail. "Exactly—as does any strong emotion. In the beginning, I was so excited about actually getting the portal to work that my enthusiasm allowed me to send the mice and rats further distances in spacetime. As my initial excitement wore off, I had less energy for the machine to use and I couldn't send them as far."

"But . . ." Kara frowned. "We weren't angry or excited yesterday. Or wait—I guess we were scared, or at least I know *I* was scared when Lilith came in and, uh, caught us."

Ethan nodded. "Exactly."

"But we weren't nearly as nervous and scared on the way back," Kara objected.

"We didn't have to be," he said. "Going back to your proper time is always easier—it's almost like a kind of temporal magnet comes into play, drawing you back to your point of origin. It's like skating downhill." He looked at Kara from the corner of his eye. "But even if we hadn't had the temporal gravity on our side, I was pretty sure I could get us back with no problems."

"Why was that?" Kara looked at him, wondering what he was trying to say.

"Let's just say I found it sufficiently exciting to be near you," he said, his deep voice soft and quiet. He stroked a lock of curly red hair out of her eyes and looked at her meaningfully.

Kara blushed. "Ethan . . ."

He sighed. "I know, I'm sorry. Now I'm the one that's being rude. You're here asking me to help you change the past because of your fiancé and I'm hitting on you." He shook his head.

"No, it's okay," Kara reassured him. "Or, well, it's not okay, but I'm not mad." She smiled at him. Oh, she really needed to be careful here. She was in serious danger of liking Ethan Robertson way too much. *I'm here for Brad,* she reminded herself sternly. *I'm not going to flush five years of a committed relationship just because Dr. Hotbody here looks good in his skivvies. Or out of them.*

"So," she said, straightening up so she wasn't leaning into his personal space. "You don't think it would be possible to get, um, excited enough to go back in time several more years?"

Ethan chewed his full lower lip thoughtfully. "It might be— I guess we could try."

"Try?" Kara said, feeling nervous. She smoothed her suddenly damp palms down her neat gray skirt. "What would happen if we failed? Would we be lost in a rip in the fabric of space-time forever?"

Ethan grinned at her. "You've been watching too many science fiction movies. No, I built the portal with several fail-safes. If we don't generate enough energy to get all the way to the time I've specified, we won't go at all."

"Oh." Kara felt relieved. "Okay, that sounds good," she said, thinking what a brilliant man he was to have provided for everything that way. "So, could we at least just try it?"

He sighed. "This is really important to you, huh?"

Kara thought of the huge fight she'd had with Brad the night before when she'd dared to bring up setting a date for the wedding. She'd come home to the tiny, but tidy condo they shared to find him sitting on the couch and drinking a low carb beer while he watched the game. When she'd cuddled up close to him and tried to talk, he'd brushed her away like a bothersome fly. The 'big breakthrough' at the therapist's office had turned out not to be so big after all. He could be such a sweet man in so many ways, she felt sure if she could just fix this one little thing about him, he would be perfect.

"Yeah," she said at last, taking Ethan's hand. "Yeah, it is and I wouldn't ask you to do it if I didn't think it would make Brad's life better, too—not just mine. See, he had this very traumatic incident happen to him when he was in high school . . ." She explained the whole head-flushed-in-the-toilet bullying episode to Ethan, exactly as Brad always told it. "So you see, the therapist thinks that's what made him fear intimacy. It's like if he lets himself get too emotionally vulnerable, he'll go back to his old, weak, pre-pumped-up self," she said.

Ethan looked thoughtful. "You know, I had things like that happen to me in high school before I got my growth spurt."

"Really?" Kara couldn't believe it.

"Oh, yeah." He shrugged. "I was never one of the popular kids. I was head of the Math League and captain of the Physics

Club—other kids called me four eyes and things like that. I guess I was kind of a geek."

Kara took the glasses off his handsome face and cleaned them gently on the hem of her skirt. "I was in the chess club," she said, "for a while until I gave it up for drama. I wasn't exactly the most popular girl in school either."

"You like chess?" He leaned forward to be able to see her without the glasses. "We should play sometime. I love it." His full mouth was dangerously close and looked kissably soft.

Kara sighed and handed him back the glasses regretfully. "The point is that we all had bad things happen in school. High school was hard for just about everybody. But I think this experience of Brad's really scarred him. He even says it had a bigger impact on him than the death of his mother."

"Really? Wow." Ethan whistled. "Okay." He sighed. "I guess we can try, but we ought to map out some kind of strategy first."

"I already thought about that," Kara said. "Here's what we're going to do . . ."

7

"Nothing's happening," Kara said. They were crammed into the small booth once again, completely naked with their clothes and Ethan's glasses in a pile in the corner, carefully out of the way. Getting undressed and into the booth together again had been more awkward instead of less than the day before, Kara thought. Maybe because of the obvious attraction between them, or maybe because they weren't rushing to get away from an angry Lilith. Fitting into the booth together, both of them averting their eyes while trying to keep certain body parts from touching, had been a nerve-wracking experience to say the least.

Kara's heart, under the electrode that was pasted on her chest, had been drumming so hard against her ribs it felt like it was trying to break its way out and she was sure Ethan felt the same way. There was enough unresolved sexual tension flowing through the crowded time booth to light up half of downtown Tampa. And yet . . . nothing was happening.

"Why, um, why aren't we moving?" Kara was waiting for the squeezing sensation to begin. She glanced over her shoulder as well as she could at Ethan who was behind her this time. He was obviously trying hard to keep a little distance between their lower bodies. She had felt something hot and hard brush the back of her thigh several times, so she knew what he was trying to conceal. She liked him better for trying to conceal it—he was a true gentleman not to take advantage of a situation like this.

"I don't know." Ethan's deep voice sounded strangled. "I'm, uh, as excited as I was yesterday—probably more so. What about you?"

Kara put her arms across her chest, feeling the brush of her stiff nipples. Ethan was so large and warm at her back. She wished she could lean back against him and ask him to wrap his strong arms around her instead of trying to keep his distance, but she knew that would only make a difficult situation worse.

"Yeah," she said at last. "I'm, uh, pretty excited."

"And yet we're not generating enough emotional current to amplify our biomechanical energy and activate the portal." He sounded thoughtful. "Maybe we should try a different emotion."

"You mean like anger?" Kara half turned so she was almost facing him.

"Exactly." Ethan grinned at her. "Go ahead—get mad at me."

"I . . . I don't think I can," Kara confessed. "You're such a sweet guy."

"You think so, huh?" Ethan got a devilish glint in his eye. "Well what if I did something to make you think differently? To make you angry?" His deep voice was dangerously soft and the look in his dark brown eyes made her shiver.

"Like what?" Kara's heart beat even harder, if that was possible. Maybe he wasn't such a gentleman after all?

"Something like this," Ethan murmured. Taking her shoulder, he turned her so that she faced him completely in the small, cramped booth and lowered his mouth to hers. The kiss was soft at first, then more demanding. Kara gasped in surprise and he took the opportunity to explore her mouth, holding her tightly against him as he marked his territory.

"Ethan!" she protested, trying to push away from him. "I can't . . . I shouldn't . . ."

"You can and you should if you want this to work." His voice was almost a growl and she felt like she didn't recognize this powerful stranger who was suddenly holding her close so that her breasts were pressed against his broad chest. Where had the mild-mannered scientist gone and who was this alpha male claiming her with such hot demanding kisses? She wanted to kiss him back but guilt held her in check. She had never cheated on Brad in the whole time they had been together.

Brad! she suddenly realized. *Brad is the reason I'm doing this in the first place. Ethan is right—if I want this to happen then I have to do anything I can to get the portal working.* It might have been a rationalization, but right then she didn't care.

She put her arms around his neck and gave in to the kiss with everything she had. She could feel the hot, hard length of his shaft rubbing against her inner thigh but she didn't pull back and this time neither did Ethan. He buried one hand in her hair to hold her in place and the other roamed over her back and sides, caressing her bare skin in long, possessive strokes.

Kara felt the heat building between her thighs as their bodies pressed together during the frantic kiss. The strength of his big body covering hers made her feel helpless—out of control. She couldn't remember ever feeling this hot, this needy. God, she just wanted more . . .

Suddenly the strange squeezing sensation came over her, robbing her of breath even more thoroughly than Ethan's kiss. It seemed to go on much longer this time, constricting her lungs in a way that reminded her of a bustier-corset type thing she'd had to wear under her dress the time she'd been a bridesmaid at her cousin's wedding.

Just as she felt her lungs would burst, the air around the glass booth shimmered and the squeezing sensation stopped. They had landed around the back of the gym at Thornton Dale High School on September 4, 1989.

"Wow," Kara sighed. Her arms were still locked around Ethan's neck and the fluttering sensation in her stomach couldn't be completely explained away by the seventeen-year time jump.

"Wow is right," Ethan murmured in her ear. He shifted against her and she could still feel him pressing against her thigh.

"Talk about an earth-moving kiss." She laughed shakily and started to disentangle herself. As hot as the kiss had been, it had achieved its purpose and she had to remember Brad. But Ethan obviously didn't want to let her go.

"Wait a minute," he said softly, still holding her close.

"Ethan . . ." She looked up at him, pleading with her eyes. "I know . . . how you feel," she said. "But I have to remember why I'm here—for Brad—for my fiancé. Okay?"

"All right." He sighed and released her reluctantly. "I'm sorry, I guess I just got . . . carried away."

"You and me both," Kara told him. She bent to get her clothes and began pulling them on quickly. "You, uh . . . you were pretty forceful there for a while," she murmured, pretending to be busy trying to get her skirt straight.

"I'm sorry." He sounded genuinely alarmed. "Did I hurt you?"

"Oh, no." Kara was quick to reassure him. "I guess I just . . . didn't expect it, that's all."

"I was trying to make you mad," Ethan confessed, with a sheepish grin on his face as he pulled on his pants. "As mad as I was that day after my fight with Dr. Sloan. I thought you'd want to slap me after I acted that way. But . . ." He shrugged. "I guess it kind of backfired."

"Kind of," Kara agreed, blushing. The truth was she'd never had such a hot, urgent kiss and the feel of his big body pinning her against the glass wall of the booth had been the most sexually charged experience of her life. Maybe it was because Ethan's kiss had been so unexpected. Brad, as much as she loved him, had never been terribly spontaneous in bed.

"So," she buttoned her blouse, still keeping her eyes down, "the only reason you kissed me was to make me mad?"

"I'd be lying if I said that." Ethan's deep voice was soft but she could feel the electricity in the air between them. She looked up, unable to help herself and saw that his deep brown eyes were filled with desire.

"You . . . you would?" she almost squeaked.

"Yes." He stepped forward and caressed her cheek with the back of his hand. "I'd be lying if I said I didn't want to kiss you all over, Kara. If I said I didn't want to taste every inch of your smooth, creamy skin."

"Oh . . ." Her cheeks flushed under his touch. She'd had no idea a buttoned-down scientist with a PhD and a head that was usually in the clouds could talk like this. Had she really thought of Ethan as an absentminded professor in the past? She put a hand to her heart, feeling it skitter like a frightened rabbit under her palm. But she felt something else, too—the hard shape of her diamond engagement ring which she'd put in the breast pocket of her blouse for safekeeping during the jump.

Ethan leaned down to kiss her again but she pulled back. "I'm sorry," she said, pulling out the ring to show him before slipping it on. "I know we had to do . . . what we had to do to get here, but I just can't do this now. I . . . if I'm right about the time, we need to go stop Brad from being beaten up."

"Of course." Ethan looked regretful but he pulled himself together and buttoned his shirt. "Let's go."

*   *   *

The Thornton Dale High School gym was a large, rectangular building separated from the rest of the red brick school by the long green oblong of the football field. Inside, it smelled like old gym socks and stale sweat. There were basketball hoops on either side of the long building and on one side of the scarred wooden floor a band of cheerleaders was doing a routine to a vaguely familiar song.

"Hey!" Kara's eyes lit up. "That's Guns 'N Roses, I used to love that band when I was in junior high." She looked at Ethan. "Remember them? What else did they sing?"

"Um . . . 'Welcome to the Jungle'?" he suggested.

"Right. You must have listened to them, too."

"Not when I was in high school, no. I'm more into classical music, actually. I know it just reinforces the whole scientist geek thing but . . ." He shrugged, grinning self-deprecatingly.

"Stop saying that. You're not a geek," Kara said fiercely, taking his arm.

He ducked his head, looking almost shy for a moment. "Sorry—must be the high school atmosphere getting to me."

"I know it's getting to me," Kara sniffed. "They need some deodorizer in here."

"Don't look now, but I think the bullies are here," Ethan said from the corner of his mouth.

Kara followed his line of vision across the gym to see three hulking football-player type boys entering the gym from the other entrance. *Goodness*, she thought, *Brad certainly didn't exaggerate their size.* One of the bullies, obviously the ringleader, nudged the other two and nodded at the bleachers across from them. Kara looked to see what they were pointing at and put her hand to her throat. A younger, much skinner version of Brad sat eating his lunch by himself on the bottom row of wooden seats. He had pimples and braces and he was ogling the bouncing cheerleaders so intently that he didn't seem to notice the bullies coming around the side to get him.

"Remember," Ethan hissed in her ear, "I'll distract Brad while you send the goon squad packing. You don't want the past him to see you or it could alter the relationship you have in the present."

Kara swallowed hard. "Got it," she whispered back. It had seemed like such a good plan when she'd come up with it. After all, she could handle a couple of high school kids, right? But they were really *big* kids, she couldn't help noticing again as they walked toward the bleachers, their footsteps echoing in the cavernous space. Really big *mean looking* kids.

"Hey, loser," the head bully yelled, striding up behind her future fiancé. The younger Brad was just turning to see who was speaking, when Ethan intercepted him neatly.

"Bradley Dodgeson?" he inquired, stepping between Brad and the bullies. "I'm the new guidance counselor, Dr. Robertson. I'd like to speak to you a moment." Looking relived, the younger Brad went off with Ethan leaving Kara to face down the bullies.

"Uh . . . Jessie Taylor?" she asked, eyeing the menacing group of bullies warily. To her dismay, the head bully stepped up.

"Yeah, lady, that's me," he sneered.

Kara looked him over carefully. She knew his type—the arrogantly handsome big man on campus who liked to pick on the weaker, nerdier kids. He was probably the captain of the football team and dated the head cheerleader too. He had carefully styled 80s hair and a sneer on his face that made it clear he considered her little or no threat. He was wearing a blue letter jacket with white sleeves and he was so big it made him look like a refrigerator dressed in a denim vest.

"Jessie Taylor," she repeated firmly, not quite sure how to proceed. Oh dear, she'd never been very good with kids except her little brother.

"Whaddaya want?" he asked.

"I, uh, want to know where the chemistry lab is," she said, finally remembering her cover story. "I'm Ms. Wilson, the new chemistry teacher." She tugged at the white lab coat, as though to verify her statement.

"Sure are pretty for a chemistry teacher." Jessie Taylor leered at her and the other boys followed his lead.

"Hey, pretty lady, what can you teach us?" the second bully said, a taunting look on his thick features. He had bright red hair which must make him Harold Cunningham.

"I think I'm feelin' some chemistry right now. Right about . . . here." The third boy with a face like a side of beef, who had to be Michael Grady, grabbed his crotch in a lewd gesture that had all three of them roaring with trollish laughter.

All at once, Kara's temper rose. She'd heard so much about these three from Brad that she'd actually done an online search on their names one night at one of those classmates dot-com sites. Put that together with the gossip she'd heard at Brad's ten year high school reunion, and she had a lot of information. Suddenly some very ugly truths rose to her lips.

"You," she hissed, poking Harold Cunningham in the chest. "You're going to flunk out of college and get some girl you don't even like pregnant. Then you'll have to marry her and you're going to live in a beat-up trailer in the bad end of town making each other miserable and having lots of ugly babies.

"You," she said, whirling on Michael Grady, "are going to end up selling used cars at your father's lot. I know that doesn't sound too bad, but then you're going to become an alcoholic and get arrested four times for DUI. Eventually you're going to get thrown in prison and, well, I'll let you *guess* what happens to you then."

"What the hell—?" he started to protest, but she had already moved on to the biggest bully of the three, Jessie Taylor.

"You," she said, slapping him on the chest, "are *gay*."

"What?" His face turned beet red and the other two boys roared with sudden laughter, this time at his expense.

"That's right." Kara leaned forward and stuck a finger in his face. "You're going to move to Quebec with your boyfriend and open a fancy French bistro. Not that there's anything wrong with that," she added hastily, seeing the stricken expression on his face. "Being gay, I mean. I never liked French food."

"But I . . . I'm not . . ." He was shaking his bullet head, a look of terror on his face. Kara almost felt sorry for him—almost. But this was the bully who had scarred her fiance's psyche. It was *his* fault that Brad didn't have the cojones to say "I do", *his* fault that she was almost twenty-eight and still childless, *his* fault that her mother called her every other day to nag and give her the 'he won't buy the cow while he's getting the milk for free,' speech.

"Oh yes, you are," she told him, grimly. "And I want you to remember this—if you and your friends don't change your ways and stop bullying the other students, I'll come back and tell everyone at this school what I just now said to you. All of you," she added, taking them all in with her reproving glare. "Is that understood?"

"Uh . . . uh . . ." Jessie Taylor couldn't seem to get a word out and the other two bullies were already backing away from the crazy chemistry teacher who could apparently tell the future. Suddenly all three of them turned and bolted for the door of the gym, their sneakers squealing and squeaking on the scarred wooden floor.

"You probably shouldn't have done that." Ethan's deep voice in her ear made Kara jump and she turned to face him, a hand on her chest.

"Oh," she said weakly. "You heard that?"

"Most of it." He was shaking his head. "You know, Kara, the idea of going back in the past is to change as little as possible. We were only going to keep your fiancé from getting beaten up—remember?"

"I know," she sighed. "But . . . well, I wanted to make sure that they didn't beat him up in the future either. Those three guys scarred Brad so badly he can hardly admit he loves me— much less ask me to marry him." She ran both hands through her hair. "I guess I did get carried away, it's just that I got so mad—so upset. Do you know how long it's been since he gave me this?" She gestured at the small diamond engagement ring as hot tears stung the back of her eyes. "It's been years," she said, gulping back a sob. "Years and he *still* isn't ready to commit."

"I'm sorry. He really hurt you, didn't he?" Brad cupped her face, wiping away a tear with his thumb.

"Yes . . . no . . . I don't know." Kara dashed away the tears from her eyes angrily. "Come on, I guess we'd better go. Is . . . is Brad okay?"

"Fine," Ethan said dryly. "He's over there, watching the cheerleaders again." He pointed over his shoulder where the past Brad was practically drooling over the bouncing breasts of the girls in the blue and white uniforms.

"Uh, what did he say?" Kara asked. It made her uncomfortable to see her fiancé acting like such a horn dog, even if it was his adolescent past self. She remembered guys like that in high school—the kind that stared at you until you felt like their eyes were crawling all over your skin like fat slugs. *Creepy*, she thought, before she could stop herself.

"He said he wanted to take some auto body classes but he was afraid those three would beat up on him." Ethan jerked his head in the direction of the door where the three bullies had beat a hasty retreat. "I told him that it was all taken care of and he should go ahead and do what he wanted to do."

"You . . . you did?"

Ethan nodded. "Yup, he says he wants to be a mechanic."

"*Really*?" Kara felt faint. Not that there was anything wrong with being a mechanic, it might even pay better than being a personal trainer, and at least he could always fix the car, she told herself. Of course, money wasn't the important thing right now—the important thing was curing Brad of his fear of commitment. And they had done that—she was certain.

"Really," Ethan said. "I hope that was okay."

"No problem," she said, trying to sound cheerful. "Of course, you could have steered him toward a career in medicine. Or he might make a good lawyer—he loves to argue."

Ethan looked mildly irritated. "That's what I mean by not changing the past too much, Kara. What if someone had come to my high school and told me I should play second chair cello in the Philharmonic instead of pursuing science as a career? It might have changed my whole life."

"You play the cello?" She looked at him, surprised—absentminded Dr. Robertson was turning out to be quite a Renaissance man.

"Only as a hobby, but that's beside the point."

She sighed. "You're right, you're right. I'm sorry."

"That's okay—I just hope this solves your fiancé's commitment issues." Ethan was frowning unhappily and she couldn't help thinking that he didn't sound very sincere.

"I'm sure it has," she said firmly. "Come on." Taking his hand, she led him out of the gym, trying not to watch the adolescent version of her fiancé drooling over the cheerleaders as they left.

8

"He's a what?" Ethan stared at her tear-streaked face in alarm.

"He's a greasy pig!" she wailed, flinging herself down on the stool beside him and running both hands through her hair. "And I don't say that just because he's a mechanic—I mean there's literally grease everywhere. He's a *slob*."

"Slow down, hold on—just start from the beginning and tell me everything." Ethan patted her back sympathetically and Kara poured out the whole story.

"I went home last night from our trip—at least to what used to be our home," she started. "But when I got there, I found out that I didn't even live there. I looked at my driver's license and found out that I live someplace else now."

"Where?" Ethan was plainly mystified.

"In a nasty little apartment complex down on South Howard," Kara said. "But it wouldn't be so bad if the place was clean inside."

"It's not?" Ethan raised an eyebrow at her.

"It's a pigsty!" Kara groaned. "I walked in and found dishes in the sink and crumbs all over the table. Everything was dirty and dusty and sticky—there were even grease smears on the couch! But . . . but that's not the worst part, Ethan."

"What's the worst part?" he said gently.

"It's Brad—he's changed too." She tried to hold back the tears and couldn't. "He was s-sitting on the couch drinking a six pack of beer, watching NASCAR and w-wearing one of those greasy jumpsuits with his n-name stitched on the pocket. And his hair was long and straggly, and he was smoking, and . . . and . . . and he had a big beer belly, too." She brushed at the tears in her eyes and took a deep breath, trying to steady her nerves.

"Ethan, for as long as I've known him, Brad's always been so particular about his personal appearance. I mean, he'd spend *hours* getting his hair just right and he works out constantly. I've never even seen him touch a cigarette and he won't drink any beer that isn't low carb. Staying in shape is like a religion with him but now . . ." She shook her head tearfully.

Ethan shook his head. "Your fiancé was right when he said getting beaten up that day was a life-changing experience. Without those bullies to make him change, he never got interested in fitness or acquired the self-discipline that comes with staying in shape and training others to get in shape."

"I thought things were bad before, but this is so much worse. Can't we go back and change him?" she pleaded.

"I'm sorry, Kara." Ethan took off his glasses and pinched the bridge of his nose between his thumb and forefinger. "But as I think I told you, any one point in history can only be tampered with once."

"But I can't stand this," she moaned. "Last night he wanted to . . . to . . ." She shook her head, unable to finish the sentence. "But I just couldn't. It . . . it would've been like making love to a stranger. And . . . and he got so mad and said fine, that he would go . . . go . . . go get it somewhere else. And he left and I haven't seen him since." She dissolved into sobs again and buried her face in her hands.

Ethan looked grim. "I was afraid something like this might happen. The only way to fix it . . ." He broke off, shaking his head.

"What? What? I'll try anything." Kara wiped her eyes with a tissue he'd handed her.

He sighed. "I don't know, Kara. It's pretty risky. I don't think we should tamper any more."

"Oh, please," she begged. "We have to do something, Ethan. I . . . I didn't just ruin my life—I ruined his, too."

"Fine." He sighed again. "The only thing I can think to do is to go further back in time, before the incident we already changed, and find another life-changing incident that might counteract the effects of what we've already done."

"Oh!" Kara put a hand over her mouth, her eyes suddenly shining with excitement through the tears. "I know! Brad's mother choked to death when he was only twelve. We can go back and save her."

"How will that—?" Ethan began, but she cut him off.

"Don't you see? He was raised without a mother—that has a big effect on a boy. If he'd had a mother, there's no way she'd let him grow up to get grease on the couch, or leave the sink full of dishes, or run out to some bar to find . . . to find what he went looking for," she finished weakly.

"I don't know." Ethan still looked doubtful. "The further back in time you go, the bigger the possible change is. It's like dropping a bigger rock into the middle of a pond—it creates more intense ripples."

"Oh, please, Ethan. We'd be saving a life," Kara pleaded. "And how could that possibly go wrong?"

"It's not just that, Kara," he said, running a hand through his hair. "It's the fact that we'd be going back even further—it puts a bigger strain on the temporal portal and a bigger strain on us.

Also we'll have to come up with some pretty strong emotions to make it work."

"Well, I mean, that shouldn't be a problem, should it?" She looked down at her hands, feeling suddenly shy. When Brad had been behaving so badly the night before, all she'd been able to think of was how much she wished she was with Ethan again. Sweet, quiet Ethan who was so sympathetic and understanding . . . and hot-blooded when the time was right. She hadn't been able to get the naked kiss they'd shared out of her mind, as much as she had tried to.

But I'm not proposing we do this just so I can get naked with Ethan again, she reminded herself sternly. *I'm doing this to fix the mess I made, to get back the man I love.* Wasn't she?

"Please," she said, raising her eyes to his. "I . . . I think we can do it if we try."

"What are you saying, Kara?" Ethan rose and leaned over her, his mouth dangerously close to hers. "That you want me to make you mad again?"

"Maybe," she breathed.

He looked toward the temporal portal. "In that case, I think we're both wearing too many clothes."

She was on her feet before she knew it, all thoughts of Brad completely gone from her mind as they ripped at each other's clothes. Part of her knew this was probably wrong but then again, giving in to the sizzling attraction she felt for Ethan was the only way to get far enough back in time to fix her mistake. It was a sacrifice she was more than willing to make.

Somehow she found herself naked once more in the small glass booth with Ethan breathing heavily in her ear. She was panting out the exact time and space coordinates to get to her fiancé's boyhood home of nineteen years before and Ethan was trying to punch them in and kiss her at the same time. They both had electrodes pasted over their hearts and, if anything, she felt hotter and more ready than she had the day before. And yet, once again, nothing was happening.

"What's . . . why aren't we moving?" Kara gasped at last, as he trailed slow, hot kisses down her neck.

"I was afraid of this." Ethan released her, panting slightly. "Not enough power . . . not enough excitement."

"I don't understand." Kara pushed her tumbled hair out of her eyes with a trembling hand. "I mean . . . just look at us. I'm so hot I—" She broke off, blushing and tried again. "I mean, I'm just . . . and so are you. Aren't you?" She peered at him anxiously. "Unless . . . you're not faking it, are you?"

"Kara . . ." He brushed against her thigh deliberately, bringing a strangled gasp to her lips. "Does this feel like I'm faking it to you?" He bent down and took her mouth again in another fierce kiss. "I can honestly say I want you more than I've ever wanted any woman before."

Kara shivered against him. It might have sounded corny if another man said it, but Ethan was so obviously sincere. Why couldn't Brad ever say anything like that to her? Then she pushed the thought away.

"So," she said, trying to get some control of herself. "I want you and you want me and still nothing's happening."

"That's true." He frowned. "We need more emotion."

"More emotion?" Kara stared at him. "I don't see how that's possible. I don't know about you, but I'm about ready to explode!"

Suddenly, Ethan grinned. "That's it, Kara—you said it. One of us has to explode."

"What?" She drew back from him a little. "You never said anything about physical violence being needed for time travel. What are you talking about—some kind of spontaneous combustion?"

"More like deliberate combustion." His deep brown eyes

were half-lidded and they had that familiar devilish spark in them. He traced a slow path over her collarbone with one long finger as he spoke. "Kara, one of us has to have an orgasm. That would certainly provide enough power to get us back nineteen years."

"Oh." She felt herself blushing all over. "An orgasm—of course, that makes sense," she mumbled. *Stop being so silly,* she lectured herself. *It's not like you've never had the big O before.* No, but big O's were few and far between with Brad, who tended to be a little too fast on the trigger, to put things nicely. It was a sad fact of Kara's life that ever since she'd been with her fiancé, orgasms had been very hard to come by, no pun intended. *But he didn't say it had to be me,* she reminded herself. *He just said one of us—why shouldn't it be him?*

"Kara?" Ethan was watching her closely and she realized she'd gotten very quiet. "Are you all right?"

She nodded stiffly. "Sure, you just . . . surprised me, that's all." She tried to smile and failed. "So . . . do you want me to . . . to touch you?" Catching her bottom lip between her teeth, she reached between their bodies and caressed the hot, smooth skin of his cock.

Ethan sucked in a breath and caught her wrist, stopping the motion. "That's . . . wonderful, Kara," he said, his deep voice a little shaky. "But it's not exactly what I had in mind."

"Oh, then what . . . ?" Kara trailed off, more embarrassed than ever. He was going to ask her to give him a blow job and Brad always complained she was terrible at that. She bit her lip again, looking up at him.

"Hey," He stroked her cheek with his fingers, touching her gently, tenderly. "Why are you looking so scared all of a sudden? I know we haven't known each other long, but I promise you, Kara, I'd never hurt you."

His soft words of encouragement made her feel a little better. "I know that, Ethan. It's just that, well . . . well . . . I'm not much good at . . . at . . . at oral sex," she blurted out at once, feeling her face flame crimson.

"You don't have to be." Ethan stroked her cheek again, unfazed by her outburst. "You see, I was hoping you would let *me* give *you* an orgasm." He leaned closer and his voice got dangerously soft. "I want to make you come, Kara. I want to touch you and taste you—I've wanted to for months, ever since you came to work here and you smiled at me every morning with that sweet, sexy smile of yours." He kissed her gently on the nose, making her giggle. "And now that I've gotten to know you," he whispered, "I want you more than ever. Please, Kara, let me make you come."

How could she refuse when he begged so sweetly? No man had ever asked if he could make her come before—not even Brad.

"All . . . all right," she heard herself agreeing.

"Good," he murmured against the vulnerable skin of her neck, kissing her again. "God, you're soft." His breath was warm and she felt goosebumps break out all over her body as his large hands roamed over her skin, exploring her completely. Long fingers tugged at her nipples, coaxing them into hard points of desire. Then he kissed lower and began to trace them with his tongue. Kara gasped and buried her hands in his thick black hair. Her heart was pounding so hard she thought it might burst.

Before, when they had kissed each other, Ethan had avoided touching her breasts or her sex despite their mutual nakedness. It was as though he was waiting for her permission to do that— well, now he had her permission and he was making the most of it. Kara could scarcely believe the wash of intense sensation as his kisses burned down her body, moving slowly from her breasts to the rounded cup of her navel. She felt like she was burning . . . melting.

He was on his knees before her now in the tight enclosure of the booth and his mouth was teasing along her hipbones, nipping and lapping at her pale, sensitive skin. Kara had an idea of what he was about to do and she sucked in a breath, biting her lip nervously as he placed a strategic kiss just above her soft red curls.

"I love that you're a redhead here, too," Ethan murmured, rubbing one rough cheek along the tender junction of her thighs. "Can't wait to taste you," he added, looking up to meet her eyes.

"Ethan . . ." Kara was trembling all over. Any second she expected to feel the familiar breathless squeezing sensation of the time portal at work, but still there was nothing. Ethan was right, she needed to have an orgasm. But did he have to do it like this?

"Hmm?" He looked up at her, his brown eyes still half-lidded with the pleasure of pleasuring her, of making her breathless and hot.

"I . . . are you sure you want to do it . . . this way?" she said at last. "I mean, it's just that . . . well, I haven't exactly had much luck with it in the past."

"Luck?" He raised an eyebrow at her in question.

"Uh, coming this way, I mean," she clarified, feeling her face go scarlet. "I mean, wouldn't you rather just, um, touch me, instead?"

"You mean like this?" Long fingers parted the wet folds of her sex and stroked gently over the side of her sensitized clit.

Kara moaned and her knees almost buckled. "Oh, God . . ." she whispered.

"No, *Ethan*," he corrected her with a tiny smile. "Do you like it when I touch you like this, Kara? Do you like to feel my fingers inside you?" He suited actions to words, pressing two long, strong fingers deeply inside her, fucking into her until she had to hold onto his shoulders to keep her balance. "Do you like that?" he persisted, never stopping the relentless motion.

"You know I do," she gasped, spreading her thighs wider for his invasion.

"Then you'll like this even better," he growled softly, lowering his head.

Suddenly she felt him parting the soft lips of her pussy, pressing her thighs wide to lay a heated kiss on her tender clit. But that was only the beginning. He kissed her sex the same way he had kissed her mouth—he was slow, hot and utterly relentless.

Kara arched her back and gave in to the intense sensation of his mouth on her in this most intimate of places. He was sucking her clit into his mouth now, tracing patterns over it with his tongue, stroking lightly at first and then more firmly, tasting her as she had never been tasted before.

"Ethan!" she moaned, digging her hands into his thick black hair. Her voice seemed to spur him on. He spread her legs wider and she felt his tongue enter her, pressing deep, as deeply as he could get to taste her to the core. To her delighted amazement, she felt herself coming closer and closer to the edge. She'd never been able to orgasm this way before, but this was an entirely different experience.

Whenever Brad tried this, it was always with a certain sense of obligation. It was as though he knew he ought to do it but didn't really enjoy it, and he always expected some sexual favor in return. But Ethan went down on her with a single-minded intensity that took her breath away. It was clear that he enjoyed it, enjoyed everything about touching her, tasting her, bringing her pleasure. It was like he was a man dying of thirst and she was a cool drink of water—the only thing that could save him—the only thing he wanted in the world.

"Ethan!" she moaned again, as he fucked her with his tongue. She was pressing against him, grinding herself against his face, riding his tongue as he pressed inside her. He was making her crazy, making her helpless to do anything but react to the intense pleasure he was giving her.

He withdrew his tongue and looked up at her for a moment, panting. His full mouth was damp with her wetness. "Come for me, Kara," he commanded in a low, urgent voice. "Wanna feel you coming all over my face."

He dove back in, spreading her wide and circling her clit with his tongue and Kara took a fresh grip on his hair, urging him on. She was close . . . so close . . . Then she felt two long, strong fingers pressing up inside her again. At the same time, Ethan sucked her clit into his mouth and began lapping the sensitive little bundle of nerves with merciless intensity.

"Oh, God. . . . *Oh, Ethan!*" she gasped as the combination of his fingers inside her and his mouth on her clit pushed her over the edge. "I can't stand it!" she wailed, bucking against him with helpless abandon. "Oh, God, I can't . . . can't . . ."

The breath was suddenly forced from her lungs as the temporal portal hummed into life. The air went cool and shimmery and Kara thought she was going to faint. She squeezed her eyes shut, trying to endure the strange but familiar squeezing sensation. *Spacetime,* she thought, still pulling Ethan to her even as they whirled backward through the years. *Who knew you had to have an orgasm to travel in the fourth dimension? I bet Einstein never made up a theory about this!*

Then the blackness took her.

9

After what seemed like forever, the horrible squeezing finally stopped and she could breathe again. Kara opened her eyes to see Ethan still on his knees before her, a smile in his brown eyes.

"Are you okay?" His deep voice was soft and gentle and he caressed her thighs lightly with his hands, as though trying to soothe her.

Kara took a deep, shaky breath. "Yeah, I mean . . . yes. Yes, I'm fine."

"Then would you mind letting go of my hair?" he asked, grinning. "I mean, I'm sure I'll probably have male pattern baldness at some point but I'd like to think I'm too young to start losing my hair just yet."

"Oh—oh, God! Sorry!" Kara withdrew her hands hastily, checking to make sure she hadn't ripped out any clumps of his thick black hair.

"Thanks." Ethan rose stiffly, rubbing his head, but he was still grinning.

"I just . . . I didn't mean to," she babbled, rubbing her palms against her thighs nervously. "I mean, I'm not usually like that. It's just that it was the most intense—" She broke off, biting her lip, her cheeks flaming.

"Hey, it's all right." Ethan stroked her hot cheek gently. "You don't have to apologize. It was wonderful. For me, too, I mean."

"Really?" She looked into his face and was relived to see sincerity in his deep brown eyes. "You mean," she laughed nervously, "Even though I nearly snatched you bald?"

"Yup." He kissed her lightly on the nose, then sighed. "Come on, we'd better get out and do what needs to be done right away. The longer we stay this far back, the greater the strain on the spacetime continuum."

"Okay." Kara grabbed for her clothes. "Let's go."

"So this is going to be your future mother-in-law." Ethan sounded doubtful and Kara didn't blame him. The woman sitting at the cheap Formica dinette set didn't look much like the self-sacrificing saint Brad was always describing to her.

At first Kara had been surprised that Ethan had taken them back to 1984 in half time, so that everything appeared like it was moving in super slow-motion, instead of real-time. Her original idea had been to go back at the exact moment Brad's mother started choking and perform the Heimlich maneuver on her. But, as Ethan had pointed out, it was much simpler to go back right before the incident and keep Brad's mother from choking in the first place.

Now, as she stared at the large, angry-looking woman with bottle-blond hair and an inch of black roots showing, Kara was glad she couldn't be seen by her or the other people at the table. Brad's mother had her mouth open, either to eat or to shout, it wasn't clear which. Her fork was suspended in midair and speared on its tines was a huge chunk of greasy, fried pork chop. Across from her sat a slight, weary-looking man with thinning blond hair that Kara supposed must be Brad's father. He had died a few years before she met her fiancé, so she had never met the elder Mr. Dodgeson, but he looked purely miserable as he sat listlessly before his own greasy plate.

Sitting between the two adults was a twelve-year-old Brad, a look of complete boredom on his preadolescent face. Whatever his parents were saying, it was clear he'd heard it all before and had no interest in hearing it again.

"I don't know," Ethan said, watching as the fork full of pork got closer and closer to the past Mrs. Dodgeson's yawning red maw. "Are you sure you want to do this, Kara?"

She slapped at his arm. "Ethan! How can you ask me that? We'll be saving her life."

He shrugged. "Okay. It just reminds me of a saying my grandfather's people have."

"What's that?" She crossed her arms and gave him a glare.

"Some souls are happier in the North. North is the direction of death and the spirit world in Navajo culture," he explained.

"I don't believe it," Kara said stoutly. "Besides, this is going to solve everything. After this, Brad will have been raised with a mother who taught him to be neat and helpful and caring and loving and *not* the least bit afraid of commitment."

Ethan scowled. "Well, for your sake I hope you're right. If you're going to save her you'd better do it now—she's almost got the fork to her mouth."

"Oh!" Kara hurriedly slid the fork out of her future mother-in-law's hand. Then she looked down worriedly. "Wait, what if this isn't the bite that does her in? I know the date but I'm not sure about the exact time she's supposed to die."

"Better be on the safe side." Ethan had taken the entire plate of greasy pork chops from the center of the cheap little table and he was quickly removing the half-eaten one from Mrs. Dodgeson's plate. Then he took the chop from her husband's plate and Brad's, too, piling them on top of the others.

"What are you going to do with them?" Kara asked, watching him curiously.

He shrugged. "I don't know. Throw them over the fence?" He nodded at the ragged backyard, which was visible through the dining room window. It was ringed with a high wooden privacy fence that no one would be able to see over without a ladder.

"Okay."

They walked outside and tossed the whole platter of whole and half-eaten pork chops, which landed on the other side in a tangle of briar bushes. Kara wondered what the family inside was going to say when part of their dinner just disappeared into thin air. It was definitely going to be an *X-Files* kind of moment, but on the whole, Ethan was right. It was much easier to simply get rid of all the pork chops than to try and explain why they were taking them away. Against her will, she found herself thinking that she wouldn't want to try and explain anything to the shrewish-looking woman they'd left inside the dumpy little house with pealing paint and an overgrown lawn.

"They weren't always like that," she said, nodding at the house. She felt a need to explain the situation out loud—the sullen-looking people and their sad life—as much to herself as to Ethan.

"Like what?" He raised an eyebrow at her.

"Well . . . so, I don't know. So white-trashy," Kara said, wrapping her arms around herself as she studied the house. "In fact, Brad told me they used to have lots of money—his father was a big time investor when he was younger."

"So what happened?" He took her hand and they started back to the temporal portal, which was parked on the ragged patch of brownish grass that passed for the front lawn.

"He got what he thought was a hot stock tip," Kara said. "So hot he decided to put not only his company's money, but all his own savings in it too." She shrugged. "But it didn't pan out and afterward, Brad's father lost his job in finance. I think he ended up selling school supplies or something."

Ethan was silent for a moment as they looked at the little house her fiancé had grown up in. Then he said, "It's not money that makes you rich, and it's not the lack of it that makes you poor."

She looked at him. Even with the glasses perched on his nose, she could see the sadness in his dark brown eyes. "What's that? Something else from your grandfather's people?"

He shrugged. "It's not a Navajo saying or anything, no. And it's not anything he ever said to me—it was just the way he lived, I guess." He sighed. "Come on, we'd better get back. We've put enough stress on the continuum as it is."

10

"So how do you like your future mother-in-law?" Ethan grinned at Kara amiably, looking up from the research; he was poring over. The temporal portal sat silent behind him, in the cages varicolored hairless rats and mice squeaked and rustled quietly to themselves. Kara thought that it was an oddly cozy scene, which just went to show how far she'd come in her thinking since she'd started getting to know Ethan, almost a week ago.

"Oh," she said lightly, sitting on a stool beside him. "She's . . . really, she's just . . ." She shook her head and the truth came out. "Oh, Ethan, she's just *awful.*"

"What?" He raised a black eyebrow at her, and pushed up his glasses, as though trying to get a better look at her problem. "But it's been almost a week. I thought you must be doing fine. At least, you didn't come back right away, wanting to go back and fix another incident in poor old Brad's formative years."

"I know," Kara said, raking a hand through her red hair, which was running completely out of control that day. "It's because, well, because I felt guilty. I mean, it's not like Brad is still a NASCAR watching, cigarette-smoking, beer-guzzling redneck any more. In fact, he's sort of the complete opposite."

"So he's back to being a personal trainer now?" Ethan asked with interest.

"Not exactly." She bit her lip. "He's a CPA in a firm downtown. He wears three-piece suits to work every day and he's almost fanatically neat. It's kind of weird, actually. He insists on pinning his socks together before he puts them in the washing machine so he never loses one of a pair and his underwear always have to be folded into a perfect rectangle when they come out of the dryer—things like that. I think having his mother around may have made him a little bit *too* disciplined."

"That can be a useful trait," Ethan said encouragingly. "Especially for a CPA."

Kara forced a laugh. "Did I say disciplined? What I meant was compulsive." She bit her lip. "Look, Ethan, I know this is all my fault and you said we shouldn't mess with the past any more but I just need one more fix."

He sighed in obvious exasperation. "Kara, where will this end? We can't keep going back further and further, trying to undo what we shouldn't have done in the first place. Brad isn't abusive, is he?"

"No, but he's still not willing to commit," she said stubbornly. "Or rather, he's not willing to commit to anyone but his mother—he's a complete mama's boy now. And I do mean complete. Ethan, she *lives* with us. Do you have any idea what that's like?" She stood up from the stool and started pacing. "Everything I say is wrong. Everything I do, she can do better and faster and more efficiently. Every time I try to cook him anything to eat, she throws it out and makes something else instead—something from scratch. I'd like to scratch her," she said, hotly. "And he won't even kiss me when she's around.

And she's *always* around." Kara shook her head. "Ethan—I'm going *crazy*. At this rate, by the time Brad is ready to commit to me, I'll be ready to be committed."

"Kara . . ." He took her hand between both of his to stop her pacing. "Has it occurred to you that maybe it just isn't meant to be?" He kissed her palm gently and suddenly all the anger she'd been feeling was changed into a hotter emotion. "That maybe there might be someone else for you besides Brad?"

"Oh, Ethan . . ." She pulled her hand away and the tiny diamond engagement ring on her fourth finger seemed to sparkle up at her reproachfully. "It's just that . . . well, I've been with Brad for five years and that's . . . that's a lot to give up. I can't just throw it all away because we've been having some, uh, problems lately. Especially when most of the problems are my fault."

He sighed and his broad shoulders slumped. "I'm sorry, Kara, I know how you feel about your fiancé. But I thought . . . after everything that happened between us . . ."

Kara felt her face getting red as she remembered Ethan on his knees before her, tasting her, touching her, making her come . . . For the past week she hadn't been able to think of anything else. But she told herself stubbornly that it was just because things were going badly with Brad at the moment. After all—he had barely laid a hand on her ever since the last change she'd made to the spacetime continuum. His controlling mother practically did everything but climb into bed with them and knowing that her bedroom was right next to theirs, Kara could hardly blame her fiancé for being a prude.

So of course with that kind of action—or lack of action— going on at home, Ethan was naturally going to look more appealing and attractive. But, as Kara's mother was always telling her, a man in the hand was worth two in the bush, or at work, or wherever. Besides, no matter how charming and hot he was, she'd only know Ethan for a week. She couldn't just throw away five years of commitment, or semicommitment in Brad's case, because she'd found someone so intelligent and handsome and thoughtful and . . .

No, she told herself firmly. *Stop thinking that way! You've got to concentrate on Brad and getting him back to normal.*

"Ethan," she said softly. "It's not that—"

He shook his head. "You don't have to say anything. I know you're committed to Brad, whether he's committed to you or not." He took off his glasses and pinched the bridge of his nose hard, as though to drive back a headache. "So. What's your latest plan?"

Kara felt like her heart was being twisted by a cruel hand, but if Ethan was willing to let it go, then she had to as well.

"Well," she said slowly, trying to take her mind off the man in front of her and get it back to the man she was engaged to, where it belonged. "I know I've made some mistakes in the past . . ."

"No pun intended," Ethan said dryly, which surprised her into a laugh.

"No," she agreed, warming to her subject. "But I know—*I know* I've got the answer this time. And I swear I will never, *never* ask you to use the portal again after this."

Ethan looked at her skeptically. "So what do you want to do this time? Go back and kill Mrs. Dodgeson after all?"

"Ethan!" Kara's eyes widened before she realized he was just kidding. "Of course not," she continued. "What I had in mind was something completely different. Remember how I told you that Brad's family used to be rich, before his father lost all their money and his job on that one bad investment?"

"Mmm-hmm." He was still looking at her skeptically. "So I guess you want to go back and stop him from doing that."

"Exactly," Kara said.

"But I fail to see how this is going to keep him from becoming a, uh, 'Mama's boy,' as you put it."

"By keeping his father in the picture," Kara said promptly. "See, apparently he died a lot sooner than he had in the past that existed before we, uh, brought Brad's mother back."

"Heart attack?" Ethan asked sympathetically.

"Suicide." Kara shook her head. "As far as I can tell, he killed himself not long after she would have died from choking on that pork chop, if we hadn't taken it away from her. She, uh . . ." She looked down at her hands. "I'm not sure but I think she might have driven him to it."

"You think so?" Ethan looked concerned.

Kara nodded. "It's all she ever talks about—how they could have been rich and comfortable, but instead they have such a hard life because Brad's father lost all their money on that bad investment. Now, if she's still talking about it twenty-seven years after it happened, think how much she must have nagged the poor man before he finally—"

"Wait a minute," he interrupted her with a frown. "How many years did you say?"

"Twenty-seven," Kara repeated.

"So you want to go back to 1978?" Ethan frowned at her.

"Well, yes . . ." She bit her lip.

"Kara," he said sternly. "How old are you?

"I'm twenty-seven," she admitted. "But, Ethan, I was six months old at the time—I already checked. So it should be fine . . ."

He frowned. "Remember that I told you it's impossible to go further ahead or back in time than your lifespan? You're really pushing it with this, Kara. And it's going to take an enormous amount of energy."

Kara felt a flutter in her stomach and her heart started to

pound. Suddenly she found she couldn't look him in the eye. "I . . . I know," she whispered.

Ethan stood suddenly and pulled her close to him. He lifted her chin with one finger, making her look at him. "Are you really sure you want to do this?" he asked softly.

"Yes." She dropped her eyes again, feeling like he could see right through her. "I mean . . . I think it's important to fix the mistake I made, Ethan. If Brad's father hadn't made that one wrong decision, then Brad's mother wouldn't have nagged him to death—literally—and they'd all be together and happy right now."

"And Brad would finally ask you to marry him, I know, I know." He sounded almost angry.

"Well, I guess so." Kara frowned. That was what she wanted—wasn't it? She met Ethan's eyes again. "Will you help me?"

"This is your last chance, Kara. If this fix, as you call it, doesn't work, there's no way you can go further back in time to change things." There was a note of sadness in his deep voice and she knew what he was really saying.

This wasn't just her last chance to fix things with Brad. It was her last chance to be with Ethan. Her last chance to give in to the electrical attraction she'd felt jump between them almost from the first minute he grabbed her to save her from falling after she'd spilled hot chocolate all over her supervisor. After this she would have no excuses left—she was a one-guy kind of girl and she had already decided that Brad was her guy. After this last trip, she and Ethan could only be friends.

"I understand," she said softly, slipping her arms around his neck. "I understand everything, Ethan. And I regret nothing."

"Then you're lucky," he said, sounding grim. "Because I regret not meeting you five or six years ago—before you met Brad."

Kara looked at him, startled. "You weren't thinking of going back in time and . . ."

He shook his head. "How would I do that without your help? I can't generate enough energy on my own to go further than a year or two back in the past. Besides, it wouldn't be right. I wouldn't want to manipulate you that way."

"The way I'm manipulating Brad, you mean," she said flatly.

"No." He shook his head. "No, you've been trying to fix something that was broken in the man you love, Kara. I respect that, I'm just not sure that what you're trying to fix is fixable."

"It has to be," she breathed, standing on tiptoe to brush a kiss across his full lips. "Or at least, I have to try." He smelled warm and spicy and deliciously male and his scent rocked her senses. Lately all Brad had smelled like was his mother's greasy home cooking and laundry starch.

"All right." Ethan kissed her back softly but she could feel the fire under the gentle gesture. Flames waiting to erupt if they only gave themselves permission to give in to the blaze. "We'll try," he murmured against her mouth. "But I can't promise that what we did last time will be enough to get us where or when we need to go."

"That's all right." Kara pressed herself against him recklessly. If this was her last chance with Ethan, then she wanted it to make the most of it. She pulled off his glasses, revealing his gorgeous brown eyes. "We'll do whatever we have to do," she whispered, kissing him again.

"Kara," he half groaned. "I—" But whatever he wanted to tell her was lost in their hungry kiss.

Kara didn't want to think about it. She didn't want to think about anything besides how much she wanted him. This time she didn't even remember giving him the correct coordinates. Her need for him was so great it was like time skipped a beat. One minute she was kissing him deeply and the next, Ethan was holding her in his arms, both of them naked with his large muscular body pinning her against the glass side of the time portal.

It was a tiny, cramped space and not the place she would have chosen for her one and only time making love with Ethan Robertson if she could have—but she wanted him so badly she was soon past caring.

"Ethan," she gasped, breaking their never-ending kiss with an effort as his large, warm hands caressed her body. "I think . . . I think we both need to have an orgasm this time."

"You're right." His mouth continued to torture her with kisses and licks, finding the sensitive spot where her neck met her shoulder and sucking fiercely, marking her. She could feel the hard length of his shaft branding her belly.

"Make . . . make love to me," she begged softly, twining her hands in his hair. "Please Ethan, just this once."

"Are you sure?" He pulled back slightly, searching her eyes with his own.

"Positive. Please, Ethan, I want you. I . . . I need you." There was no thought in her head now of Brad's mother or father or fixing the past. No thought of her fiancé at all. There was only the man in front of her, the man she wanted more than she'd ever wanted anyone.

"Kara," he whispered. "I've dreamed of this. I wish we had time to make it last, to take it slow . . ."

"Don't want it slow," she whispered, giving him another hot, urgent kiss. "I just . . . I just want you inside me. Please, Ethan." She ran her hands over his arms, feeling his muscles flex with tension. It was the only warning she got.

He lifted her suddenly, supporting her thighs with his hands and parting her legs. Kara felt the broad head of his cock swipe against her wetness once and then he sank into her in one smooth, long thrust.

"Ethan!" She threw back her head and wrapped her legs around his waist, feeling utterly supported by his strong arms around her. He was in her so *deep.* She bit her lip and bucked against him, needing more. He thrust again and she moaned at the slick motion of his thick shaft piercing her sex.

"Kara, look at me." His voice was low and strained.

She opened her eyes and looked, seeing the emotion in his face. This was more than just sex for him, too, she could tell. But she pushed the thought out of her mind. Instead, she caressed his cheek gently with her palm. He thrust into her again and she gasped.

"Tell me what to do," he growled softly, holding her eyes with his own. "Tell me how to make this good for you—how to make you come."

Kara couldn't imagine it getting better. He was pressing her back against the cool glass side of the time booth with her legs locked around his waist and his cock buried to the hilt in her body. It was like making love in a phone booth but the cramped quarters didn't matter. Having sex with Brad had never been this intensely emotional, this achingly hot.

"Just . . . just don't stop," she begged breathlessly. "Just fuck me, Ethan. *Please.*"

Her words seemed to release some tension inside him because he took a fresh grip on her thighs and pulled back, nearly leaving her body, before thrusting in again, so hard and deep Kara thought she might faint.

"God, Ethan, please!" she moaned again. He pulled back and thrust in again, setting up a steady, relentless rhythm that seemed designed to drive her wild with pleasure, his muscular arms supporting her easily as he fucked into her again and again. Kara cried out in wordless acknowledgment as he plowed into her, deliberate and delicious.

There was pain as his thickness opened her wide and the head of his cock pressed hard against the mouth of her womb, but there was pleasure as well. The pleasure of being well and truly fucked and Ethan was doing it right, the way it ought to be done. He didn't let up for an instant, refusing to give ground even when she whimpered and writhed against him. He only held her more firmly, spreading her wider as he stroked into her wet sex relentlessly, filling her with his thickness until she felt ready to scream.

Kara felt herself getting closer to that edge she'd been searching for from the moment he entered her. Ethan was helping her reach it, giving her just what she needed by filling her over and over with his thick cock, ramming it into her now at a faster pace. He was getting closer to the edge himself, Kara could tell by his unsteady breathing and the way he forced himself deeper and even deeper into her body.

"Ethan, oh God, Ethan," she moaned, feeling the first waves breaking over her as she began to come harder than she ever had in her life. "I'm coming, you're making me come. Don't stop, fuck me harder!" she begged, all restraint torn completely away as he pounded into her, answering her pleas the only way he could.

Kara felt her orgasm break over her like a tidal wave, drenching her in pleasure so sharp she screamed. *Godohgodohgod* . . . her mind moaned and she could feel her sex clenching all along Ethan's thick length still impaling her so deeply. Apparently he could feel it too, because his rhythm abruptly dissolved into a wild bucking inside her as he pulled her closer, trying to get even deeper into her body with each rough thrust.

"Oh, God, Kara, I love you," he groaned as he allowed her orgasm to trigger his own. His words tore at her heart, even as Kara felt the familiar squeezing sensation, taking her back to the past for what was certainly the last time.

11

Being seen bare-assed naked and wrapped in the arms of another man was not her first choice for how to meet her future father-in-law. Unfortunately, Ethan's coordinates were disastrously accurate, landing the time booth in the middle of the senior Dodgeson's office, right in front of a desk piled high with papers. His mouth open in astonishment, Brad's father watched as she hurriedly disentangled herself and pulled on the white lab coat Ethan offered her.

"Who . . . how . . . ?" Brad's father stuttered, plainly at a loss.

"*You* are about to make the biggest mistake of your life." Kara emerged from the time booth and sat down beside her future father-in-law in an ugly orange naugehyde chair. She took the big clunky phone from his sagging hand and put it back on the receiver. It was a rotary dial, she noted in passing. The last time she'd seen one like it was at her grandma Louisa's house. Grandma Louisa refused to throw anything away, no matter how outdated the technology was.

"Who are you and how did you get in my office?" Mr. Dodgeson stared at her, one wispy blond eyebrow raised to his already receding hairline. He was wearing a brown and green checked polyester leisure suit that was loud enough to make her eyeballs bleed and he had on chunky platform boots that made him a good three inches taller than he would otherwise have been. Obviously Brad had inherited his diminutive height from his father.

"Who I am isn't important, what I tell you *is*." Kara crossed her legs and leaned forward. "Now, listen up, because I don't have much time. Right now you think you have a hot tip—a stock that's supposed to go through the roof. You're thinking you'll put everything you have in it—for your company and yourself, too."

"Well, yes. But how—"

"Don't do it," she interrupted him. "It's going to crash and you'll lose everything, and I do mean *everything*." She ticked it off on her fingers. "Your money, your job, and eventually, your life."

"But . . . but how—"

"See that booth behind me with the naked scientist in it?" She nodded over her shoulder. "It's a time machine," she said casually. "And yes, I am from the future. The future—not the *Twilight Zone*," she emphasized, seeing the alarmed look in Dodgeson's mild eyes. "Now look, I'm going to give you a tip on what's *really* going to be hot in a few years." She mentioned the name of a famous software company.

"Micro-who?" Dodgeson looked confused.

"Here, I'll write it down for you. You may not have heard of them yet but they're going to be big—huge. I promise you."

"All right but I—"

"And another thing," Kara lectured him, deciding she might as well go whole hog. "You and your wife need counseling. She's a very unhappy, controlling woman and she's going to make you very unhappy unless you do something about it."

For the first time Dodgeson lost his expression of disbelieving bewilderment. "She's *already* making me unhappy," he admitted. "And we haven't even been married for ten years yet."

"Do something about it—work on it. Also, don't let her eat pork chops. But that's just a precautionary measure." Kara stood to leave. "Oh, and I almost forgot the most important thing. Your son Brad is going to need some serious self-defense classes."

Dodgeson's face creased in a frown. "Brad? But he's only five."

She nodded. "I know that, but as soon as he gets old enough enroll him in some tae kwon do classes."

"Ti-what?" Dodgeson shook his head.

"Oh." Kara racked her brain. "I mean karate—like the Bruce Lee movies?" she asked hopefully. "Um, what's that one, *Enter the Dragon?*"

"Oh, yeah." Comprehension lit his face. "Bruce Lee—*groovy.*"

"He's far-out, all right," Kara agreed without batting an eyelash. "So get Brad into something like that so he can defend himself and gain a sense of self-confidence and self-worth early in his life—before he goes to high school and those bullies put his head down the toilet."

"Before they what?"

"Oh, sorry. Getting ahead of myself." She glanced over her shoulder and saw Ethan making hurry-up gestures with one hand. She only had a minute or two left. "Okay, that's all I've got," she said rapidly. "But look, before I go, I have to know. Are you going to take this advice? I hope I didn't make this trip for nothing. A twenty-seven year time hop is no piece of cake, you know. It requires considerable . . . uh, energy." She felt herself blushing at the thought.

Dodgeson still looked dazed. "I don't know—this is the strangest thing that's ever happened to me."

Kara felt frustrated—the senior Dodgeson was proving to be as indecisive as his son. But her time was up. "I have to go," she said, standing up. It was up to Brad's father now. Either he believed her and would follow her advice or he wouldn't.

"Wait—will I see you again?" Dodgeson half rose as she put her hand on the knob.

"That depends." Kara leveled him with a last warning glare. "If you don't act on what I just told you, you'll be dead in the next ten years," she said, in what she hoped was an ominous tone.

"Wait, wait," he gabbled, half rising from his seat. "Let me just get this right. Uh . . . put money in this Micro-something company," he waived the small slip of paper where she'd written the name, "take my wife to therapy and keep her away from pork chops, get Bradley Bruce Lee lessons, uh . . . is that all?"

"That's pretty much it," Kara agreed, slipping off the lab coat and climbing into the booth beside Ethan. "Look, I really have to go. If I stay any longer I'll screw up the spacetime continuum."

"The what?" he asked almost plaintively, but she was already gone.

12

"Well, do you think it worked?" Ethan averted his eyes considerately while Kara slipped into her clothes. It was strange, she thought sadly, that not two hours or twenty-seven years ago, depending on how you looked at it, they had been making passionate love, but now he was treating her like a friend again. Just a friend and nothing more.

"Only time will tell," she said dryly. "Pun definitely intended that time."

"Yeah." He sighed. "Kara, I—"

"Look, Ethan," she started at the same time. They were both dressed now, standing around his lab with the temporal portal between them. Ethan had replaced his glasses but even through their lenses, Kara could see the look of misery in his dark brown eyes.

"You first," he gestured for her to continue, but whatever she had been going to say had suddenly left her brain.

"No, you." She felt around in the pocket of her skirt, looking for her engagement ring.

"Kara, I just want to say that these last couple of weeks, getting to know you, has been the best time of my life. And, well, I know it may sound silly since we've only really known each other as . . . as more than coworker for a few days, but . . . I care about you. A lot."

Kara closed her eyes. "Oh, Ethan, please don't say it," she whispered.

"I care about you and I wanted to ask . . ." He cleared his throat. "Wanted to ask you if you wanted to accompany me tonight to the Tampa Theater."

Her eyes flew open. "Huh? What's at the Tampa Theater?" The theater was an old, one-screen movie theater downtown that had been lovingly restored to its former glory and showed Indie films and old movies rather than the latest popcorn blockbusters.

Ethan grinned at her. "There's a *Star Wars* marathon tonight that starts at eight and runs until two AM. They're going to show the first trilogy back to back to back. I thought maybe you'd like to go. You, uh, can even wear your hair in the Princess Leia cinnamon rolls if you want. I promise not to laugh."

"Ethan, that's so sweet of you." Kara didn't know what to say. She'd been dreading a declaration of undying love which she couldn't possibly allow herself to return, and instead, he was inviting her out to a sci-fi film festival. Actually, she thought, it sounded kind of nice. Brad would certainly never take her anywhere like that. In fact, he wouldn't take her anywhere there wasn't a large-screen TV showing the latest Bucs game. Then she quickly pushed the disloyal thought out of her head. *He's changed now,* she reminded herself, *I'm sure he has.*

"So you'll go?" Ethan looked even more hopeful.

"I'd . . . really like to," she said carefully. "But Ethan, I . . . what the hell?"

"What is it?" Ethan came to her quickly, crossing the distance that had somehow grown between them to hold her clenched fist in his. "Are you all right?" he asked anxiously.

"I . . . I'm fine." Her exclamation had been caused by the fact that she had finally found her engagement ring, which she had been fishing for in her deep pocket as they spoke. But this definitely wasn't the ring she had taken off her finger before getting into the temporal portal the last time with Ethan. This was . . .

"Completely different," Kara breathed, opening her palm to see the glittering, three-carat pear-cut stone that was perched in an elaborate white-gold setting.

"Well, it looks like you changed something all right." Ethan's voice sounded grim. "That certainly isn't the ring you used to wear."

"It certainly isn't," Kara breathed, slipping it on. It fit perfectly. Just then a respectful knock sounded at the door.

"Ms. Wilson?" came a familiar voice. It was Lilith, her supervisor.

Kara felt herself go pale, remembering the last time Lilith had caught her with Ethan inside his small, private lab. "Quick," she hissed, making shooing motions at him. He looked amused.

"We're dressed this time," he reminded her, in a low voice. "So it should be all right."

"Oh. That's right." Kara took a deep breath and smoothed back her hair before going to the door. "Ms. Buchanan," she began. "I'm sorry if I overstayed my lunch hour but I was just helping Dr. Robertson . . ." She trailed off because Lilith was giving her an odd look.

"Since when do you call me 'Ms. Buchanan?'" she asked, frowning slightly.

"Well—" Kara floundered but Lilith didn't give her a chance to answer.

"I just came to ask you if I could leave a little bit early today.

I have a doctor's appointment and since it's Friday . . ." She looked at Kara hopefully.

"Well, but . . . why are you asking me?" Kara asked, feeling bewildered. Lilith gave her a confused stare.

"Because you're my supervisor, of course. Who else would I ask?"

"Me? The supervisor?" Kara put a hand to her chest, surprised. The huge diamond on her finger sparkled importantly.

"Ms. Wilson, please." Lilith looked slightly exasperated. "Can I leave early?" she repeated.

"Well . . . sure. Go ahead, knock yourself out." Kara still felt dazed. How could she be the supervisor now? Had she changed her own reality as well as Brad's? Could it be that in this new present she found herself in, she had actually been able to complete her business degree and become more than a lowly receptionist who was always late for work?

Lilith turned to go, then turned back. "Oh, I almost forgot. Your fiancé, Mr. Dodgeson called. He said he'll be sending his car for you around four and that he got reservations at La Deaux, so be sure you change into something nice."

"Oh." Kara felt even more confused. La Deaux was an exclusive French restaurant that had only two tables. It was hideously expensive and nearly impossible to get into, from what she had heard. *But I don't like French food,* she thought. *Brad knows that, doesn't he?* Then again, in this new reality, maybe she *did* like it and she just didn't know it yet.

"Good-bye. I guess I won't see you Monday." Lilith said.

"Why not? Where am I going to be on Monday? Why won't I be at work?" Kara felt slightly panicked now. What else did Lilith know about her new life that Kara herself had no idea about?

Lilith stared at her. "Are you sure you're feeling all right, Ms. Wilson? You're acting very strangely if you don't mind me saying so."

"No, no, I don't mind. Just tell me what I'm doing on Monday," Kara said urgently. She wished she was the kind of person who kept a dayplanner so she could look up her schedule. Then again, maybe she *was* that kind of person now . . .

"After you go to La Deaux you're flying to Hawaii to be married tonight," Lilith said, obviously truly mystified now. "And you're going to be on your honeymoon for the next two weeks. So *of course* you won't be here on Monday. I assure you, we'll handle everything just fine though, don't worry."

"I . . . I'm sure you will." Kara suddenly felt so faint she thought she might fall over. She swayed weakly and strong arms caught her.

"Whoa—maybe you'd better sit down." Ethan's voice was low and soft in her ear. Kara realized she'd forgotten all about him—he had been standing so quietly behind her while Lilith revealed her new future in that bland, no-nonsense way of hers.

"Are you all right?" he asked softly and the look in his deep brown eyes was concern and some other emotion she was afraid to name.

"Fine . . . just surprised, that's all." Kara put a hand to her neck to rub the tension headache that was throbbing up from the base of her skull. "I just—" she began, when another voice interrupted her.

"Kara, darling, here you are!"

She looked up in a daze to see Brad striding into the room. But not the Mama's boy neurotic Brad or the mechanic redneck Brad, or even the old, over-pumped and over-primped, self-centered personal trainer Brad. No—this Brad was *perfect*, she thought with faint surprise. His blond hair was thick and wavy and his pale blue eyes gleamed from a tanned, handsome face. The crisp dark suit he was wearing must have cost more than the monthly rent on their old condo and he was neither over-nor under-pumped. He even looked taller.

"Just right," Kara muttered to herself, feeling like Goldilocks in the fairy tale. She could feel Ethan stiffen behind her. But even as she turned to catch his expression, Brad was holding out a tanned, well-manicured hand and smiling politely, showing perfectly capped, brilliantly white teeth.

"Dr. Robertson," he said, still in a familiar slightly nasal voice. At least *that* hadn't changed. Kara felt obscurely relived. She saw Ethan take the offered hand with obvious reluctance.

"Mr. Dodgeson," he replied, dropping Brad's hand as soon as he possibly could.

"I've heard so much about you from Kara, I almost feel I already know you." The new Brad smiled winningly. "My father and I have seriously discussed funding some of your private research. Kara says you're a brilliant innovator and she should know."

"I should?" Kara looked up at her new and improved fiancé wildly. What did he know about her and Ethan?

"Of course you should, darling," he said, still smiling. "You're a brilliant judge of people—that's why you're marrying me." He laughed as though it was a wonderful joke and Kara managed to join in weakly. Ethan was conspicuously silent.

"Well, it's nice to finally meet you," Brad said to him. "I actually just came to collect Kara a little bit early." He turned to her. "I know I told your assistant that I'd send the car at four but then I thought—why wait? I called La Deaux and moved up the reservation so we can take the jet to Hawaii early. We'll be married before you can say aloha. Isn't that wonderful?"

"It's . . . it's nice," Kara managed.

"Just nice?" He pulled her out of her chair and put an arm around her protectively. "You must have been working too hard. Come on, maybe we have time for a mini shopping spree before La Deaux." And before she knew it he was leading her away. Away from the small lab with its cages of squeaking multicolored mice, away from the temporal portal that had served her so well, and away from Dr. Ethan Robertson.

Kara turned her head helplessly as Brad marched her firmly out the door, wanting one more glimpse. The look in Ethan's dark brown eyes behind their thick lenses twisted her heart but then they turned the corner and he was gone.

13

Dinner was a blur of creamy sauces and flaky pastry that turned Kara's stomach. Or maybe it was more than the rich French food that was bothering her. But what could it possibly be? Brad was perfect in every way. He was rich, handsome, charming and obviously completely devoted to her. He had taken her on a shopping spree and dropped over ten thousand dollars on her in the space of an hour before their early dinner. What more could a girl want?

"Darling," he said anxiously as Kara picked morosely at her wild blueberry crème brûlée. "Are you all right? I thought you loved French food."

"I . . . I'm fine," Kara said, wondering why she wasn't. For some reason she kept thinking of Ethan, alone in his lab with the rustling mice and rats, and the temporal portal standing empty and quiet behind him. She lifted her left hand to her face to rub her temple and caught the muted gleam of the huge diamond on her fourth finger. It seemed to weigh down her hand somehow. *It's not money that makes you rich, and it's not the lack of it that makes you poor,* whispered a voice in her brain. Kara lowered her hand to the tablecloth hastily

"I'm worried about you." Brad peered at her anxiously. "You're so pale—even paler than usual, my redheaded beauty."

I love that you're a redhead here, too, whispered the voice. Ethan's voice. Kara felt herself blushing dull red with shame. *I only did what I had to do,* she argued with herself. *To fix everything.* And she had fixed it all right. Fixed it good. Aloud she said, "I'm fine, just a little tired. But . . . do we really have to go straight to the airport from here?"

Brad looked surprised. "Well, I guess not—after all it's my jet so we can go whenever we want to. But I thought you couldn't wait to get married."

"I . . ." Kara hesitated, twisting the heavy ring around her finger. "There's a *Star Wars* marathon at the Tampa Theater tonight," she said at last. "I just thought it might be fun to go."

"What?" Brad made a face. "My practical Kara wants to go to a *Star Wars* marathon? But you *hate* science fiction. You always say it's junk food for the mind."

"Do I?" Kara stared at him, wondering if it could possibly be true. Was she really the über-organized, French food-loving, sci-fi-hating woman that this new and improved Brad had apparently fallen in love with? *I can't be,* she thought wildly. *That can't be me. There must be some mistake!*

"Of course." He frowned at her, looking even more concerned. "Look, Kara, just tell me if you're getting cold feet."

"No, no," she said hastily. "I just . . . I just remembered that I forgot to do something at work. Would you . . . do you mind if we stop by there on the way to the airport?"

Brad laughed. "Now that's the workaholic Kara I know and love. Sure we can, darling. In fact, why don't you take the car and I'll take a cab to the airport to get things ready. That way the minute you get there we can take off."

"Sure," she muttered, rising from the table. "I, uh, guess I'll see you there."

"Don't be long." He pecked her lightly on the cheek and Kara stumbled out of the restaurant on legs that felt like old dry sticks.

Ethan was not at the lab. In fact, no one but the custodial staff was there at this time on a Friday evening. A glance at her watch told Kara that the shopping spree and dinner at La Deaux had taken longer than she'd thought. It was almost seven o'clock. She wondered if Ethan would be going to the marathon without her. For some reason the thought made tears sting the back of her eyes.

She wandered up to the little private lab, thinking of all the adventures she'd had there in the past couple of weeks. *These last couple of weeks, getting to know you, has been the best time of my life,* Ethan's voice whispered in her head.

"Oh, Ethan," she whispered to herself, feeling the tears start to flow. She wished he was still at the lab, so she could talk to him. So she could be sure she was doing the right thing.

This is foolish, Kara argued with herself. *I've only known him a little over a week. I can't throw my life with Brad away for a two week-long infatuation. Can I? Should I? If only there was a way to be sure . . .*

Suddenly Kara snapped her fingers. What an idiot she was. Of course there was a way to be sure—she had a freaking time machine at her disposal!

It was the work of a moment to get into Ethan's private lab; he'd never hidden the code from her. A second later Kara was standing naked inside the three-sided glass booth with an electrode stuck to her skin right over her heart, punching dates into the controls.

Two years ought to do it, she thought to herself. Ethan had told her he couldn't gather enough energy on his own to send himself either forward or backward in time more than one or two years but Kara was certain that would be enough. Surely she could muster the energy to send herself forward two years. *Only one way to find out.*

Closing her eyes, she tried to think of the happiest thoughts she could. She was marrying Brad—finally, at last getting married! And they were going to have an elaborate honeymoon in Hawaii, staying at the best resorts and sparing no expense. Her mother would stop nagging her and she could settle down and have those two-point-four kids she'd always dreamed about and . . .

And none of it was working. Kara hadn't felt even a tiny squeeze and the temporal portal remained quite and unmoving. Desperate, she tried again. *Brad holding me on our honeymoon night, moonlight and champagne, making love on a tropical beach.* But somehow, all she could see was Ethan making love to her. Right here in the cramped little booth, the touch of his large warm hands, his mouth on her body, his words as he finally lost control, *Oh, God, Kara. I love you!*

Without realizing she was doing it, Kara's hand crept between her thighs as she pictured Ethan's handsome face. He was so sweet, so caring . . . so *hot.* She thought of the way he'd pressed her against the glass side of the booth and rubbed lightly over her clit, pretending her fingers were his. God, when he touched her, her whole body exploded. It felt so good, so right . . .

The temporal portal hummed to life and the familiar squeezing sensation signaled success as her orgasm overtook her. Before Kara could think about the fact that thoughts of the wrong man had gotten her there, she was already two years in the future.

14

A glance at her new driver's license had let Kara know that her new address was now on Bayshore Drive, the most expensive and well-established neighborhood in Tampa. The houses that wound along the length of the meandering road that followed Tampa Bay counted their worth in the multimillions.

She had decided to come in real time, hoping to be able to sneak in the huge white house that was now her residence and catch a peek at her future self. There was no doubt she would have a harder time explaining her nudity if someone saw her, but as a wealthy citizen of South Tampa, Kara was hoping to be able to pass it off as an eccentric whim on her part if anyone saw her. She could say she was just sunbathing in the nude— that was it. After all, a naked sunbathing millionaire was much more likely to be excused than say, a naked street person.

Luckily for her, she landed in the backyard instead of the front. She gathered her clothes into a bundle and sneaked quietly onto the back porch of the mansion, fumbling for the key in her pocket as she did. As soon as she snuck inside she would get dressed—she felt too exposed to try and wriggle into her clothes standing outside in the backyard.

The back door opened into a kitchen that was as large as her entire old condo. Luckily it was empty and Kara concentrated on easing the door closed quietly, still clutching the bundle of clothes to her chest.

"Kara, what the hell are you doing?"

The voice behind her startled her so much that Kara dropped her clothes on the floor, and then had to scramble to pick them up. She looked up to see a very disapproving Brad standing over her. He looked pretty much like the Brad she had left two years in the past, except his hair was a little shorter and he had an ugly scowl on his handsome face.

"I, um . . . I was, um . . ." The nude sunbathing story went right out of her head and Kara couldn't think of a thing to say to explain her current state of undress. But Brad didn't give her a chance to explain.

"What would the neighbors think? You know how important it is to keep up a good front—even if we are getting a divorce."

"A divorce?" Kara was wiggling into her clothes as fast as she could, but hearing Brad's last statement stopped her cold. "But we've only been married for two years," she protested. "Why would we get a divorce?"

Brad laughed, a bitter, angry sound. "Oh, I see what this is all about. Your lawyer probably told you that most of my assets were tied up and untouchable. So now she's advised you to try and play up to me—maybe put it off a few weeks so she can try and untangle some of the legal knots."

"No, I—"

"Well, you can forget it, sweetheart." He laughed again and gave her a condescending once over. "Whatever charms you had for me were exhausted long ago. Showing up naked in the middle of the day isn't going to make me want you again." He frowned. "Especially when it looks like you've been slacking off on your crunches lately. Better keep up with those, Kara. How else are you going to find another rich husband to take care of you?"

"But . . . but Brad . . ." His nasty remarks stung but Kara tried to shrug off her hurt and get to the bottom of the matter. "Honey," she started, laying a hand on his arm. Brad shrugged it off angrily.

"Don't 'honey' me. You know, Kara, you have only yourself to blame for this mess."

"I do?" Kara racked her brain. What could she have done to provoke Brad into asking for a divorce?

"I mean, if you hadn't hired that damn detective to follow me around you never would have known. You could have kept on living in blissful ignorance. None of those girls really meant anything to me—it was purely physical."

"Girls?" Kara felt faint. Had Brad been cheating on her?

"Yes, girls, all right? I admit it—there was more than just the one your damn detective got on film." Brad was striding angrily back and forth across the huge expanse of the kitchen floor now. "Go tell your bloodsucking lawyer, I don't care," he shouted. "You can have the house and the Jaguar but not a penny of my money, you ungrateful little bitch!"

"Brad, please." Kara put a hand to her head, not caring anymore that she was only half dressed. "Are you telling me that you've been cheating on me the whole time we've been married?"

He rounded on her viciously. "Since day one, sweetheart. Remember that cute little Hawaiian maid in our honeymoon suite?"

"Oh, Brad, you didn't!" Kara felt like he was cutting into her chest with a sharp knife and removing her heart. At least the old Brad had been faithful to her—hadn't he? She realized she really couldn't be sure.

"I did and I enjoyed it." He laughed at her again. "So go back and tell your lawyer that we're going to court as scheduled." He turned on his heel and left the kitchen, his shoes making angry sounds on the highly polished parquet floor.

"But I . . . I . . ." Kara shook her head, stunned. How could he? *How could he?* She stumbled back to the time machine, ripping off her clothes carelessly as she went. Only one thought pounded in her brain—she had to get back. *She had to get back!*

She stuck the electrode over a heart that felt like it was made of lead and punched in the coordinates with a shaky hand. How stupid she had been to think she could change Brad for the better. Everything she had done had only made things worse.

If only she could talk to someone who would understand. But there was no one who would believe her crazy story—no one except Ethan, who thought she didn't care about him. *But I do care,* she thought helplessly. *Oh, Ethan, I do care so much, but I've been too blind and stubborn to see it. And now it's too late.*

15

It was a good thing going back to her original time didn't take much energy because Kara couldn't manage a single happy thought. She felt tired and hurt and emotionally exhausted. When the squeezing sensation finally stopped, she climbed out of the glass booth feeling like an old woman.

"Kara, what's wrong?"

She looked up to see Ethan standing in the doorway to the small private lab, a look of concern in his deep brown eyes. Kara took a step toward him and stumbled. Before she could fall, he was beside her, taking her in his arms. Not caring that she was naked, Kara buried her face against his chest and just let him hold her.

"What is it?" he murmured against her hair. "What is it? Why are you crying?"

"Am I?" She reached up to touch the wetness on her cheeks. "I guess I am. Oh, Ethan, I've made such a mess out of things!"

"Have you?" He held her closer. "What's wrong now?"

"I . . . I've created a monster," Kara admitted tearfully. "It's Brad—he's worse than ever. I went forward a few years just to check on us because, well . . ." She looked up at him, trying to read his face. "Because I couldn't help feeling like I was making a big mistake, marrying him."

"And what did you see?" Ethan asked gently.

"We . . . we were getting a divorce," Kara choked. "Because . . . because he'd been cheating on me. And, oh, Ethan, he was so hateful about it. And not a bit sorry that he'd done it, you know. He was just mad that I'd found out and I was getting the house and the Jaguar and I guess my lawyer was trying to get more because . . . because . . ." But she couldn't continue. She shook her head and pressed her hot face against Ethan's chest. He stroked her hair quietly, letting her cry.

"I was afraid of this," he said at last. His deep voice was grim and sad. "I wish I could help you, Kara, but this time there's no fixing it. We can't go further back than we did—it's too dangerous and too close to the start of your lifespan."

"I . . . I know it's not fixable." Kara sniffed and looked up at him. "But that's not the reason I'm upset. Or the *only* reason I'm upset, I should say."

"No?" Ethan looked at her and despite the glasses, she thought she could see a small spark of hope in his dark brown eyes. That little spark gave her hope, too, and the courage to speak her mind.

"No," she said softly. "I'm crying because I've been such an idiot—trying to fix things with Brad when what I really wanted . . . what I really *needed* was here under my nose the whole time."

"You mean . . . ?" Ethan looked down at her, hope and tenderness in his face.

"Yes," Kara said softly. "I mean you were right when you said it wasn't meant to be for me and Brad. And Ethan . . . I . . . I know I must have hurt you, going off with him without even saying good-bye. But I kept telling myself that I couldn't give up on a five-year relationship, that I couldn't throw everything I had with Brad away on a whim."

"A whim? Is that what I am?" But there was no anger in his voice as he said it.

"No," Kara whispered, looking up at him. "You're a lot more than that. Ethan, can you forgive me for being so blind and stupid?"

"Stop calling yourself stupid," he said fiercely. "You've very intelligent. And beautiful, and sweet, and—"

Kara laughed through her tears. "Does this mean you still want me to go with you to the *Star Wars* marathon at the Tampa Theater?"

Ethan blushed. "You know, that was so stupid of me. What I wanted to say was that I loved you, but I was afraid I'd scare you away. So instead, I invited you to the marathon. After you left, I could've kicked myself for not saying what I wanted to. I was thinking, 'what kind of a geek am I, that I couldn't even tell her how I feel?'"

"You're *my* kind of geek, and don't you forget it," Kara whispered. She pulled him down for a kiss, winding her fingers through his hair and putting everything she felt into the gesture.

When they finally came up for air, Ethan had a grin on his face that was bright enough to light up the city. "Kara," he murmured, "I don't think I need a time portal to know that we're going to have a happy ending."

"Oh, Ethan." She kissed him again and grinned back. "Come on, if we hurry I bet we can still make the beginning of *The Empire Strikes Back.*"

"I don't think so." Ethan bent down and swept her up into his arms, making her giggle with the sudden movement. "I want to take you home—back to my house."

"Why," Kara asked, feeling her stomach flutter with anticipation. "What's there?"

"A king-sized bed," Ethan growled, kissing her again. "I want to make love to you somewhere we can stretch out. The time portal is wonderful for traveling through the spacetime continuum, but it's definitely lacking in the romantic ambiance department."

"I couldn't agree with you more," Kara sighed happily. "And I have the feeling, we'll never have to use it again."

Mirror of the Heart

1

It all started with the dream.

Large hands were touching her, undressing her, caressing her body. They were making her naked—making her hot and frightened at the same time. Who was touching her and why? Why couldn't she move to stop them?

Her breasts were bared, the cool night air whispering over her heated flesh, and rough fingers pinched her nipples to attention. She wanted to gasp but the breath was caught in her lungs—wanted to scream but her voice was locked in her throat. Helpless, she felt the man's hand travel lower, pushing aside the flimsy silk nightgown she wore, exposing her thighs.

"Nice," said a voice. Did it belong to the man who was touching her? She couldn't move her head to find out, couldn't see anything but the plain white ceiling above her, gilded by a watered-silk pattern of moonlight.

"Perfect. Just perfect." The hand was tracing the curve of her hip, the length of her thigh. She itched to slap it away even as her body heated to his touch. What was wrong with her?

He was spreading her thighs now, warm, rough hands sliding upward from the inner curve of her knees to the tiny silk triangle that barely covered her sex. She was wearing the panties that Miles had given her, the ones with the see-through lace panel and the intricate little silk flowers sewn on the sides. But the hand touching her didn't belong to Miles. Whoever was touching her this way was a stranger.

Thick fingers teased aside the fabric, baring her completely and a cool whisper of night air stroked her naked sex. She was wet. She fought to struggle, to close her legs, to dispel the unwanted sexual heat that was twisting in her belly like a live thing. Need burned down her nerve endings like lightning and she knew she wouldn't be able to resist him even though he was a stranger.

Thick fingers were touching her, spreading her, she wanted to close her legs, to roll away. Suddenly a sharp pain pierced her thigh and she jerked . . .

Taylor woke up with a gasp and sat bolt upright in bed so fast she made herself dizzy. The pain in her thigh was from an open safety pin she'd been using to hold the too-small sheet to the puffy pillowtop mattress. She must have thrashed around in her sleep and rolled over it, spiking herself in the leg. But it wasn't the small smear of blood on her leg that concerned her— it was the bizarre dream she'd been having before she woke up.

For a moment she could still feel the warm rough touch on her body. She ripped up her nightshirt and stared down at herself, as though expecting to see the phantom hands still touching her. But there was nothing. Nothing but the strange ache between her legs—a ghost of the hunger that had threatened to consume her in the dream.

"What the hell?" she said out loud. The sound of her own voice melted the few remaining cobwebs that were clouding her brain. Taylor realized she was sitting up in her bed with her nightshirt raised almost to her chin, looking down at herself stupidly. Her nipples were hard from the chilly morning air. She pushed the blue nightshirt down, smoothing it past her thighs quickly, as though there was someone there to notice or care.

What had she been dreaming about again? Something about some stranger touching her while she wore the special peek-a-boo panties that Miles had given her on their last Valentine's Day together. But she only wore those on special occasions. And there were no more special occasions with Miles. Not since the pregnancy scare when he'd decided he wasn't ready to be a father. The pregnancy test at the clinic had dispelled Taylor's doubts, but not her fiancé's. Or should she call him her ex-fiancé now? Taylor supposed that would be more accurate.

Her alarm went off in a series of staccato chirps like a chorus of crickets gone berserk. Taylor slapped at it until she hit the snooze button and cut it off. She was really awake now—awake enough to remember everything. Such as the fact that she was due in to work today although her two week vacation was officially only half over. That was her own fault, though. She shouldn't have answered the phone when she was supposed to be away on a cruise to Cozumel. A cruise for which she had already paid her half, even though Miles made three times as much as she did. A cruise that he had taken her best friend on instead of her. Ex-best friend, she reminded herself.

"Ex-fiancé. Ex-best friend." Taylor said the words aloud, rolling them in her mouth, tasting them the way she had used to taste the words, 'Mrs. Miles Hearn.' They tasted bitter, or maybe it was just the residue of the Ben and Jerry's pity party she'd been throwing herself for the past week.

"Get up, Taylor," she told herself, suiting actions to words as she slid out of bed. A glance at the window confirmed that the rainy spell was continuing. The light painting her ceiling was the color and consistency of a runny egg white. Even in the sunshine state a little rain must fall, she reminded herself. Or in this case, a hell of a lot—Tampa was beginning to resemble the lost city of Atlantis. She'd be lucky if the front sidewalk of her condo wasn't flooded again. She made a mental note to wear shoes she didn't care about and headed for the bathroom.

"It's not the end of the world," Taylor lectured herself in the shower, letting the steaming water run over her head as the rain pounded outside. She'd been telling herself the same thing all week between pints of gourmet ice cream, but today she had to go back to work. Today was the day to believe it.

She toweled herself dry vigorously, reminding herself of all of Miles's bad qualities. He was cheap, for one thing. The tiny quarter-carat diamond engagement ring she'd thrown back in his face during the big fight was proof of that. He pulled down the big bucks as a biomedical consultant, but he always insisted that they split the cost of everything equally.

At first it had made Taylor feel like a liberated woman to pick up half the tab at dinner, to buy her own ticket to the movies, to split the cost of the miniature golf game down the middle. By the time she'd realized she didn't want to be quite so liberated, there was no graceful way to broach the subject.

Also, she reminded herself, attacking her too-thick dark blond hair with the blow-dryer and round-headed brush, Miles was *boring*. Stay at home on Friday night and watch the football game he'd Tivo'ed boring. Never go to parties or try anything new boring. Taylor had considered it a major achievement to get him to eat a piece of sushi and the salsa classes she'd wanted to sign up for were out of the question.

She brushed her teeth, noting that the inside of her left cheek was sore. Had she bitten herself in her sleep? Maybe she was getting scurvy from a steady diet of junk food and regret. Her mirror showed bloodshot green eyes and hair that was a blond bird's nest. She squirted in some Visine and shoved some combs in her hair to keep it in line. The show must go on. Where had she been? Oh, yes, the boring thing.

The boring thing had extended to the bedroom too, she reminded herself, while slapping on some makeup. Not that she demanded perfection in bed, far from it. She wasn't exactly the most experienced person herself, but a little effort once in a while might have been nice. The most exciting thing Miles had ever done was buy her those damn panties and she'd worn them maybe twice.

Thoughts of the panties, which were among the things she'd gotten rid of after Miles had asked for his ring back, made Taylor think of the dream again. What the hell had *that* been about, anyway? Maybe her subconscious mind was trying to tell her she needed to go out and get some. What she needed was a little excitement—a strange man with large, knowing hands to drive her to the brink of pleasure again and again . . .

Taylor snorted at her own purple prose as she dug through her closet in search of something that would fit after a week of self-indulgence. The tan skirt was out—it was tight through the hips even on a week when she'd been good. Likewise the burgundy pantsuit. After huffing and puffing for two solid minutes trying to get her all-purpose black A-line skirt buttoned and zipped, she had to admit defeat. There was only one thing in her closet that would do after a week of Chunky Monkey and Phish Food. Taylor dug to the back of the rack and pulled them out. The dreaded fat pants.

She wanted to cry as she pulled them on but she made herself hold it in. She'd done enough crying in the past week to last a lifetime and it was time to dry it up. The pants looked like a dull black polyester hide stretched over her ample ass. As though she'd skinned some ugly beast with a non-breathing fabric skin to get them.

"Back to the gym tonight," Taylor told herself out loud,

watching the too-curvy blonde in the bathroom mirror mouth the words with her. Unless she wanted to be stuck in the land of size fourteens forever, she'd better make good on her promise. She buttoned her blouse and stuck in some earrings, then took in the total effect.

A blond girl in her midtwenties with sad green eyes and flyaway hair stared back. She was five-seven, tall enough to carry some weight, but not nearly as much as she was currently packing. Taylor sighed. She might as well have opened the tubs of Ben and Jerry's and spread them directly on her thighs. It would have saved her some trouble.

Enough with the pity party already. She would go to the gym and work it off. Hell, she might even sign up for those salsa classes herself. It might be a good way to meet someone new. Someone exciting and unpredictable.

Taylor grabbed her kissy-lips umbrella and slid into some shoes she didn't like very much. They matched the fat pants to a T. Then she slipped her purse over one shoulder and let herself out the front door, into the rain. She picked her way through the sodden mess that was currently her condo's front lawn, trying not to get wet to the ankles.

She had no idea she was being followed.

2

Reese stared as the curvy blond girl raised the pink umbrella that was covered in red and white lip patterns. He compared her to the tiny 3-D scan he had in one hand while navigating his vehicle with the other. She was the one, all right—Taylor Simms.

She was wearing typical early twenty-first century clothing and her face had the open look of someone who'd never suffered poverty or disease. Reese knew that made some of the Chrono Patrol he worked with mad. All they wanted to talk about were the privileged classes of the past. The citizens of the time before the Last Great War and the plagues of 2086.

Reese didn't feel that way, though. He didn't time hop much, being assigned to the Genetic Crimes Unit instead of the Chrono Patrol, but he liked the looks of openness that he saw on most peoples' faces here in 2006. The fearless way they walked down their streets, heads held high, reminded him of Leena. Then he pushed the thought away—Leena was a long time ago and better left forgotten.

But just because she wasn't in any apparent physical danger, didn't mean his subject wasn't in pain. Even as he watched,

Taylor ducked her head and wiped at her eyes, obviously upset about something. Reese had a sudden urge to comfort her, which he fiercely suppressed. She was just another subject. The only thing special about her was the fact that she was going to lead him to Ycaza and his crew. Then he would finally get revenge.

He started to open his door—there would never be a better time to grab her than here on the mostly deserted suburban street. But suddenly a boy on an early twenty-first century two wheeled conveyance rolled by. He was tossing rolls of gray paper at the doors of the domiciles he passed. Reese hadn't time gazed enough to figure out what the purpose of this was, but the boy's presence on the street was enough to stop him cold. There must be no witnesses, if at all possible. Only if it looked like there was no other option would he grab her in public. Cursing under his breath, he got back into his vehicle.

He drove by her car as she climbed in and then time looped to get behind her again while she was well on the way to work. Several people in the vehicles he passed seemed to be staring at him, or maybe it was just the outer appearance of his own vehicle that was attracting attention. Most of it was safely in the fourth dimension, but he had done his best to make the part of it that showed match the appearance of the other twenty-first century conveyances. Maybe he had gotten it wrong, he thought. He had been in such a hurry to get to his subject that there hadn't been much time to prepare. Maybe the pattern he had picked for his vehicle was one that was unacceptable for transportation devices.

Ahead of him, Taylor Simms's car swerved suddenly, breaking his train of thought. He watched her anxiously, ready to make an emergency grab if he had to, but she had just been changing lanes. Reese shook his head. He had to get to her soon. Her primary clone had been active for one week now if his information was correct. At any time she could begin experiencing the neural fugues that would incapacitate her completely for as long as they lasted. If she had one while she was operating her vehicle, it would be a very bad thing.

He followed Taylor carefully, keeping an eye on her, ready to make the grab at any time.

3

Taylor cast another glance behind her as she took the Franklin Street bridge to downtown. She had never seen a plaid car before and the guy that was driving it didn't look like the type to own something so eccentric. He had a grim expression on his dark face and a white scar under one eye that she could see even in her rearview mirror.

On any other day the blue and green plaid car and its serious driver might have caught and held her attention. She might have started making up stories about him in her head—it was a pastime she frequently indulged in. Such as . . . the little old man she saw walking the tiny terrier in a pink sweater vest was actually a Russian spy from before the Cold War ended and he was still passing secrets to the supposedly defunct KGB in exchange for the latest in doggie haute couture . . . that kind of thing. Silly but fun. Taylor had an active imagination and liked to keep herself amused.

But today, not even the weird plaid car could jump-start her creative motor. It was all she could do to keep driving in the right direction, making her way toward her job in the stuffy downtown law firm of Peters, Peters, and Richards (sometimes called Peters, Peters, and Dickhead by disgruntled employees), instead of away from it.

She was an underpaid, overworked paralegal for Richards, the senior attorney who made up the 'dick' part of the firm in every sense of the word. The minute she had picked up the phone yesterday and heard her boss's voice on the other end of it, she knew she had made a mistake. But before she could protest, he had been calling her in to work. Taylor hadn't put up too much of a fight. After all, what else was there to do but lie around her house eating herself into oblivion? If she'd been allowed to go on binging on Ben and Jerry's for another week, even the horrid fat pants wouldn't have fit her.

The rain was letting up a little so she parked in a lot that was several blocks from the building that housed her office. If she was going to work off the ice cream she'd been eating, walking was as good a way to start as any. Besides, she wanted a few minutes to clear her head before she had to face the staff of P,P, & D and explain why she was still in town instead of having the time of her life in sunny Cozumel.

She stepped out of the car and hit the fob on her key chain, hearing the reassuring double 'bloop' that let her know it was safely locked. There wasn't much need for her kissy-lips umbrella now but she raised it anyway. The bright colors gave her a slight, but much needed, boost. Keeping her head down, she began the five block trek to her building.

Downtown Tampa usually had a dirty charm that enchanted Taylor and sparked her imagination, but today it just seemed dirty. She barely noticed that the strange, plaid car was still behind her, idling along in the right-hand lane down the confusing one-way streets.

In the middle of the first intersection she felt a strange tingle at the back of her neck—almost as though someone was tickling her with a feather. Or maybe a bug had landed on her skin?

She reached back to slap at the annoying sensation and the dream hit again, bludgeoning her brain with the force of a grand-slam driving baseball bat. It knocked her to her knees right between the white lines of the crosswalk so that she was face to face with the grinning silver grille of a late model Cadillac.

She was vaguely aware of people around her exclaiming and the rough blacktop digging into her knees through the shredded material of the fat pants. She tried get up and lost her balance. She fell sideways so that she was staring at the Cadillac's tires instead of its grille. Everything seemed to be happening in slow motion.

Someone with a deep, authoritative voice was shouting. "I'm a doctor—let me through." Then she dropped her kissy-lips umbrella with a muted clatter and the world around her faded into oblivion.

Someone was showing her off. The same rough hands she remembered from before were undressing her again. Her nipples were peaking as his fingers ran over her body in a careless caress.

"See what I mean? Perfect in every detail. Think how much they'll pay." What was he talking about? Who would pay? For what?

The hands on her again, making her hot despite her fear. Where was she? This time she couldn't see anything at all—not even a ceiling. She tried to blink her eyelids and felt a thick band of some heavy material obscuring her vision. Blindfolded—she was blindfolded. Why?

The hands were moving her limbs, posing her in different positions. Someone was stroking her breasts, pinching her nipples. Then the hands were moving lower, parting her thighs again.

"Take a look at this pussy and tell me it isn't the prettiest thing you ever saw." Harsh laughter again. Rude fingers between her thighs, spreading her open for some obscene inspec-

*tion. She trembled with the indignity of it, the horror, even as
her body responded like a cat in heat.*

"Damn, she's so wet."

"Hot, isn't it? Strap her down now. Gotta make the jump."

*Rough straps of some flexible material were being drawn
over her nude body. Taylor could feel the scratch of them
against her hyper-sensitive skin—a low-grade, intensely pleasurable agony. There was a low click as something locked them
into place. Where were they taking her?*

A jolt of pain shot through her, interrupting the dream like a
new radio frequency taking over the station she'd been listening
to. Taylor jerked and gasped, coming back to the reality of blacktop beneath her cheek and the stinging pain of her skinned knees
even as desire rolled through her. What was going on?

"I *said* I'm a doctor. Move back—give her room to breathe!"
That deep, authoritative male voice again. The same one she'd
heard right before the dream had taken her. Then the man in the
plaid car was bending over her, his dark face grim with concern.
The scar under one eye was very white against the dusky tan of
his face. He was wearing a long, black leather duster and didn't
look like any doctor Taylor had ever seen before.

"I . . ." She opened her mouth to protest but the man cut her
off.

"Fight it, Taylor. Try not to give in." Strong arms were
scooping her off the street, pulling her away from the damp,
steaming blacktop and close to a broad leather-covered chest.
How did he know her name?

"Hey man—I don't think you're sp'osed to move her," one
of the other pedestrians was protesting.

"Shut up and get the fuck out of my way." He was striding
across the street, carrying her as though she weighed no more
than a kitten.

Taylor saw that traffic was backed up in all directions, horns blaring and people staring at the place where she had been. How long had she been out? Her kissy-lips umbrella was lying forgotten on one side of the street. Where was this man taking her?

"Where . . . ?" She looked at him, the dark face, the white scar, wishing she could be more articulate. But her brain was still fogged from the dream and her body still throbbed with desire. Suddenly she wanted to kiss him—wanted to taste the narrow but sensual mouth she could see when she raised her eyes.

"Someplace safe," he said, sparing her a glance. He had serious eyes the color of steel and a dark fall of blue-black hair partially obscured his high forehead.

"Safe?" She looked around and saw that he was heading for the plaid car. The same one she had seen this morning on her way to work. Its vivid colors seemed to blob and run in the misty air as though it was melting somehow—bleeding itself onto the dirty street. She looked back at the dark man. "You're not a doctor!"

"Quiet." His voice was stern but not angry. "I told you I'm taking you someplace safe. Don't worry, I'll get you back to your proper time unharmed."

"Proper time?" What was he talking about? Taylor felt her eyes go wide and fearful. She wanted to struggle but her limbs still felt loose and disjointed from her fall and the strange dream, or had it been more of a vision?

The weird car got closer and it came to her that he was going to put her in it and drive away. He was abducting her. Something from a long-ago self-defense lecture surfaced in her foggy mind. *Never let a strange man take you anywhere. Once he gets you from point A to point B, you're dead.* The desire she'd been feeling was abruptly extinguished, drenched in cold dread.

"Let me go!" she demanded, beginning to struggle weakly. "Help! I don't want to go with this man! I don't know him!"

Heads were beginning to turn but they were almost to the plaid car. The man, who was carrying her with some difficulty now, suddenly made a motion and the door of the car disappeared. It didn't open outward or slide to the side like a minivan door either. It just simply *disappeared*.

Taylor watched as the door evaporated before her eyes, feeling a scream rise in her throat. What the hell was going on?

"Relax," the man was saying. "I don't want to hurt you." Not, "I'm *not* going to hurt you," but, "I *don't want* to hurt you." Taylor's brain recognized the difference at once. She opened her mouth to let the scream out, pressing against the broad leather clad chest as the man struggled to feed her into the hole in the side of the plaid car.

And then the dream took her again.

4

Reese phased the rest of his vehicle into the fourth dimension, ignoring the startled looks its sudden disappearance caused. The walls around him went opaque as the familiar interior of his ship took form. It was just a few rooms, but for the time being at least, it was home.

In his arms, Taylor Simms went rigid, then limp as another neural fugue overcame her. He laid her carefully on one side of the double blast couch, frowning. The fugues could be dangerous if allowed to go on for too long. He needed her link to the primary clone to find Ycaza and his crew of Multiple Men, but he didn't want her injured in any way.

First things first—he had to prepare for the jump. Time hopping grew more complicated and difficult the further one went either backward or forward in time, and they were about to jump a solid century.

Trying to remain dispassionate, Reese began undressing her. Any kind of objects or implements from a previous time could not be brought into the future. Only living flesh could make the jump forward, although objects from the future could be brought into the past with no ill effects. His own clothing and weaponry were simply going back to their point of origin and would remain intact. But if he let Taylor remain clothed, the fabric she was wearing might melt into her skin or worse, mutate her DNA. He couldn't have that.

When she was naked, he couldn't help himself—he had to take a moment to admire her body. She was a true endomorph, what the people of the early twenty-first century had called full figured. She had large breasts and curving hips—not to mention an ass that a man could really sink his teeth into. Endomorphs were rare to the point of extinction in his time. The human race was on a more even keel now, but the diseases, wars, and famines of the late twenty-first century had killed off all but the hardiest of people, mostly the more muscular mesomorphs like himself.

Reese was used to the flat chests and lean bodies of the women of his time, but Taylor's softly rounded breasts capped with pale pink nipples stirred something in him. It was probably the reason Ycaza had picked her out in the first place. Endomorph clones consistently fetched the highest prices at the illegal auctions which usually went down on the dark side of the moon.

She stirred again and moaned, her long eyelashes fluttering rapidly against her flushed cheeks. Reese frowned as he watched her breathing quicken and her nipples harden. When she moved her legs, he could see that the small patch of blond curls between her legs was damp with her arousal.

No one knew why the neural link between a genetic subject and their primary clone affected the pleasure centers of the brain so radically, but it was dangerous. The body quickly became addicted to the sexual arousal the link engendered, and higher and higher levels of either pleasure or pain were needed to break it and end the fugue states.

Reese fingered the electroshock pen he'd used to break her

free the first time. It delivered a simple, painful charge of controlled electricity, severing the connection between subject and clone. But he was reluctant to use the pen on her again. For one thing he knew how painful it was, having tested it on himself to be sure he wouldn't injure her with it. For another, he didn't want her to associate him with pain. He needed Taylor's cooperation if he was ever going to catch Ycaza. For years now revenge was all he'd had to live for. He couldn't screw it up now—not when he was so damn close . . .

Taylor stirred again, and moaned under her breath. She had to be brought out of the fugue soon—such an extended linking was dangerous. Reese shook his head. Pain or pleasure were the only options, and he had ruled out pain. There was only one thing to do.

Taking off the black duster, he draped it over a chair and climbed onto the blast couch beside her. She was warm and soft against him and her hair smelled like flowers. Reese gathered her close, pressing his face to the side of her neck and breathing her scent in, trying to control his reactions. It had been a long time since he'd been with a woman he really desired—not since Leena, but he didn't want to think about that right now.

He wanted to kiss her soft pink lips, wanted to take that vulnerable mouth with his own and explore her with his tongue—but he knew he couldn't. *Just touch her,* he told himself sternly. *Just do what has to be done—nothing more or less.* This wasn't about stealing a quick grope—it was about breaking her free of the fugue before her link with the clone caused permanent damage.

Her breasts were soft, filling his hands, and her nipples were highly responsive. Reese wanted to suck them but again he restrained himself. She was already in a state of advanced sexual arousal so bringing her to orgasm shouldn't be too difficult. He ran his hand down her body, feeling the soft curves, the skin like silk beneath his calloused fingertips. God, but she was beautiful.

Despite his best efforts, his cock was throbbing angrily in his pants when he finally reached her thighs. He could tell himself that he was only trying to help, but Reese knew there was another reason he'd chosen to use his hands on her instead of the electroshock pen. He wanted to touch her. Had wanted to since the first minute he looked at the 3-D scan of her and knew what he had to do.

Taylor made a little mewling sound in her throat and her eyelids fluttered rapidly as he stroked her inner thighs. She spread her legs responsively, as though begging for his touch, although Reese knew she was probably just reacting to the pleasurable stimulation of the link. Still, as he cupped her damp mound in the palm of his hand, he couldn't help enjoying her heat and moisture. She was so wet . . . so hot . . .

She moaned and pressed up against him as he spread the sweet lips of her pussy. At the center of her pink folds he could see the small, darker pink button of her clit. He had a sudden urge to do more than touch her—he wanted to drop to his knees before her and caress that little bud with his tongue. He wanted to taste her hot, salty-sweet flavor and press his tongue deep inside her velvety depths and feel her coming all over his face. Reese shook his head, reminding himself of what he was doing and why. This wasn't exactly a consensual situation—he needed to do only what was necessary and no more.

He touched her gently, mindful of the way physical sensation was multiplied by the stimulation of the link. Taylor gasped and moved under his hand. Reese gathered her closer with one arm, supporting her head so that she wouldn't knock it too hard against the minimal padding of the blast couch. With the other, he continued to stroke along the side of her clit, enjoying her slippery heat as he built her to the breaking point.

Taylor cried and pressed up against him, her cheeks heated as she whipped her head from side to side. She was close, Reese could see it in her face and feel it in the way her sex pulsed under his fingers. Her small hands fisted at her sides and her thighs spread wider—mutely begging for more.

Reese couldn't help himself. He dipped his head and pressed his mouth against the side of her neck, lapping at the vulnerable flesh there, tasting the sweet sweat of her desire. She was bucking too wildly—he was losing his place. Reaching lower, he penetrated her with two fingers, fucking into her hot depths as she cried aloud.

God! So hot . . . so wet . . . He wished savagely that it was his cock her sweet wet pussy was sucking instead of his fingers. He wasn't sure how much longer he could stand to have her naked and helpless in his arms as she writhed with the pleasure of the link and his added stimulation.

Finally she was coming. With an inarticulate cry, she pressed up against his fingers and he felt her warm wetness contract around him. He drew back to watch her face, enjoying the expression in intense pleasure that moved over her delicate features. He couldn't remember wanting a woman so much. But there was no point in thinking like that, he reminded himself sternly. No point in getting involved in any way. He could only keep her out of her own time for a week without risking a serious rift in the Continuum.

She was letting go completely now, giving him everything as she surrendered to the power of her orgasm. Her breath was coming hard as he pressed his fingers deep inside her, helping her ride out the waves of pleasure. The link must be about to snap—she should be coming out of the fugue at any second, he thought. That was good because it was nearly time to make the jump.

"That's right, baby," he whispered softly under his breath. "Let it go. Come back to me, Taylor."

Suddenly her eyes flew open and she stared at him, breathing hard. "Who . . . what . . . ?"

"Helping you," Reese answered her questions as well as he could. It was an inadequate response at best. He only hoped she would understand when he explained the situation.

"Were . . . were you touching me?" She looked down at their entwined bodies, at his hand which looked so large and tan on the pale skin of her inner thigh. Reese withdrew it hastily.

"Yes," he said shortly.

Her eyes clouded with fear. "Why am I naked? Why were you touching me?" She looked around at the bare metal walls of his ship. "Where am I?"

"Look, I'll—" The chronometer on his wrist beeped suddenly and he realized he didn't have time to explain. "I'll tell you everything after the jump," he promised, releasing her reluctantly and sliding off the blast couch.

"After the what?" She looked like she wanted to run but the aftermath of the fugue had left her weak.

"The jump. Hold on, I'll need to strap you in. We're hopping a whole century." He started to cross the pollychroma fiber bands over her body and was surprised when her large green eyes filled with tears. There wasn't much time but her obvious distress made him stop despite the urgency of the situation. "What?" he said roughly, pausing as he was about to secure the bands.

"Just like the dream. Strapping me in. Holding me down." She shook her head, her blond hair loose on her shoulders like a silk shawl. Suddenly he understood. She had been seeing the events that were happening to her primary clone, just as the clone was no doubt seeing what was happening to her. Ycaza and his Multiple Men must be making the jump forward, too.

"That was no dream—it was a fugue," he told her. "Listen, I'll explain everything as soon as we make the jump." He hesitated for a moment, wanting to wipe the tears from her flushed cheeks. Wanting to touch her again. The insistent beeping of his chronometer saved him from being stupid.

"Please." The look in her eyes was pure terror. It tore at him.

"No time—we're going to miss our window." He finished securing the bands and went to the time hopper he'd had installed specifically for this reason. The counter was zeroed out and the red warning light was on. They had to make the jump *now*. Reese manipulated the controls which were pre-set for his time and jammed an impatient thumb to the activator. Behind him, he heard Taylor struggling against her bonds.

"Hang on," he said. "This is going to be a rough ride."

5

The strange man with the dark face and the white scar under one eye who had abducted her was saying something about a rough ride. Before Taylor could really grasp his words, everything around her turned inside out. She wanted to scream but the sound went down her throat instead of up and out of it. The breath in her lungs felt like it was rushing out of her when she tried to breathe in. When she exhaled, her lungs felt full enough to pop. What was going on?

She tried to look around but her head and the rest of her body was being held in place by some horribly strong force. It reminded her of the one and only time she'd been brave enough to get on one of the centrifugal rides at the fair. It was one of those rides where you stand with your back against the rounded wall and the ride starts spinning and spinning until you're stuck to the wall by the sheer pressure and speed. Then the bottom drops out but you can't fall because the momentum of the ride is holding you in place like a large fist, squeezing and squeezing . . .

"It's all right! It's almost over." The man who had abducted her was shouting over the unbearable pressure that was pressing against her eardrums. Taylor wouldn't have answered him even if she could have. Suddenly, everything around her rainbowed into a blur of light and motion. She opened her mouth and swallowed another scream that should have pierced the air instead of rolling back down her throat. She couldn't stand it. She was going to be sick. She was going to die.

Then, suddenly . . . nothing. The pressure was gone. One moment she felt like she was being squeezed flat by the hand of a sadistic giant and the next she could breath normally again. There was no in between state. The sudden lack of constriction was almost too wonderful to bear. Taylor took in a deep, whooping breath and let it out in a shrill, piercing shriek.

"Whoah—wait a minute. Stop it—*stop* it!" The man was suddenly beside her, a frown on his dark face. He shook his head but Taylor shrieked again. She didn't know where he was holding her but she was damned if she wasn't going to at least try to get some help.

He clamped a hand over her mouth suddenly and Taylor bit him. His steel-colored eyes narrowed as she dug her teeth into the meat of his palm until she tasted blood, but he made no move to get away from the pain. He seemed to be waiting her out. Her jaw began to get tired.

"You finished?" he said at last when she released her grip.

Reluctantly, Taylor nodded.

"Good." He looked at her seriously. "I'm going to take my hand away and I don't want any more screaming. Understand?"

She nodded again but he must have seen the determined look in her eyes.

"The screaming gets on my nerves and hurts my ears," he said. "So I'd prefer you don't do it. Besides, it won't do you a damn bit of good. There's nobody here to hear you."

He took his hand away and Taylor felt her breath whoosh

out in a silent gasp instead of the scream that she'd been planning. Maybe it was the stoic look on his dark face or his flat, uninterested tone, but she believed him when he said that no one could hear her.

He walked away for a moment and then came back, spraying something from a small metal canister on the bite mark she'd made on his hand. He looked up and saw her watching him treat the wound.

"I deserved this," he said, gesturing with the wounded hand which now had an opaque pink latexlike patch on it. "I should have explained everything but there was no time. We were about to miss our window."

Taylor licked her lips nervously and tasted blood. She spat to one side, wishing her hands were free so that she could wipe her mouth. "Window?" she asked.

"For the time jump. I've just taken you from your time of 2006 to my own of 2106." He spread his hands and made a mocking little bow. "Taylor Simms, welcome to the twenty-second century."

Taylor closed her eyes briefly and tried not to panic. Okay, she had been abducted by a crazy guy who thought he was from the future. She supposed the plaid car should have been a major tip off. Then she remembered the way the door of the car had disappeared in front of her—how could she explain that? But she pushed the thought away. Much easier to write this guy off as insane than to start wondering if they had cars with meltaway doors in the twenty-second century.

"Did you hear me?" he asked.

When she opened her eyes he was looking at her. What could she do? *Humor him.* Taylor tried to meet his eyes and sound calm.

"I heard you. You took me on a trip to the next century. That's so . . . nice."

He frowned. "It's not permanent so don't worry that you'll be stuck here. I can only keep you away from your own time for a week without risking a Continuum rift."

Taylor perked up a little at this. Was he saying he would let her go in a week? Then she shivered, remembering that she was naked and that he had been touching her while she was unconscious. She could think of all kinds of horrible things he could do to her in a week. *Stay calm,* she told herself.

"I'm glad to hear that," she said, keeping her voice neutral. "But you know, I'm kind of cold and my arms and legs are going numb from these straps. Do you think you could untie me and give me back my clothes?"

"Your clothes are history—literally." He grinned slightly at his own joke. "But I can unstrap you. The jump is over."

"The . . . jump. Right." She nodded.

He frowned. "Yeah, the jump. Sorry I didn't tell you more about it but there's really no way to explain it unless you've been through it. The further you go, the worse it is." As he spoke, he was loosening the straps around her with quick efficiency.

The minute she was free, Taylor slid off the side of the high, padded platform he'd had her on, eyeing him mistrustfully. She backed away, keeping the platform between them. Now that she could see him standing up, she realized what a large man he was. He was wearing black pants and a black shirt with sleeves that came down to his elbows. His arms bulged with muscles.

"Here." He tossed her the long black leather duster he had been wearing when she first saw him. Taylor jumped back as though he'd thrown a snake at her. Then, realizing it was better than being naked, she bent stiffly, never taking her eyes off him, and picked it up.

"Can't I have my own clothes?" she asked, wrapping the coat around herself. It wasn't really leather, she saw, but some synthetic fabric that she had never seen before. "Please?" she added. She remembered her horrible fat pants with a longing she never dreamed she'd feel for them.

He sighed impatiently. "Look, I told you, your clothes are gone. Nothing from the past can make the jump into the future. Nothing that isn't alive, that is. That's just the way it is. I'll synthesize you some new clothes later—as soon as I get your measurements."

"Okay, fine," she said, thinking that there was no way she was going to get close enough for him to measure anything. She put her arms through the sleeves of the coat which was ridiculously large on her and started to look around the strange, metal lined room they were in. Besides the raised padded platform there were a few chairs, a table, and counter with some weird appliances on it in one corner. In another corner was a control bank that made her think of old *Star Trek* re-runs. Great, the guy was so crazy he had built his own science fiction spaceship set. She was in big trouble here. *Big* trouble.

He was casually peeling away the latexlike pink rubber he had sprayed on his hand after she bit him. Taylor saw with surprise that the wound she had made with her teeth was gone—his skin was already completely healed. How had he done that? She had never heard of any medical product that worked that quickly.

He looked up and saw her eyes darting around the room. "If you're looking for the door, don't bother," he said

Taylor had a sudden inspiration. "Of course I'm looking for the door," she said, trying to smile at him. "You went to all the trouble of taking me into the future, so of course I want to see it. What does Tampa circa 2106 look like?"

"It's a blast zone," he said flatly. "Has been since the Last Great War of 2055. Why do you think I came in a lead-lined ship?" He strode to the control bank and thumbed a button. "Here, see for yourself."

"I . . . I . . ." Taylor searched for words but none came.

Around her, the dull gray metal walls suddenly melted away to nothing. She was standing in the middle of a bleak, gray field filled with rubble. Nothing moved in the field and no birds flew in the sky. The sky was a flat, ashy gray without a single cloud. Or rather, the whole thing was one solid cloud, she realized. A cloud so thick that not a single ray of sunlight could penetrate it. The rubble-strewn ground was frozen solid and rimmed with ice. She couldn't feel the cold but she shivered anyway. Everything here was dead.

"Nuclear winter," he said. "Have you seen enough?"

Mutely, Taylor nodded. Her mind was trying to put the pieces of the puzzle together, but it was showing her a picture she didn't want to see. *The plaid car with the melt-away door . . . the pink skin stuff that heals almost instantly . . . transparent walls that show total devastation . . .* One thought kept pounding in her brain. *My God—it's true. He's telling me the truth.* Mercifully, the walls returned, blocking out the dead gray field. She looked at the man who was now leaning against the padded platform with his arms crossed over his broad chest, staring at her.

She licked her lips. "All right," she said at last. "I . . . I guess I believe you. But . . . but why me? I mean, why did you come to get me?" A suspicion flashed through her brain. "Is there . . . I mean, are we supposed to repopulate the earth? Restore the human species?"

He threw back his head and laughed—a deep and surprisingly pleasant sound even though it was apparently at her expense. "No," he said at last, shaking his head, a slight smile tugging at the corner of his mouth. "No, Taylor, we're not going to repopulate the earth. I came through time to get you because I need your help. You see, I'm with the Lunar Peacekeeping League, Genetic Crimes Unit. You've been cloned."

6

"I've been *what?*" She stared at him in surprise and Reese couldn't help feeling some sympathy. It was, after all, shocking news. The worst form of identity theft.

"Listen," he said, indicating a chair. "Sit down and I'll explain everything."

She wrapped his duster more tightly around her shoulders and lifted her chin defiantly. "I prefer to stand."

Reese shrugged and took a seat at the table himself. "Suit yourself." He decided to start at the beginning. "A quick recap of history," he said. "The Last Great War of '55 pretty much leveled everything on Earth. Only the people on the lunar and Martian colonies survived."

"What?" She shook her head and drifted a little closer to the table.

Reese nodded. "You heard me. There wasn't much left of humanity at that point and the Earth was pretty much ruined. We tried to rebuild but then came the plagues of '86."

"You mean 2086?" She had drifted even closer, her eyes never leaving his face. Reese thought of offering her a seat again but then thought better of it. She would come when she was ready. She didn't trust him enough yet.

He nodded. "Right. It was after the plagues ran their course that the government lifted the ban on cloning. Right around 2020, the entire science had been outlawed—even the research was punishable by life imprisonment. But they were forced to rethink that after the devastation of the plagues of '86. You see, everyone had lost someone."

"You?" She finally sat down at the table across from him. Reese concentrated on not making any sudden moves.

"I lost my parents," he told her. "I was ten at the time."

"I'm sorry," she said at once. Her eyes were dark with sympathy.

Reese shook his head. "Don't be. Like I said, everyone lost someone. So the human race turned to cloning."

"Did they . . . were they able to clone your parents?"

Reese felt his face harden. "No. It took years to revive the research and develop the technology that was illegally used on you. And it was found that only one true-to-life clone could be made—a primary clone. Any other . . . copies were mindless, soulless hunks of meat. Secondary clones." He closed his eyes briefly as thoughts of Leena flashed through his head. Then he made himself continue. "They were . . . worthless to anyone but the Multiple Men."

She frowned. "Multiple Men?"

"A prostitution agency that specializes in secondary clones. They're headed by a bastard named Ycaza. They stole your DNA to make a primary clone. From the primary they'll make as many secondary clones as they can to sell all over the solar system." He noticed she was looking rather green. "Look, would you like something to drink?"

She shook her head. "No, but I could sure use some ice cream right about now."

Reese frowned, combing his memory for the lost early twenty-first century word. "I scream? What's that?"

"Oh, my God." Taylor ran a hand through her tousled blond hair. "Okay, first you've abducted me from my own time and brought me forward a whole century. Fine, I can handle it. Next, you tell me I've been illegally cloned for prostitution purposes. That's all right—I can deal. But now you tell me the future has no ice cream?" She shook her head. "I'm telling you, I'm about to lose it here, Mr. . . . ." She looked at him. "What is your name anyway?"

"Reese," he said. He could see she was trying to make a joke about the 'I scream,' whatever it was, but the information he was giving her was tough to take.

"Mr. Reese—"

"Just Reese," he cut her off.

She looked momentarily confused. "Is that your first or last name?"

"It's my only name," he said shortly. "Look, we don't have much time before we have to get out of here. Let me finish telling you what you need to know. Later on you can play with the nutrient simulator and see if you can get it to make you some I scream. All right?"

"Sure, fine, whatever." She gestured at him. "So I've been cloned."

He nodded, glad to be back on track. "You have."

Taylor shook her head. "But I don't understand. Why me? Why come back in time and pick me to clone? I mean, for genetic diversity or what?"

Reese looked at her for a long moment—she really didn't know. "Taylor," he said, trying to be gentle. "They picked you for your beauty." He leaned forward, caressing a silky strand of blond hair out of her eyes, pleased that she didn't pull back from his touch.

"Sure . . . right," she mumbled, her cheeks coloring.

"I'm serious," Reese told her. "You see, the plagues of '86 pretty much wiped out all the endomorphs and—"

"Endomorphs?"

He described a curving shape in the air between them. "You know, soft, curvy . . ."

"Fat," she said flatly.

Reese shrugged. "Call it what you want. Most of the people in my time are like me." He gestured at himself. "Spare, muscular. All flat planes and angles."

Taylor stared at him, uncomprehending. "But that's what we all want . . . all *wanted* to look like in, uh, in my time. I mean— buns of steel, six pack abs—just look at you. If you've finally achieved it, why bring back what we were all trying to get rid of?"

Reese shrugged. "Because it's human nature to want what you can't have? What you thought was lost forever?" He leaned forward again and cupped her cheek in his palm. She flinched a little but didn't pull away. Her green eyes were filled with doubt. "You're what I want. What *they* want, I mean. The Multiple Men." He suddenly realized he was touching her too much and pulled back. "The fugue states you're experiencing are a result of the neural link you have to your primary clone."

Taylor frowned. "You mean the strange dreams I keep having where I'm somewhere else and I can't move are . . . ?"

"You're seeing through the eyes of your clone. Just as she's seeing through your eyes." He looked at her intently. "We need the information they produce, but these instances of connection—the neural-fugues—are dangerous, Taylor. As long as you're in the same time frame as your clone, they can happen at any time. You have to be brought out of them or risk permanent damage." He cleared his throat, feeling uncomfortable. "That's why I was touching you."

"I'm sorry, *what?*"

Reese sighed. He had known it was going to sound bad. "Once you're deep in a fugue only two things can bring you out of it: extreme pain or extreme pleasure. When I first got to you lying on the street, I used pain." He produced the electroshock pen and showed it to her, pressing the activator to cause a small spark of electricity to jump from its tip.

Taylor recoiled, obviously remembering the pain. "A tazer," she said.

Reese shrugged at the unfamiliar word. "Whatever you want to call it. But I didn't want to keep hurting you—didn't want you to associate me with pain. So the next time you entered a fugue, well, I used pleasure to bring you out. To break the link between you and the clone."

"So you . . . you . . ." She shook her head, cheeks flushed, obviously unable to say it.

"I made you come," Reese said bluntly. "It was that or use this again." He made the pen produce another, larger spark and she jumped. "I'm sorry if you thought I was taking advantage of you."

"I thought . . ." She bit her lip. "I thought you were some crazy guy and that you were going to take me away somewhere and . . . and . . ."

Reese saw the fear in her eyes plainly and once again it tore at his heart. "I want you to understand something, Taylor. I would never willingly hurt you. All right?"

She studied his face for a long moment before nodding. "All right. But let me understand this—when I go into one of those . . . those fugue states, it's almost like having a seizure?"

He nodded, pleased. It was an apt analogy. "One you have to be brought out of if you don't want to fry your brain. Only pain or pleasure can break the link between you and your primary clone and end the 'seizure,' or fugue, as we call it."

"When I first had the dream . . ." she murmured.

"What?" he asked.

"Well," She looked at him, twisting her fingers together. "The first time I had a, uh, fugue, I woke up because I stuck myself in the thigh with a pin by accident."

"You were lucky," he said grimly. "If you hadn't had that pain to break the link . . ." He shook his head.

"But what if . . . what if I get stuck in a fugue again? Are you going to . . . ?"

Reese frowned. "I'll do what's necessary, nothing more. Do you prefer pleasure or pain?" He waved the pen at her and she went pale.

"I've never been much of a masochist," she confessed. "And I'm on the pill. But I don't have any, uh, protection."

"Protection?" He frowned at her, then understood what she was trying to say. "Look, Taylor, you're going to have to trust me on this. I wouldn't make love to you without your permission."

"Make love?" She was still looking at him mistrustfully.

"Would you rather I said 'fuck'?" Reese asked roughly. "That's one word that's survived from your time to mine and I'm sure it still means the same thing. You have my word, Taylor, I'm not going to fuck you if you don't want me to."

She recoiled from him, her green eyes dark, and he regretted his angry words. He didn't want to frighten her but he kept doing it just the same.

"Look," He ran a hand through his hair. "I'm sorry. It's just . . . I'm a man of my word. I'll touch you if I need to, but I won't take advantage of you. You can trust me."

She lifted her chin and looked him straight in the eyes. "You can talk about trust all you want, but I think I'll take my chances with that." She nodded at the electroshock pen he still held in one hand.

"Fine. I won't touch you again unless you ask me to." Reese put the pen away. He was disappointed, of course, but he admired her spirit. To choose pain over pleasure was never an easy decision. He ran a hand through his hair and decided to go on.

"So this is what we're going to do," he said. "We'll use the information you gather through your primary clone's eyes to track Ycaza and his crew. Then we'll get the primary clone and any secondaries we find along the way, and once I've got them taken care of, I'll return you to your own time."

"What will we do with her when we find her? My primary clone?"

Reese shrugged. "Destroy it—humanely, of course."

She put a hand to her chest. "Do we have to? I mean . . . I've never had a sister . . ."

Reese leaned forward. "It's not your sister, Taylor. It's an exact duplicate of you right down to your most intimate memory—to the last hair on your head. The only difference is the duplication mark on its arm. And as long as you remain in the same time frame you'll be subject to the neural fugues because of it."

"It," she muttered. "You keep saying 'it'."

"Because that's all it is. It's not a real person, Taylor—it's an illegal clone. System regulations dictate that cloning is only lawful in the case of wrongful and unnatural death. The same regulations bind me to destroy any illegal clones." He tried to make his voice gentle. "Look, if it makes you feel any better, I'll use a lethal injection. It won't feel a thing."

"Right." She frowned and crossed her arms over her chest as though she was cold. "She won't feel a thing."

"Exactly." Reese leaned forward again. "So, I need you to tell me what you saw during that last fugue."

7

The next few days were some of the strangest Taylor had ever experienced. They were traveling to the Moon, according to Reese, in order to intercept the bad guy who had cloned her in the first place. Reese thought he was probably trying to sell the secondary versions of her for sex at the illegal clone auctions and whore houses. He explained that his ship was capable of traveling in both time and space, but not at the same time. As soon as the mission was complete, he promised he would put her in a more advanced space-time continuum shifter and send her back to the exact moment he had grabbed her. She would have no memory of what had happened to her and her life would go on as usual.

Taylor spent her time trying to get more information out of the close-lipped Reese and trying to get his nutrient simulator to make something resembling ice cream. She had once spent two weeks on the Atkins diet and the stuff that came out of his simulator tasted pretty much like all the low-carb food she'd eaten during that time. It was no wonder, she thought ruefully, digging into a pile of what tasted like a frozen protein shake, that everyone in the future was lean and muscular. Everything they ate was high protein and low carb. There wasn't even so much as a baked potato in sight.

At least the bland protein paste didn't hurt the inside of her cheek, which was still tender for some reason. The other benefit of the boring future diet as she was beginning to think of it, was that she was beginning to lose her Ben and Jerry's weight. If she'd had her dreaded fat pants on hand, Taylor knew she would soon have been swimming in them.

Not that her weight seemed to bother Reese. He spoke bluntly, almost roughly to her most of the time, but Taylor had caught him looking at her several times with what could only be described as a hungry expression on his face. He had given her clothing simulated by one of the machines on his ship, a tight black jumpsuit that was made of the same fabric as his duster, and it showed her every line and curve. She might have been reluctant to wear such a revealing outfit if it wasn't so obvious that Reese liked what he saw whenever he looked at her.

But it wasn't just the way he looked at her—it was the way he touched her during the fugues. Several times in the voyage from the decimated Earth to the Moon, Taylor was overcome by what Reese had called her neural-link. The jolt of pain from the tazer pen he carried was getting harder and harder to bear, but she always woke with his arms around her and several times he had wiped away the tears that leaked from her eyes after an agonizing jolt to her nervous system.

The pain was intense but it was almost worth seeing the look in his dark gray eyes while he held her afterward. That look was making Taylor re-evaluate her choice of the tazer over his hands on her, bringing her to orgasm to end the fugues, but she didn't see how in the world she could broach the subject with him.

Matters came to a head on the third day of their journey when she was trying once again to get the nutrient simulator to make something that didn't resemble freeze-dried cardboard. Reese had just shocked her out a particularly disturbing fugue in which her clone was being molested in ways that Taylor didn't even want to think about, much less experience, even vicariously. In addition to the horrible things she had seen and experienced, the jolt from the tazer pen had been terribly painful. Reese had explained to her that as the fugues continued, they would be harder and harder to break, requiring a greater level of pain or pleasure to bring her back to herself and Taylor understood and accepted his explanation. But that didn't make the fiery jolt of electricity any easier to bear.

"Damn thing," Taylor muttered, working the controls on the blocky silver contraption as another blob of inedible paste came out the sharp spout at its bottom. The way the nutrient simulator worked was you had to hook yourself up to its interface module and imagine the food you wanted it to make. The first few days, Taylor had tried for something like Chunky Monkey or Cherry Garcia; now she thought she'd be satisfied with just plain vanilla. The electrode pasted to her forehead was giving her a rash and she had a throbbing headache from trying to picture the perfect scoop of ice cream in her head. It didn't help that her brains felt scrambled from the electrical shock Reese had been forced to give her to break her out of the last fugue either.

"Creamy," Taylor muttered under her breath, concentrating again. "Smooth, rich, delicious. High butter fat content. Melts in your mouth." She poked the nonmelting lump of supposedly edible material away from the sharp silver spout to make way for her next attempt. "Icy, silky, voluptuous pleasure across your tongue," she whispered, beginning to really get into her ice cream fantasies now. It was going to work this time—she could *feel* it. "Orgasm in your mouth," she murmured, as she pictured that first perfect spoonful of creamy vanilla passing her lips and melting on her tongue. "Little specks of vanilla bean on its satiny white surface. Sweet and perfect and—"

The unromantic *splurt* of the nutrient simulator interrupted her concentration and she looked down to see the worst mess yet. A sloppy glop of black-flecked matter was oozing out of the machine's silver spout, looking more like bird shit than anything ever manufactured by a premium ice cream company.

"No, no, *no!*" Taylor cried. She slapped at the offending mess and hit the serving spout instead. There was a white-hot pain as the sharp metal edge caught her hand and then she was staring down stupidly at the blood that was suddenly filling her palm. *Cut myself,* she thought blurrily. The sharp pain on top of the disappointment and her earlier frying by the tazer was too much. Taylor felt a sob welling up in her throat and couldn't keep it down she began to cry.

"Taylor?" Reese was suddenly by her side, his gray eyes full of anxious concern. "Are you all right?" he asked, cupping her hurt hand in his.

"N . . . n . . . no," Taylor moaned. She wanted to stop bawling but there didn't seem to be any way to turn off the waterworks now that they had started.

"Let's get that treated," Reese said practically, but gently. He led her to the blast couch and tended to the small wound which looked much worse than it was, then sat beside her and put and arm around her shoulders. Taylor leaned against him and just cried. All the fear and pain and frustration of the last three days seemed determined to come out and she just couldn't help herself.

Reese didn't say anything but he held her close and let her know that it was all right. His big frame was so comforting, his hard, warm chest so perfect to lean on, that Taylor found she didn't want to move when the tears had run their course.

"Are you that upset about the I scream?" he asked at last, his deep voice rumbling in the ear she had pressed against his chest.

"No," Taylor said softly. "I just . . ." She held up her hand which now had a coating of the pink wound-healing agent. "It hurts," she said simply. "Not just this, I mean. But . . . when you have to bring me out of a fugue."

"Taylor, I'm so sorry." Reese tilted her chin up so their eyes met and the look on his dark face was genuinely distressed. "You know I don't like hurting you over and over again. But I can't let you stay in the fugue state when your connection to the neural link kicks in. You might fry your brain and it's my job to protect you."

"I know," she whispered, looking down at her hand again. "It's just . . . I'm tired of being tazered all the time, Reese. Couldn't we . . . could we try it, um, the other way, for a while?"

"Taylor," he said softly. "Are you asking me what I think you're asking? Do you want me to touch you instead of using the pen to bring you out of the fugues?"

Taylor bit her lip, shame and need warring within her. She knew the pain of the tazer wasn't the only reason she was asking him to do this. She was beginning to care for the tall, dark man who had kidnapped her from her own time—probably much more than she should. She hated to admit it, even to herself, but she wanted his large, warm hands on her body. Wanted to feel him touching her, caressing her, pleasuring her.

"Yes, Reese," she said at last. "Yes, I . . . I want you to touch me. Touch me and . . . and make me come." She blushed as she said it, and could barely meet his eyes.

"Taylor," he whispered and his voice was rough with emotion. Bending down, he kissed her lightly on the lips.

The gentle touch made her shiver with need and Taylor expected him to take things further. But instead, he drew back, breaking the kiss after a timeless moment. He didn't say anything and neither did she. But the next time she lapsed into a fugue, she woke up in his arms with the slinky black jumpsuit open, baring her breasts and her sex for his large, warm hands. He had touched her gently, spreading her pussy and stroking lightly along the side of her clit until she came, her orgasm severing the link between her and the clone. The aftershocks of her orgasm were intense—as intensely pleasurable as the jolt of the tazer had been painful.

It felt wonderful, but Taylor squeezed her eyes shut in embarrassment. She had barely known him for three days and she was asking him to do this with her—to touch her like this. Reese seemed to sense her feelings because he was quick to refasten the suit he had given her and leave her in privacy to recover. She spent the rest of the day unable to get the memory of those large, warm hands out of her head. Those hands, undressing her, caressing her, invading her body so gently to make her come.

The next time it happened, Taylor felt less self-conscious—more comfortable in his arms for some reason. She let herself meet his eyes and saw the yearning look on his face. Were women scarce in the future or was it only women like her—endomorphs, as Reese had called them? She had to admit that their bodies fit well together. Her soft curves seemed to complement his hard, angular planes.

For whatever reason, she saw a depth of loneliness in the steel-gray eyes that moved her to pity even as his gentle touch moved her to orgasm. He never asked for more or tried to go further despite the throbbing urgency of his cock, which she could feel against her thigh when he held her close.

Taylor wanted to get inside his head—wanted to understand him and the secret pain she saw in his dark, handsome face. She dared to ask him once about the white scar he carried under one eye, but he put her off, saying it was just from an occupational hazard. She was well aware that they had less than a week before he had to return her to her own time and she had just about decided that she would never learn his secret. Then they landed on the Moon.

"What do you mean I can't go with you?" Taylor stood with her hands on her hips, furious at the frowning Reese.

"Just what I said—you can't go with me," he repeated, as though that settled everything. "It's too dangerous, Taylor. The Sea of Tranquility doesn't exactly live up to its name—it's the roughest of the lunar colonies. I can't do my job while I'm trying to watch out for you."

"I'll be fine," she said through gritted teeth. "You won't even know I'm there. Look, my fugue states are what led you here in the first place."

"Speaking of which, what if you have one in the middle of the action?" Reese took a step closer and ran one warm hand down her arm, making her shiver with desire despite herself. "I've already had to help you twice in the last several hours, Taylor. I couldn't drop everything to do that if we were in the middle of a brawl at one of the brothels I'll be searching."

Taylor felt herself flush at the memory of his hands on her body. "It wouldn't be like that," she muttered resentfully. "I can feel them coming on now—I can almost fight them off."

Reese lifted her chin with one finger. "So you're saying you could have fought the last two fugues off on your own but you chose not to?"

It was closer to the truth than she wanted to admit. No one had ever touched her the way Reese did and Taylor had grown to crave it. But she couldn't tell him that. She shook her head and dropped her eyes, unable to meet that steely gaze.

"Fine." Reese's deep voice sounded disappointed somehow. Had he wanted her to admit how much she wanted his touch? "I'm going now," he said. "Don't leave the ship. I'll be back in an hour."

8

Reese strode down the crowded streets of Trank, as the Sea of Tranquility lunar colony was known to its natives. The slight artificial breeze had the familiar stale smell of air that has been breathed by a hundred thousand different people a hundred thousand times before. He had grown up here and he knew every inch of the hundred square kilometers covered by the aging atmosphere dome—every crumbling building and crooked alley. As an orphan of the plagues he'd played in the gutters here and nearly starved to death before a kindly woman who had lost her own son had taken him in. He had lived with Nana Tessa until he was fifteen and old enough to be sent to the Lunar University for early vocational training. Even then he had known he wanted to be a cop.

After graduation, he'd been assigned to the Lunar Peace-keeping Academy, which was where he'd met Leena. She was a sweet girl with large brown eyes and full hips. Reese had fallen for her hard. They had been planning a joining ceremony with Nana Tessa's approval when Leena disappeared.

Reese closed his eyes at the memory of that agony. Leena

was a smart girl who knew how to protect herself but still they had taken her. Ycaza and his Multiple Men. They had taken her and by the time he had found what was left of her . . . He shook his head. No use thinking this way. Not when the end was finally in sight. *Soon, Leena my love. Soon you'll be able to rest in peace.*

Reese opened his eyes to find himself right in front of The Cat's Meow, a low-level whorehouse that specialized in secondary clones. Most men wanted the women they bedded to at least have a semblance of a personality, but not the ones that patronized this place. To walk through the pitted and scarred plasti-steel door of The Cat indicated that you barely cared if the woman you fucked had a pulse. It was the lowest of the low.

Reese frowned as he studied the 3-D holo image of a half naked woman with whiskers and a tail cavorting in front of the door. Taylor had received a very clear image of this image in her last fugue. It was almost as though Ycaza was taunting him—daring him to follow. But then, there was no way that the illegal cloner could know that Reese had picked up his original subject and was following him. It had to be a coincidence—one that worked in Reese's favor.

Sighing, he pushed open the door, hearing the chime that sounded like a purring cat which announced his entrance.

"Yesss?" A woman appeared almost before the chime had faded to silence. She was tall and thin to the point of emaciation and she had been genetically altered to grow long bristly cat whiskers and a bushy tail. The madam, Kitty M.

"How long since Ycaza came through here?" Reese demanded. If he was lucky the son of a bitch might still be on the premises, but he doubted it.

"Don't know what you're talking about, *dahling*," the madam purred gently. "That name means nothing to me."

"Like hell it doesn't." Reese frowned. She was denying things as a matter of course but she was too calm. If Ycaza and his crew were still on the premises she would have been more anxious. He pulled out his badge, flipping it open so she could see the logo on the bottom.

"Lunar Peacekeepers, Genetic Crimes Unit," he told her, in case she missed the point. "Just show me what you bought from him."

The woman groomed her long whiskers angrily. "Look, I don't care who you are, I paid good money for those whores and my license is up to date." The playful purr had left her voice, replaced by a hard-edged, back-streets lunar accent.

"Secondary clones can't be classified as sex workers and you know it, Kitty. They can't even be classified as human because they have no brain function." He flipped the badge closed and pushed it into the inside pocket of his duster. "Now, do you want to show me what you bought or should I go through room by room and give all your secondaries lethal injections?" He pulled out the small silver needler he used for such purposes and set the dosage on lethal.

"Fine." Kitty looked mad enough to spit. "Come with me." She turned and stalked down the narrow, dark hallway, which was lined with flimsy synthi-wood doors. Her tail was swishing angrily, Reese noted.

They had just reached a room at the far end of the hall when the door chime purred again.

"With you in a second," Kitty called over her shoulder. She turned to Reese, one hand tipped with long red nails on the knob. "Make it quick in here, whatever you want to do. I'm just glad I only bought one."

"We'll see about that." Reese stopped her when she would have turned to attend to her new customer. "How long ago did you see him? Did he say where he was going?"

"Why would he tell me where he was going?" she spat. "He comes with a new batch every few weeks and leaves, that's all I know. It never takes longer than a few minutes."

"So he was here how long ago?" he pressed.

Kitty shrugged her rail-thin shoulders. "I don't know. A few hours? Maybe more."

"Fine." Reese shouldered his way past her and into the dank, squalid area that passed for a pleasure room at The Cat. Inside, a man so filthy his skin was gray was pressing a blond girl who looked exactly like Taylor into the dirty padding of the bed platform with rhythmic thrusts. The secondary clone's eyes were open but unseeing, her head lolling to one side as it knocked against the wall with each rough motion. There was a fine shining line of spittle suspended from her bottom lip which seemed not to bother her patron at all.

The rage that washed over him was so intense Reese thought he might be sick. So many memories flashed through his brain, so much hurt and horror at the sight in front of him that it was all he could do not to give the bastard that was riding her a lethal shot in the back. Better yet, he wished he had a blaster, so he could blow a hole in the sick son of a bitch.

Instead, he grabbed the man by one shoulder and pulled him off, throwing him to the floor.

"Hey—what the fuck?" The man looked up, his dick still exposed.

"Show's over, buddy. Move it along," Reese ground out between gritted teeth.

"You sonuvabitch—I paid good money for that and I ain't finished." The man staggered to his feet, tucking himself back inside his filthy jumpsuit with quick, jerky motions.

"Lunar PK, Genetic Crimes Unit," Reese told him flatly. "You're finished now. Got it?" He pointed the deadly bore of the needler at the man who turned suddenly pale beneath his coating of grime.

"Uh, yeah, sure. Whatever you say, officer." He stumbled out of the room, leaving Reese alone with the mindless clone.

He walked over to her slowly. Her limbs were in disarray and the duplication mark—the small purple blood blister no bigger than the moon of his smallest fingernail—was evident on the inside of her left forearm. It was the one obvious physical imperfection that all clones, both primary and secondary, bore, although the mental imperfections of the secondaries were far more glaring in Reese's opinion.

He looked down at the clone. The blond hair he had begun to love was a tangled mess and the sharp green eyes were blank and empty. *Stop it,* he told himself sternly. *This isn't Taylor. No more than the other one was Leena.* Still, what he had to do hurt. Hurt deeply.

He arranged her neatly on the bed platform, closing her legs and folding her arms. He pulled the ragged blanket that was bunched at the foot of the bed up to her chin, covering her nudity, and wiped her mouth gently with the corner. He stroked her hair into place, arranging it around her shoulders and closed the staring green eyes. *So beautiful, so hopeless.*

Reese pinched the bridge of his nose sharply, fighting the burn he felt behind his eyelids. This was part of the job but it never got any easier. If anything it was harder this time because he'd stupidly begun to let himself care for the woman whose genetic material had made this clone.

Forget it, he told himself. *Just finish what you came here for so you can concentrate on finding Ycaza.*

He put the muzzle of the needler against the creamy skin of her neck and pulled the trigger. The clone drew one last ragged breath and then the full breasts stopped rising and falling. She was gone.

It was then that he heard the muted gasp behind him. He whirled to see Taylor—the real Taylor—standing in the doorway with her hand pressed to her mouth, her eyes wide.

"Taylor . . ." Reese took a step toward her.

She shook her head and backed away from him. "So this is why you didn't want me to come with you. This is what you didn't want me to see." Her tone was thick with accusation.

"Look," he said, trying to keep his voice even. "I had to do it. It's just a secondary clone. You don't understand."

"You're right." She was still backing away from him, a look of horror in her beautiful eyes. "I *don't* understand, Reese."

"Taylor," he stared again, but she was gone.

9

She ran for an unknowable length of time down the twisted streets of the city, dodging the sullen people who barely moved to let her past. The grayness of their everyday lives was apparent to her, or had been when she was thinking about it on the way to the whorehouse she'd followed Reese into. Now all she could think of was the muzzle of his strange silver gun pressed to the neck of the girl that looked just like her. The girl that Reese had killed.

How could he? The thought kept beating in her brain as she ran through the crooked streets, feeling the tears push at the back of her eyes. He had spoken of humanely doing away with the clones when he found them, but hearing him say it and watching him do it were two different things. All Taylor knew was that the girl he had killed looked exactly like her—could have *been* her.

She ran until the breath tore in her lungs and she thought she would collapse. No workout at the gym could have prepared her for the blind panic she felt when she saw Reese kill the clone.

At last she reached a dead end at the back of a narrow alley and was forced to stop. She had a stitch in her side and she was beginning to see gray spots in front of her eyes. She felt like she would never be able to catch her breath.

"Taylor."

She turned at the sound of his voice, one hand pressed to her pounding heart and the other held up in front of her to keep him back. He took a step forward and she backed against the wall, shaking her head.

"Don't . . . don't touch me," she panted, trying to get enough air into her lungs to speak. "Don't . . . want you anywhere near me."

His gray eyes held a depth of pain she had never seen before. "Just let me explain."

Taylor shook her head. She seemed to be getting more out of breath rather than less and the gray spots that had been dancing in front of her eyes were turning into large black holes eating into her line of vision. She realized she was going to faint.

He took another step forward. "Try to slow your breathing. There isn't as much oxygen in this atmosphere as you're used to."

"No . . ." She shook her head again but the gesture made her dizzy. She stumbled and would have fallen, but Reese caught her.

"No!" She beat weakly against his broad chest. She was reminded of the way he had picked her up off the street of downtown Tampa and carried her away with him to the future, which seemed like a hundred years ago. Then she almost laughed at her ridiculous thought—it *was* a hundred years ago—literally. Her laugh came out as a sob and then she was weeping against him, the tears coming too thick and fast to stop, the sobs tearing in her throat and shaking her entire body.

"All right, it's all right." His deep voice was soothing as he carried her easily through the streets of the lunar city. Taylor had run with no thought of anything but getting as far away from him as possible and she realized through her tears that she was completely lost. But Reese found his way quickly and without confusion back to the port where his ship was docked, holding her close like a frightened child all the way.

He let them into the ship and laid her down on the blast couch, then went to fix something at the counter. He came back with a glass filled with a brown liquid that smelled strongly medicinal.

"Here." He shoved the glass into her hand and nodded at her. "Drink."

"I don't want it." She tried to give it back to him but he glared at her.

"I said drink it."

"How do I know it's not poison?" she demanded. She regretted her words as soon as they were out of her mouth. Reese's dark face turned so pale that the white scar under his eye almost faded completely.

"Do you really think I would hurt you?" he asked softly, sinking onto the blast couch beside her. "Don't you know that I . . ." He shook his head, unable to continue.

"I don't know what to think anymore," Taylor said. Feeling like a sullen child, she took a small sip from the glass. Surprisingly, the liquid tasted strongly, and not unpleasantly, of vanilla. It burned going down, giving her a warm glow in the pit of her stomach and she had a brief thought that it was too bad she couldn't get the nutrient simulator to make it in frozen form.

Reese sighed and ran a hand through his hair. "I should have explained everything to you from the start," he said in a low voice. "But I thought . . . well, I knew we'd only be together for a week and it's . . . hard to talk about."

"I'm listening." Taylor took another small sip.

"Ten years ago, I was engaged to be joined . . . married I think you call it in your time." He sighed again. "Her name was

Leena and she was beautiful." He looked at Taylor. "You remind me of her a little. Not the way you look—Leena was a brunette, but your spirit, the way you act and talk. I loved her so much . . ." He broke off, shaking his head. "Anyway, she was kidnapped for her DNA."

"Ycaza?" Taylor asked, pronouncing the name she'd heard him speak with such loathing carefully.

Reese nodded. "Yeah. Ycaza and his Multiple Men. They took her but she fought them. After they made the primary clone they killed her. But the primary fought them, too—she was, after all, exactly like Leena and my Leena was a fighter." He looked down at his hands and then back up at her. "I tracked her, of course. I spent months looking for her. But by the time I found her . . ."

"They killed the primary clone, too?" Taylor guessed.

"Long before I found them." Reese bowed his head. "But I didn't know that. I had convinced myself that there was still some hope—if not for Leena then at least for her primary. I managed to catch Ycaza off his guard in an abandoned warehouse where he'd set up shop, but I didn't have any backup. We fought." He gestured to the scar under his eye. "That's how I got this. I asked him what he'd done with Leena and he laughed at me—told me to look next door. I stunned him. I should've killed him but I wasn't thinking straight. I wanted my revenge, wanted to take my time making him pay. So I set my needler to a lower level before I shot him." His face hardened. "At least I shot him where it counts."

"You shot him in the . . ." Taylor made a motion below his belt.

Reese nodded grimly. "Then I ran to find Leena."

"She . . . was she already dead?" Taylor guessed, hesitantly. She sat the glass, which was still half full of the vanilla-flavored liquid, carefully down on the platform beside her.

"Worse." Reese pinched the bridge of his nose between finger and thumb, his eyes closed tightly. He was silent a long moment before continuing. "Next door was a whorehouse—one a lot like The Cat's Meow, the place you followed me to today. The only thing left of my Leena was one secondary clone and she . . . *it* was almost dead."

"I'm so sorr—" Taylor began but he held up a hand to cut her off.

"The madam of the house was using her as 'the special of the day'. Ten credits a ride." His voice was low and choked. "I half killed the man that was with her and I took her home. I knew it was useless but I couldn't leave her there and I couldn't bring myself to kill her. She looked exactly like Leena—just like the one I injected today looked like you, Taylor." He looked up at her, his eyes red.

"I . . ." Taylor shook her head, at a loss for words. She had noticed that Reese had stopped saying 'it' and started saying 'her' and 'she' instead.

"I took her back to my apartment, cleaned her up, tried to get her to eat . . . I thought maybe she could be taught somehow." He shook his head. "Nothing. She was an empty shell. I couldn't get any food into her—she was starving to death. I'd try to feed her and she'd just look at me with Leena's eyes. Just look with no recognition, no comprehension . . . no love."

He pinched the bridge of his nose again and looked up at her. "I finally had to give up. I let her go as gently as I could." He shook his head. "No, I didn't let her go. I killed her. Put a needler to her neck and gave her a lethal injection. The same thing you saw me doing at The Cat." The gray eyes were tormented—filled with guilt. "I had to, Taylor. There was no other way. There's no other way with any of them."

Taylor bit her lip. "I guess . . . I just didn't really understand."

Reese sighed. "I don't blame you for being upset," he said. "It's part of my job but every time I have to do it . . ."

"Then why keep doing it?" Taylor asked gently. She put a hand on his arm, feeling the tension thrumming through his muscular bicep. "Why not find another profession, let it go?"

"Revenge." Reese looked at her again and this time his steely eyes were red with rage instead of grief. "I'll make him pay if it's the last thing I do. Do you know how many innocent girls— girls like Leena—he's taken?" He stood abruptly and began striding around the small metal-lined room. "We cracked down on him and the disappearances stopped, but not the flow of secondary clones. We couldn't figure it out until the Chrono Patrol started seeing some Continuum anomalies. Then we knew. He'd gotten hold of a time hopper and was going back in the past, taking DNA from girls that lived a hundred years ago. He'd make a primary clone and bring her forward to our time to make secondaries to sell."

"But what about the fugues? The link between the girl whose DNA he used and her primary clone?" Taylor asked.

Reese shook his head. "He doesn't give a damn what happens to the original subjects. Although for commercial reasons they sometimes change the DNA sequence a tiny bit when they're done making secondaries and they want to sell the primary. You won't have to worry about that though—by the time I send you back, your primary clone will be terminated."

"But . . . but the primary clone is just like me," Taylor said. "If what you've said is true she can think and feel as much as I do. Why not change her DNA and let her live in this century while . . ." she swallowed. "While I go back to mine?"

Reese sighed wearily and stopped pacing to stand in front of her. "Taylor, I'm not going to fight with you about this. Your primary clone is illegal—it has no rights and it's not even technically a person. It's my job to terminate it as soon as I find Ycaza. And no matter how hard it is, I *always* do my job. Do you understand?"

She nodded, feeling a lump in her throat. "Yes. Yes, I do."

She didn't know how she felt about this aspect of his job, but now that she knew the reason for his pain, she wanted to comfort him somehow. Wanted to take some of the agony from his steely gray eyes.

He was still standing in front of her and since she was seated on the raised blast couch, their eyes were nearly level. Hesitantly, she reached out to touch him. "Reese," she said softly, cupping the side of his face in her hand. She could feel the bristle of his five o'clock shadow against her palm.

"Yes?" He looked at her, the hunger in his eyes unmistakable. Taylor wondered if she was making a mistake, but she couldn't seem to stop herself.

"I just . . . I didn't know. I'm sorry I lost it."

He took a step closer and shook his head. "It's an ugly thing. I don't blame you for being upset. What you need to know is that it isn't easy for me. I don't . . . don't like to do it. Especially when it looks like someone I . . . someone I know," he finished lamely.

"I understand," she said softly. She had been watching him for a long time in The Cat's Meow before she gave herself away by gasping when he killed the secondary clone. She remembered the way he had looked arranging the blond girl on the bed, the tender way he had closed her legs and folded her arms. The gentleness in his large hands as he closed her eyes. *He was thinking of me,* she realized. *Hating what he was doing because the clone looked like me.*

Her eyes locked with his and she couldn't look away from the heat she saw there—the need she saw every time he touched her. "Reese," she said again, but then his mouth was covering hers in a hot, breathless kiss.

Taylor moaned into his mouth and tangled her fingers in his blue-black hair, giving herself to the kiss. Giving herself to Reese. His tongue was demanding entrance to her mouth and she willingly granted it, wanting him with a heated intensity she hadn't known she was capable of. Kissing her ex-fiancé, Miles, had never been like this. It was as though all the emotions she had been holding in check every time Reese touched her had sparked a match somewhere inside her, igniting her soul.

He tasted like some exotic spice she couldn't name and hot, aroused male. She felt his hands on her body, large and warm, exploring her, communicating his need as he cupped her breasts through the tight black jumpsuit, rolling her nipples until she gasped.

Just as she was about to start pulling at his clothes, wanting to feel his skin against hers, Reese tore himself away from the kiss.

"What?" Taylor looked at him with passion clouded eyes, not sure what was happening.

He stood before her, head down, breathing heavily, like a man who had finished a difficult race.

"Reese?" she asked, wondering why he had stopped.

He shook his head. "We . . . Taylor, we can't do this. I'm on assignment here. It isn't right."

"It *is* right," she protested, unable to help herself. "Reese," She looked at him seriously. "I was with my fiancé back in 2006 for two years and I *never* felt anything like what I felt just now with you."

He looked at her, his gray eyes anguished. "I felt it, too, Taylor. And that's exactly why we need to get back to business. Besides it's . . . been a long time for me. I don't know how gentle I could be. Do you understand?"

"I'm not afraid of you," she said, meeting his eyes without hesitation. She reached for him again but he pulled away.

"Well, maybe you should be." His voice was low and rough.

Feeling hurt and bewildered, she sat up and straightened her clothes. To have something to do she picked up the glass of vanilla liquor and took another sip before placing it back on the blast couch beside her. "Fine," she said, trying to sound normal. "So what are we doing then?"

Reese cleared his throat. "We need to start thinking about where we can find Ycaza. We only have a few more days before I have to send you back. So the next time you have a fugue—"

It was almost as though his words triggered it. Before he could even finish his sentence, Taylor felt the familiar tickle at the back of her neck and then she was falling. Her arm knocked over the half full glass of vanilla liquor. It smashed on the metal floor and shattered into pieces with a musical crash. She would have fallen right off the table and gouged herself to ribbons on the shards but once more, Reese caught her.

"Go with it this time, Taylor," she heard him saying urgently. "Don't fight it. I'll bring you back in a few minutes . . ."

"Yes," she tried to say, but then she was gone as the fugue took her.

She could see this time, her eyes weren't blindfolded and her head was turned toward a window. No, not a window, but a port in the side of a ship, she realized. Outside there was the blackness of space and far in the distance she could see a round red speck.

"Mars," a man's voice said in her ear. He wasn't touching her this time but, as always, she could feel the heated desire beginning to flow through her limbs. A side effect of the linking with her clone, Reese had told her. She was almost used to it now, the fear and disorientation of being trapped in another body she couldn't control mixed with the hot need that filled her completely.

"How long till we get there?" another voice asked. Taylor couldn't see either speaker and she wondered which one was Ycaza.

"Not too long. Two days maybe. I talked to the crew on Apollinaris—they're all ready to go," the first voice answered.

"Good." A rough hand gripped her chin suddenly and her

face was turned to look at the man. He was large and muscular like most of the people of the future and he had the lightest blue eyes that Taylor had ever seen—they were almost white.

The man grinned at her, pale bloodless lips parting to reveal a perfect row of gleaming silver teeth that reminded her somehow of a shark. "Did you hear that, my dear? We'll be there before you know it. And then you and I are going to have so much fun . . ."

His laughter chilled her even as the sexual need flowed through her veins.

"Leave me alone!" she tried to shout, but as always, nothing came out. And then the scene was fading before her eyes . . . fading into the bright pleasure of orgasm as her mind switched channels to see . . .

Reese stared down at her, his steel-gray eyes filled with hunger as he stroked her naked body.

"That's right, Taylor," he murmured, when he saw her eyelids flicker and realized she was back with him. "That's right, baby. Give it up—come for me."

"Oh, God! Reese!" Taylor clutched at him, riding the waves of the fierce orgasm he was bringing her to. She gasped as she felt his fingers press deep inside her, fucking into her open pussy as he pushed her to the edge and beyond.

"Taylor . . ." Her name sounded like a prayer on his lips and she couldn't stand it anymore. The heat from her recent linking mixed with the incredible sensations he was subjecting her to made her feel like she couldn't get a deep enough breath. She needed him and there was too much distance between them— too many clothes. She reached up and wound her fingers in his hair, bringing him down for a searing kiss. He came willingly and this time he didn't pull away.

He hadn't just opened the tight black jumpsuit this time, he had taken it off completely. She reveled in the feeling of his hard, still-clothed body pressed against her naked skin. He was so big on top of her, pinning her down, holding her in place while he explored her mouth thoroughly.

They broke the kiss at last, panting. "Please," Taylor whispered, wanting him even though she knew she shouldn't. There was no point in getting involved with a man she'd never see again after this week was up. No point in falling in love. *So I won't fall in love,* she promised herself, knowing already it was a lie. *What does love have to do with what I want now?*

"God, Taylor, I shouldn't do this." Reese's tortured groan in her ear was belied by the way his large hands continued to roam over her body, molding her breasts and pinching her nipples.

"Do it anyway," she gasped, wanting him more that she cared to admit.

"All right." He stood suddenly and grasped her wrists, pinning them above her head so that she was helpless under him. His gray eyes had regained their steely glint. "All right, Taylor, but if we do it, we're going to do it right."

"I . . . don't understand," she panted, feeling like she might explode if he made her wait much longer.

Reese didn't answer her. Instead, he leaned down and sucked one hard nipple into his mouth, rolling it with his tongue until she moaned her submission. After a long moment, he released it and began to kiss and suck a hot trail down her quivering stomach.

"Reese!" Taylor struggled against him but he was still pinning her down, using one large hand to hold both her wrists with ease to one side of her body. "What are you doing?" she gasped as he reached her lower abdomen and showed no signs of stopping.

He looked up at her, his eyes blazing with heat. "I've been wanting to do this from the first moment I saw you." His deep voice was hoarse.

"But . . . I don't . . ." Taylor struggled ineffectually at the hand holding her in place. This wasn't what she'd had in mind at all. She'd wanted to push Reese into taking her—into *fucking* her, to be honest. She didn't want to give in to her emotions and let herself really feel—she just wanted to react to being taken. Fucking was safe but this . . . what he was about to do to her most certainly was not. This was much too intimate. It was something she had never even tried with Miles, and she'd been with him for two years before they broke up.

"Please, Reese. I don't do this," she protested as his mouth moved lower, nuzzling the soft pale fuzz that decorated the top of her slit.

"I don't care if you don't do this—I *do*." He stared at her, holding her eyes with an intensity that made her blush all over. "Now are you going to hold still for me or do I have to strap you down?" He indicated the scratchy fibrous straps he'd used on her the first time when they were making the jump from her time into his. Taylor felt her stomach clench with a mixture of terror and pleasure. Would he really tie her down?

"I . . . I can't—" she began.

"Fine." Reese cut her off. "If you can't promise to hold still, I'll have to use the bands.

"Please, no!" Her begging and promises fell on deaf ears. Reese reached above her and wrapped one of the rough straps around her wrists, binding them over her head to hold her in place. Taylor struggled against the bands but it was no use—she was bound too firmly to wiggle free. She gasped as she felt her arms stretched over her head, holding her in the compromising position with her naked body spread like a feast before him. Her nipples hardened in the chilly air of the ship and she could feel her sex getting slippery with need. She had never felt more helpless or more hot.

"That's better." Reese looked at her approvingly, then stepped back to shed his own clothes so that he was as naked as she was. The dim overhead light cast his muscular torso in shadows, making him seem even larger and more intimidating than usual. Taylor bit her lip at the size of his cock which jutted fully erect from between his thighs. Maybe he was only going to fuck her after all.

The half formed hope was dashed when he stepped back between her legs and began to caress her in long strokes, from her breasts to her inner thighs. Taylor trembled beneath his large warm hands, helpless to stop him. Reese paused for a moment and pinned her with his eyes.

"Are you afraid of me now, Taylor?" he asked softly.

Wordlessly, she nodded. Then realizing he was waiting for a verbal reply she said, "A . . . a little."

"Don't be." His hands resumed their gentle stroking along her body as she tugged uselessly at the strap around her wrists. "I'm not going to hurt you," he told her, his deep voice soothing. "I'm just going to taste you."

"Reese!" His name left her lips as a plea even though she knew it was no use. He had her helpless now and he would do whatever he wanted with her. As if to emphasize that fact, he bent his head and once more began to trail those soft, hot, maddening kisses down her quivering stomach and abdomen. He stopped for a moment to circle her navel with his tongue until he drew a muffled groan from her, then continued down to her inner thighs.

Taylor tried to close her legs but he held them open easily, his large palms warm on her thighs. "I told you if we did this we'd do it right," he said sternly. He stroked her thighs, spreading her open, emphasizing her helplessness to stop him. "Relax," he almost whispered, holding her eyes with his. "Just relax and let me taste you, Taylor."

She bit her lip and stilled under his firm touch and the commanding tone of his voice. His breath was hot against her slit as he kissed her softly, then lapped gently at the place where her right thigh met her body. He took his time, teasing her with his tongue and lips, kissing everywhere but her heated sex as she writhed under his touch. Finally he looked up at her, catching her eyes again.

"Ready?" he asked, his deep voice soft and serious.

Taylor shook her head. "I don't know," she whispered.

"I think you are." With his thumbs, he parted the soft lips of her sex, swollen with desire. Spreading her open, he bared her completely to his gaze. "Look how hot you are, Taylor. How wet," he said. "I can't wait to kiss you here, to taste your sweet wet pussy. I want to put my tongue inside you and suck your clit until you come."

"Oh, God!" His hot words and the way he was keeping her in a state of agonized anticipation were making her feel almost faint with desire. Taylor swore she could feel her heart beating in every part of her body.

"Watch me," Reese commanded, still holding her eyes. "I want you to watch me eat your soft little pussy. I want you to watch me make you come." Then he lowered his head and suited actions to words, sucking the throbbing bud of her clit between his lips and lapping gently along the side until Taylor nearly screamed with the intense sensation. Having his hands on her was nothing compared to this—this was like nothing she had ever felt before. Nothing she could ever explain.

Reese spent a long, slow time, tracing magical patterns around her swollen clit, bringing her close to the brink and then backing her off again and again. Taylor bit her lips, trying not to scream at the intense sensations. He was torturing her so sweetly—as though her pleasure was the only thing he cared about in the world.

Then he pressed lower and she felt his tongue enter her, penetrating her quivering sex as he spread her thighs wide and tasted her thoroughly. He'd been touching her for a while—using his talented fingers to make her come, to bring her out of the dangerous fugue states the link with her clone brought on.

But now Taylor realized how much of himself he'd been hold-ing back—how careful he had been with her before. His fingers on her clit had always been gentle and slow; deliberate and quickly withdrawn when his purpose was accomplished. His mouth was a complete contrast: it was hot and delicious, and utterly relentless as he spread her open and pushed her towards orgasm with his lapping and sucking.

"Oh, God! Reese!" Taylor felt herself falling over the edge, quivering around his invading tongue, losing herself completely in the pleasure he was giving her. At last he raised his head.

"Love to make you come, Taylor." His voice was a low rasp. "You taste so sweet coming for me."

"Reese, please!" She had no shame left. She needed him— needed him filling her, taking her, *fucking* her. He seemed to understand. Rising, he positioned the head of his cock at the slippery entrance of her sex, sliding flesh over flesh, teasing her but never quite fulfilling his threat. Taylor writhed beneath him. He was making her crazy with the delicious friction.

"Let me see," he rumbled, looking down at her as he contin-ued the slow, deliberate stroking without actually penetrating her. "How should I do this, Taylor? How do you want it? Hard and fast or long and slow? You decide."

"I don't care!" Her voice was a breathless sob. "I don't give a damn—just do it!"

"Hard and fast it is," Reese growled, beginning to press in-side her. "Later we'll take our time. I'm gonna want to spend hours fucking your sweet little pussy. But for now . . ." He let his actions finish the thought, ramming into her in one smooth thrust that made Taylor scream.

He didn't take it easy with her—didn't hold anything back. His mouth on her had been soft and giving. His cock inside her was absolutely merciless.

"God!" she gasped as he withdrew and pressed forward again, fucking her relentlessly, filling her to the limit and beyond with the thickness of his shaft as though he would never stop. Was this what he had warned her of when he said she ought to be afraid of him? When he had warned that he couldn't be gentle? Taylor gasped with each thrust, trying to be open enough to take him, to give everything he was demanding of her with each pounding thrust.

She had often wished for passion and spontaneity when she was with Miles, but she had never even dreamed of the scenario she found herself in now. Strapped naked to the bed and spread open for the massive man between her legs to fuck as long and as hard as he wanted . . . He twisted her nipples ruthlessly as he drove into her, his roughness and her own helplessness pushing her closer and closer to another orgasm.

"Godohgodohgod . . ." Someone was moaning aloud and it was her—she couldn't have shut up if she tried. Taylor closed her eyes at the intensity of the pleasure he was forcing from her body but Reese's voice rang like a shot.

"No! Open your eyes, Taylor."

She looked up at him, at the straining muscles of his chest and arms as he pressed inside her, fucking her.

"I want to watch your face and see it in your eyes when you come for me," he growled softly. "I want to watch you come all over my cock."

Once more the hot, dirty words seemed to intensify the effect he was having on her body, pushing her over the edge into the most intense orgasm she had ever had. Taylor sobbed her release as he thrust into her, holding her eyes with his in a moment of fierce intimacy unlike anything she'd ever experienced.

"That's right, baby," he growled softly, watching her come. "That's right, Taylor—let it all go and come for me. God! I can feel you all around me. Love to watch you come."

He thrust deeply into her and Taylor knew he was letting her orgasm trigger his own. He pressed hard inside her, never losing eye contact as he bathed the inside of her sex with his seed, filling her with his cum. Every muscle in his upper body was hard with tension and she could feel his immense strength in his grip. His large hands flexed on her thighs, holding her open, spreading her wide to take as much of him as she could.

Reese held her there for a long, intense moment before finally relaxing and withdrawing from her. "God . . ." Taylor heard him mumble and then he reached up to untie the strap that was holding her hands above her head. He lowered her wrists, massaging the faint red marks the band had made on her flesh. There was an anxious look in his gray eyes and his dark face was lined with worry. "Did I hurt you?"

"I . . ." She shook her head. She was a little sore, but it was a pleasurable kind of ache—the aftermath of being ridden hard and skillfully. "I don't think so." She was still trying to catch her breath. "It was just . . . really intense."

A slight grin quirked at the corner of his mouth. "I'd say that's an understatement." Then the smile faded and he looked grim. "Shouldn't have done it."

"Why not?" Taylor struggled to sit up and he gave her a hand, looking at her intently. Feeling suddenly shy, she wrapped her arms around herself, covering her breasts from his gaze. "Will it . . . I don't know," she shrugged, "Will it mess up the space-time continuum or something science fiction-y like that?"

"No." He frowned but his eyes were sad. "Nothing like that," he said softly. "But we only have three more days together. Then I'll have to let you go."

"Can't you come and visit me once in a while?" She looked at him hopefully but Reese shook his head.

"I'll be returning you to the exact point in time I took you—you'll have no memory of any of this . . . or of me."

"Introduce yourself." Taylor put her hand on the hard muscle of his arm. "*Make* me remember."

He shook his head again. "If I keep coming back to the same spot I could cause major ripples in the fabric of the Continuum.

That kind of thing is strictly regulated by the Chrono Patrol. It wouldn't be allowed."

"Oh." She didn't know what to say, didn't know why she felt a lump in her throat at the thought of leaving him. *The future sucks,* she tried to remind herself. *No Earth to live on, everybody gray and unhappy, crowded into those big dirty atmosphere domes. Not to mention there's not even any ice cream . . .* But somehow all she could see was that the future had Reese, and her past held only pain.

"I'm sorry." His eyes were dark and unhappy. "I should have controlled myself, Taylor. I never should have—"

"Don't be sorry." She tried to smile at him. "So we've only got a few days. Let's make the most of them. Come here." She pulled him down for a long, lingering kiss. Reese kissed her back, his mouth gentle but urgent and she sensed he hadn't gotten nearly enough of what he needed from her yet.

"God . . ." He pulled back at last reluctantly. "I wish I could take you to bed and keep you there but I have to figure out where Ycaza is going next."

"Mars," she said, remembering what she had seen in the last fugue.

"What?" Reese looked at her, plainly startled. "Are you sure? Most of the illegal clone auctions and brothels are in the lunar colonies."

"Positive," Taylor said. She told him what she had seen and he shook his head.

"It doesn't make sense. The Martian colonies are mostly residential. I should know—I live there."

"What?" Taylor frowned at him. "I thought you lived here—in the Sea of Tranquility. I was feeling sorry for you. It seems so, I don't know, gray and hopeless."

Reese nodded. "It is—mostly because it's a mining colony, I think. I did grow up here but after my parents died I was adopted by a woman who had land here as well as an estate on

Mars—Nana Tessa. When she passed on, she left it to me. It's nothing like this—it's clean and bright like most of the more recent colonies. The atmosphere dome is much newer." He shrugged. "Not that I get a chance to stay there very much. Leena and I were going to settle down there but now . . ."

"You spend all your time chasing Ycaza," Taylor finished for him.

Reese nodded. "Yes, I guess so."

"So is the place they mentioned—Apollinaris—anywhere near your home?"

"Not too far—the next dome over." He frowned. "I don't like this—the way you could see out of the window, the specific details of where they were going and how long it would take to get there . . . It feels like a trap. But, damn it!" He brought the flat of his hand down hard on the blast couch, making Taylor jump. "There's no way Ycaza could know that I picked you up to help me track him through your primary clone. It's never been done before—I had to wade through a shitload of bureaucracy to get the permission to do it. There's no way he could know you were watching. And besides, why set himself up to be caught?"

"What can we do?" Taylor asked.

Reese looked grim. The scar under his eye was very bright in his dark face. "Go anyway and be damn sure we have backup to cover our asses. In fact, I'll call ahead and have the Martian PK out in force to surround him as soon as he makes orbit." His face brightened slightly. "There is one good thing though . . . on the trip to Mars we'll have nothing to do but . . ."

"This?" Taylor suggested, pulling him close for another kiss.

"Exactly." He wrapped his arms around her and took a long, leisurely time exploring her mouth. "This."

It was on their last morning together, when they were already in orbit around Mars, that the emotions Taylor had been repressing finally caught up with her. Reese was holding her close on the blast couch, which doubled as a bed, when she lost it.

Their last night had been spent making love gently for hours. He had explored her entire body with his mouth, licking and kissing all her most sensitive and ticklish places, making her gasp and giggle and moan until he drove her to the brink and she begged him to let her come. Maybe it was the long, sweet assault on her senses or the gentle way he was stroking her hair as he held her, but Taylor finally felt herself going into a meltdown.

She tried to hold back the tears, hold back the knowledge that this was their last time together forever, but somehow she just couldn't anymore. It was almost time to get up and get dressed and head down to the planet's surface. There she would be put into the space-time shifter and sent back to her own time forever. Feeling like her world was coming apart, Taylor sobbed.

Reese held her, her face pressed into the hard warm wall of his chest, as she cried out her grief and he sorrow and he had the good sense not to ask her what was wrong. Instead, he stroked her hair gently until her sobs died off into unhappy sniffles and she finally looked up.

"Reese," she said, her voice thick and unhappy. "Isn't there any way? Any way at all?"

His gray eyes had darkened to almost black with sorrow and he shook his head curtly. "Not that I can think of. And believe me, I've been thinking."

"Where . . . what do I do with the rest of my life?" Taylor meant the question to be rhetorical, but Reese answered matter-of-factly.

"I did some time gazing when I was preparing for this case and I think you get back together with your fiancé. Then you get joined on a big boat in the middle of the ocean." He looked pained at the thought.

"What?" Taylor raised herself on one arm and looked down

at him. "I get back with Miles and he takes me on a cruise to get married?"

"A what?" He looked puzzled.

"It's . . . never mind. I just can't believe he'd have the nerve to take me on a cruise after he broke off our engagement and took the last cruise with my best friend without me. And I can't believe I'd be dumb enough to go back to him after he ran out on me with that red-headed bimbo." She closed her eyes briefly. Miles's defection had been bad enough—she hadn't even allowed herself to think about the loss of Susan, her best friend since middle school.

Reese frowned. "You say your best friend—"

"*Ex*-best friend."

"All right, ex-best friend, has red hair?"

Taylor nodded. "So?" she asked, seeing the look on his face.

"It's just that . . . well, I seem to remember that a red-haired woman is your honor attendant."

"What?" Taylor yelled. "Not only am I stupid enough to take Miles back but I let Susan attend my wedding too? And as my maid of honor? I don't think so!"

Reese shook his head. "I'm only telling you what I saw when I looked to make sure taking you wouldn't cause a rift in the Continuum."

"Can I look?" Taylor sat up eagerly.

He shrugged. "I'm sorry but I don't have a time gazer here—just the rudimentary time hopper. Strictly no-frills."

Taylor sagged, disappointed. "I just can't believe I'd go back to him. After all the things he said to me when the clinic called and said my pregnancy test was negative."

Rees frowned. "You went to a public laboratory and gave bodily fluids?"

She shrugged. "It's the only way to be sure. I mean those little home pregnancy tests where you pee on a stick are just not . . . Why? Is it important?"

"Not now, but it's probably how Ycaza got your DNA in the first place. I'd say that you should remember not to do it in the future except that—"

"I know, I won't remember anything," Taylor finished for him dully. "It's just—"

She was interrupted by a dull buzzing that indicated a call on the com-link. The first time she'd seen the 3-D hologram of a disembodied head floating in the middle of the ship's control area, she's screamed. Now she took it as a matter of course when Reese had a call.

He sighed. "I'd better get that. It's probably my backup." He slid off the blast couch reluctantly and pulled on a pair of black pants as the com-link buzzed again.

Taylor made sure she was covered from the neck down and tried to make herself inconspicuous. From what Reese had told her about his job, he had a remarkable amount of leeway, but she was pretty sure his coworkers or supervisors would think the relationship between them was inappropriate.

She was wondering if sex in the workplace was as big a deal in 2106 as it was in 2006 when Reese pressed the button to accept the call and a large 3-D head appeared in the middle of the ship's control area.

Taylor put a hand to her mouth as the head's features became clear. Spiked blond hair and pale blue wintry eyes stared back at her. Bloodless lips parted to reveal shiny silver teeth that reminded her of a shark.

It was the man from her fugues.

10

"Ycaza," Reese barked, moving instinctively to put himself between the holo's line of view and Taylor. "What do you want?"

His enemy grinned, showing that hateful grille of silver teeth. "Why simply to say hello, old friend. And to issue an invitation."

"I don't need an invitation to bust you, Ycaza." Reese felt the rage pounding in his head. "And this time I'll set my needler to lethal. What you did to Leena carries an automatic death sentence and I'll be more than happy to act as your judge and jury."

Ycaza shook his blond head sorrowfully. "Such aggression, Reese. I can't believe you still hold that ancient history against me. Speaking of which, how is your own personal little piece of history working out?" He nodded at the space behind Reese, clearly indicating Taylor. "I wondered if they would give you permission to bring her along. To track me, as it were."

Reese felt a nasty jolt of surprise but he tried not to let anything show. How had Ycaza figured out that he was using Taylor's fugues to track him through the clone? "How did you—?" he began, but Ycaza cut him off.

"Think about it, Reese. How else would the Martian Peace-keepers be alerted to my presence before I even made orbit? But I have my own piece of history right here." The holo winked out to be replaced by a scene instead of Ycaza's face. Reese realized that he must have drawn back to give the com-link a larger field of view to work with.

Lying with its arms bound behind it on a blast couch was Taylor's primary clone, a look of terror in the large green eyes. That look twisted Reese's heart even though he knew the clone wasn't technically a person. Though he was duty bound to de-stroy it, it still had the same fears and joys and pains as the woman behind him—the woman he had come to love—and he didn't want to see it hurt or mistreated. But why was Ycaza showing him this?

"What the hell do you want, Ycaza?" he growled, when the familiar hateful blond head appeared again.

"To strike a bargain," Ycaza said flatly. "As I said, I found a little welcoming party when I reached my base of operations here on Mars. The Martian PK have demanded I surrender and I, in turn, have demanded that you should be the moderator in this awkward situation I find myself in."

"Me?" Reese frowned at the floating head mistrustfully. "Why the hell do you want me there?"

"We started this journey together." Ycaza grinned at him, al-most leering now. "Your sweet Leena was the first subject I ever cloned. She made well over a million credits for me, did you know that, Reese?"

"You son of a bitch!" Reese wished fiercely that the bastard was actually there instead of just a holo. He wanted to beat Ycaza to a bloody pulp.

"And we should end it together, too," the blond head finished. "You, Reese, have been my most worthy adversary. I want you by my side at the end as you were at the beginning." The head disappeared suddenly, and the bound clone became visible once more. "Come and I'll surrender without a fight. If you don't, I'll kill her," Ycaza's voice announced. "And I know you don't want anyone killing illegals but you, Reese. Besides, I won't be nearly as humane as you would be." The head reappeared. "Oh, and bring your pretty little piece of history too," he said, nodding again at Taylor. "I want her to meet her double face to face before you do away with her."

The head blinked into oblivion before Reese could reply. The transmission was over.

"I'm going with you." The look in Taylor's green eyes was mutinous, and this time Reese sensed he wouldn't be able to overrule her. Even if he did, she'd just ignore him as she had before and leave the ship without him. He loved her independence but sometimes it was inconvenient.

"Taylor," he began helplessly but she shook her head. She slid off the blast couch and came to face him.

"No arguments, Reese. This concerns me, too—after all, it's *my* DNA that bastard stole in the first place. I have a right to confront him." She lifted her chin defiantly. "Besides, didn't you say we'd have backup?"

"We'll be surrounded by half the planet's PK League," Reese said dryly. "But that's not the point. The point is . . ." He shook his head, then forced himself to go on. "The point is that I'll have to terminate the primary clone." He brushed a strand of hair out of her eyes tenderly. "I don't want you to see that, Taylor. Sometimes they beg for their lives and it's . . ." He sighed. "I just don't want that to be the last memory you have of me before you go back."

"It won't be." She caught the hand that was stroking her hair and placed a soft kiss in his palm. "Please, Reese, it can't be any worse than what I saw at The Cat's Meow. I just . . . I want to spend every minute I can with you before you have to send me back. Please?"

He looked at the pleading green eyes and knew he couldn't refuse her. "All right," he said grimly. "But you may be sorry you asked."

"Thank you." She pulled him down for a kiss. Reese buried his hands in her hair, trying to lose himself in the sweet taste of her. He had a feeling that he was going to regret not sending her back to her own time immediately, but he just couldn't bear to let her go one second before he had to.

11

The Martian atmosphere domes were, as Reese had explained, newer and brighter. Taylor found herself admiring the scenery as they walked through the space port and out into the city of Apollinaris. Everywhere she looked there were potted plants and growing things, contrasting vividly with the rust-red Martian soil. The space port was full but not crowded and the people around her looked happier and moved with more purpose than the people on the lunar colony she'd seen so briefly. Maybe the future wasn't so bad after all, she thought. Not that she'd be around to see much more of it.

They took a sleek silver monorail to the large city's convention center where Ycaza was supposed to surrender himself and the primary clone. They had word from the Martian Peacekeepers that he was holding a blaster to the clone's head and was refusing to speak to anyone until Reese appeared. Since Reese was the only one who could legally terminate the clone, it was an effective threat.

Taylor still didn't know how she would feel about seeing him kill the primary clone, no matter how humanely he did it.

She knew it was part of his job and Reese had explained at length about the cloning laws that were in effect for the lunar and Martian colonies.

She also knew that if the clone wasn't terminated, she would go on having the debilitating neural-fugues forever—unless one of them was willing to change their DNA to break the link, that was. Since gene therapy was still in its infancy back in her time of 2006, there was no way she could manage that herself. She could imagine what her life would be like if the fugues continued—it would be like living with an untreatable, uncontrollable form of epilepsy. But no matter what she told herself, it still seemed like a heartless thing to do.

Taylor tongued the tiny sore spot on the inside of her cheek thoughtfully as they stepped out of the monorail in front of the convention center. As soon as she got home, she'd have to see a doctor about it. It was small but annoying and if she'd had to eat anything but the bland 'future' food that was excreted by Reese's nutrient simulator, it would have been bothering her a lot more.

The Apollinaris convention center was a large round building surrounded by curving steps. It was surrounded by men and women in rust-red uniforms with shiny silver badges that projected holographic displays of their names and ranks. They held sleek, impressive looking weapons that Reese assured her were blasters—much messier than the small silver needler he always carried.

At the top of the long set of curving stairs, they were met by a man wearing a red uniform of the Martian PK. He was wearing a gold badge instead of a silver one. *Captain Jorge P'tresson,* declared the spooling holo-letters displayed above it. The captain gave Reese an elaborate two handed salute which Reese returned. Then, to Taylor's surprise, the two men embraced.

"Reese—damn good to see you." The captain's voice was a

clear, pleasant tenor that fell easily on the ears. He had brown hair and dark eyes.

"Good to see you, too, Jorge." Reese released him and looked the other man in the eye. "Where is he?"

"Holed up in the conference room at the end of the first hallway with two of his men. We've got guards stationed all around it but he swears he'll kill the clone if any of us come in without you. Since that's your department, I decided it might be best to go along with him until you showed. I don't even want to *think* about the red tape involved if anyone but you does the termination."

"All right." Reese made a face. "I'm going in and so is she," he nodded at Taylor. "I want you with me, too, Jorge, but no one else. We know how slippery Ycaza can be. If he thinks he smells a rat . . ."

"Right." The captain nodded solemnly, then turned to Taylor. "I assume this is the original subject of the primary Ycaza is holding?"

"Oh, I'm sorry." Reese shook his head at his thoughtlessness. "Jorge, meet Taylor Simms." He turned to put a protective arm around Taylor and she was glad to see he wasn't all business, even at a time like this. "She *is* the subject and she's been helping me track Ycaza from the first." He squeezed her gently. "She, uh, has to be sent back as soon as we're finished with this business. I'm assuming your space-time shifter is in working order?"

"Tip-top shape," the captain nodded and smiled at her. "We'll have you home in no time, Ms. Simms. And you have our undying gratitude for helping to track and capture the most notorious cloner our solar system has ever known."

"She has a lot more than that," Reese muttered, squeezing her again before letting go reluctantly. Taylor felt tears sting her eyes and she turned her head, looking away from him for a moment.

The captain seemed to sense that something was wrong between them because he paused awkwardly for a moment before saying anything else. "Well," he said at last. "I think we'd better get in there."

"Of course." Reese gave a quick, jerky nod and they walked together into the cool interior of the convention center.

The glossy rust-red Martian marble floors and arching ceiling couldn't keep Taylor's attention as they made their way to the room where Ycaza and her clone were waiting. More and more she was beginning to feel that she didn't want to be here. That she didn't know how she could stand to see Reese do what he had to do. Seeing him kill the mindless secondary clone was one thing. But to watch him terminate the primary who was an exact replica of Taylor herself, right down to the last little memory . . . no, it was going to be bad. Really bad.

But before she could opt out of the situation, she found herself on the other side of a thick synthetic wood door staring down a long glass-topped table at the face of the man she had only seen in her fugues.

Ycaza was flanked on either side by two of his Multiple Men, large, brutish looking guards with muscle-bound arms crossed over their chests. He was holding the primary clone, who looked just like Taylor, in the crook of one arm. The muzzle of a large black blaster was pressed casually into her right temple and her green eyes—Taylor's eyes—were dull with fear and pain.

Taylor felt a lump rise in her throat at the pain in her clone's eyes. She could almost feel the thick choking arm around her own throat and she raised her hand to her neck in mute sympathy. Then Reese stepped in front of her, putting himself between her and Ycaza with muttered instructions for her to stay back.

"All right, Ycaza," he said, when they were all facing each

other across the glass-topped table. "I'm here to take you in myself, for what it's worth."

"Oh, I assure you, it's worth a great deal to me, Reese." Ycaza grinned lazily, showing his double row of metal teeth. "More than you can imagine. And, as per our deal, I am willing to surrender without a fight, but *only* to you."

"Fine." Reese fingered the snub-nosed needler he was holding that Taylor knew was set at its maximum dosage. "But one wrong move and you're dead, Ycaza." He motioned curtly with his weapon. "Put the blaster down, come around the table and assume the position."

"Not so fast," Ycaza said sharply. His pale blue eyes narrowed as he looked between Reese and Taylor. "First there is the little matter of terminating the primary clone. I want to see it."

"You want to watch?" Reese shook his head. "You're a sick bastard, you know that?"

"It's a small request to make when you consider that I'm giving myself up with no trouble," Ycaza said mildly. "You know you're duty bound to do it anyway as Captain Jorge P'tresson here is duty bound to witness it."

Reese's dark face hardened until it looked like a block of granite and the scar under his eye looked very white. Taylor could see him struggling with himself and she suddenly understood how much he hated this part of his job.

"Fine," he said, jerking his head at Ycaza. "Let her go and send her around the table."

"Oh, no, I don't think so." Ycaza's grin widened and his grip on Taylor's double tightened. "You see, what I have here is the original subject. *You*, my dear Reese, are in possession of the primary clone."

Taylor saw every eye in the room turn in her direction and she felt suddenly, horribly naked.

"You're lying," Reese said flatly. "I took her from 2006, not far from her domicile."

"You took her from where I left her," Ycaza corrected softly. "The real Taylor Simms was out on a large boat celebrating her joining to one Miles Hearn when I snatched her. Her clone had already been in place for a week. I used a minor memory adjustment and she thought she had been left at the alter, as it were, by the man who was already joined to the real Taylor Simms."

"*No.*" Taylor put a hand to her mouth.

"Oh, yes, my dear." Ycaza grinned at her with malicious good humor. "You must forgive me the abject misery my little memory implant caused you but I'm afraid it was necessary to keep you ignorant of what your double, the real Taylor Simms, was doing."

For the first time, the girl across the table who looked exactly like her spoke. "He took me on my honeymoon. Stole me right out of the bed in the stateroom Miles and I were sharing." She had Taylor's voice and her mouth trembled just the way Taylor's did when she was trying not to cry.

"Oh my God." Taylor felt like she couldn't get a deep enough breath. She remembered the first fugue she'd ever had—the one she'd thought was a crazy dream on the morning of the day Reese had gotten her. Hadn't she been dreaming of wearing the panties Miles had bought her for special occasions? A honeymoon would certainly count as a special occasion, she thought. And the pattern of water and moonlight that had been reflected on the ceiling was exactly like what you might see on a cruise, out on the ocean. Beside her, Reese, who had seemed almost frozen, suddenly came to life.

"You're lying," he said harshly, gripping Taylor's arm and turning it over to pull up the black sleeve of her jump suit. His grip on her hurt as he showed the underside of her forearm. "She has no duplication mark."

"Oh, doesn't she?" Ycaza laughed. "We've been working on that for a while, you know. That ugly little mark—it's such a giveaway. And while it cannot be entirely eliminated, we've found that it can be hidden quite neatly in a place where no one would think to look." He nodded at Taylor. "Check the inside of her cheek, my friend."

Once more, all eyes focused on her. Taylor put a hand to her face, feeling cold all over. Reese had explained to her that the duplication mark was a part of the cloning process that couldn't be hidden or faked. That only true clones had one. But she couldn't have one, could she? Inside her cheek?

She explored the cheek Ycaza had pointed at with her tongue, finding the small sore spot she had there. She'd had it for two weeks now, ever since Miles had broken off their engagement. But then, apparently, he'd changed his mind and taken her on the cruise after all, with Susan, her best friend, as a surprise addition for their wedding at sea.

Or at least, Taylor acknowledged with a sinking heart, he'd taken the *real* Taylor Simms. While *she* had lain in bed eating gourmet ice cream thinking she had a broken heart, when in actuality she'd only been in existence for a week. She was vaguely aware that Ycaza was rolling up the other girl's sleeves to show that she had no duplication mark on either arm. Did that mean he was telling the truth?

Oh, God, it was all so confusing. How could she not be herself? How could she be the clone while the other girl across the table from her was real? *But I'm real,* Taylor argued with herself. *As real as she is. I have thoughts, dreams, memories, emotions. . . .* As she was thinking this, Captain Jorge P'tresson was suddenly in front of her.

"I'm sorry, ma'am," he said formally. "I'm sure Ycaza is lying but it's my duty to verify your identity."

"No!" Reese thrust himself between the captain and Taylor. "No, he had to be lying. There's no need to look."

"There *is* a need, Reese. I'm sorry." The captain's pleasant tenor was quiet but firm and Taylor knew he wouldn't be denied. She could try to make a break for it but every man in the room was heavily armed and Reese might get caught in the cross fire. No, if she was the clone and the other girl was real, there was nothing to do but admit it, she decided numbly.

"It's all right, Reese" she heard herself saying. She stepped forward and opened her mouth, feeling like she was about to have a dental exam that could mean life or death. The captain and Reese both peered at the inside of her cheek for a moment before backing away.

"I'm sorry, Reese," she heard the captain say in a low voice. "But you saw it and so did I. I don't know how the bastard did it, but he's managed to get the mark on the inside of the cheek instead of the inside of the arm. The girl he has is real and this one is the clone."

The clone. I'm a clone, Taylor thought. Ycaza's voice from the other side of the table broke into her thoughts.

"Do it, Reese. It is your duty to terminate the primary clone. I want to see you do your duty." He grinned maliciously.

"What?" Taylor raised her head, staring across the table at the hateful metal grin. Surely he couldn't mean . . . The numbness that had clouded her emotions began to melt and her heart began to pound. Surely Reese wouldn't kill her—would he?

"As much as I hate to admit it, Ycaza is right." Captain Jorge P'tresson's voice was sympathetic but firm. "I'm sorry, Reese."

"No." Reese stood in front of her. "No, I won't do it."

"If you don't, then I'll kill the real one." Ycaza's voice was flat and humorless. Taylor could see that he was shoving the muzzle of his blaster hard against the real Taylor's head. "I'll blow her head off right here in front of all these witnesses. How will you explain that, Reese?" He laughed harshly.

Reese looked at her and then across the table to Ycaza.

"Why?" His deep voice was rough with emotion. "You planned this well in advance. Why?"

"Why?" Ycaza laughed again. "Maybe because it's so much fun to torment you, Reese. Or maybe, just maybe, it's because I, too, have a little souvenir from our last encounter." He gestured at the white scar under Reese's eye. "My sonic blade cut your face. But where you shot me . . ." He frowned. "Do you know what the long-term effects of a direct blast from a needler at close range are, Reese, my friend?"

Taylor put a hand to her mouth again, understanding. Reese had said he shot Ycaza 'where it counts.' "You're impotent?" she asked aloud, before she thought about it.

Ycaza scowled. "Well, well, the little clone has more brains than the rest of you put together. Too bad she's scheduled for termination. Yes, I am impotent. I can have any beautiful woman in the solar system—in *history*, for that matter, but I'm unable to do a damn thing with them. I decided I would rather die than live the way I am now. Oh, yes," he nodded, "I know they'll execute me for my crimes against humanity. But first, I intend to have my revenge." He shoved the muzzle of his blaster against the real Taylor's temple until she cried out. A thin trickle of blood was running down her cheek. "Do it now, Reese," he said. "You shoot her or I will, as soon as I kill the real one."

"Reese." Captain P'tresson stepped forward, shaking his head. "We can't let him kill the original subject. You'll be scheduled for execution yourself if you let it happen. Gross negligence, fiduciary misconduct . . ."

"I can't." Reese's steely gray eyes were dark with agony as he turned to Taylor. "I can't lose her, not like this."

"If you can't then I will." The captain's pleasant face was grim. "I'm sorry, Reese—you and I go all the way back to the academy but I can't let you flush both our lives over a clone." He pulled out his shining silver blaster and aimed it straight at

Taylor's head. As if in a dream, Taylor stared down the bore of the weapon which looked as wide as a subway tunnel. She wondered if it would hurt very much to have her head blown off. She thought she might faint.

"No!" Reese stepped between her and the captain's blaster. "No, Jorge. If it has to be done I . . . I'd rather do it myself."

"All right." The captain withdrew but didn't put away his blaster, Taylor noticed. He must have seen the desperate look in Reese's eyes and he wasn't taking any chances.

Reese stepped forward and caressed her cheek with one hand. His large palm was warm and rough against her tear-stained face. Taylor realized she was crying.

"Please, Reese," she whispered. "Please, I . . . I don't feel like a clone. I have memories . . . emotions. . . ."

"They all do, Taylor." Reese's voice was hoarse but steady and he was fingering the snub-nosed needler restlessly. Taylor remembered what he'd said when he tried to keep her from coming with him: *sometimes they beg for their lives.* She raised her chin defiantly. There was no way out of this situation and she refused to beg. Still, she had to let him know how she felt.

"Reese," she said softly, keeping her eyes locked on his, shutting out everything else in the room. "I haven't known you long but, well, I guess it sounds silly to say it, but this week has been the best time of my life. You made me feel things I never thought I'd feel. I . . . I guess I love you."

"Taylor . . ." He broke off, shaking his head. His steel gray eyes were dark with pain.

"Let me finish," she said. She reached up to cup his cheek, feeling the rough scratch of his whiskers and the warmth of his skin against her palm for the last time. "Reese," she continued. "I know it's your job and I don't really have any rights, but I want you to know something. I'd rather be dead than go back to 2006 and marry Miles and never see you again. I don't want to live the rest of my life without you. So just . . . go ahead and do it."

Reese leaned down and kissed her softly, taking her mouth for the last time. Taylor gave in to the kiss, offering herself as passionately as she had the first time he kissed her. When he drew back at last, Reese's gray eyes were suspiciously bright.

"I love you too," he whispered. Then she felt the chilly silver muzzle of his needler against the side of her neck. "Close your eyes, baby." Reese's voice was rough with emotion. "I don't want you to see this."

There was a sharp moment of shooting pain in the side of her neck and then everything went black.

Taylor opened her eyes to darkness and the sound of a deep, worried voice.

"Come on, Taylor, come back to me," someone was saying. It was exactly the way Reese had spoken to her whenever he was helping her to escape one of the fugues. She blinked her eyes, confused. Had she been having another moment of linking with her clone? She couldn't remember any of the details. But wait . . . memories came rushing back to her. She couldn't be linked with her clone because she, Taylor, *was* the clone. She was the clone and Reese had to kill her.

She tried to sit upright in a moment of blind panic, only to find that someone was holding her down.

"Shh, it's all right. Everything's going to be all right now." The deep voice was gentle and suddenly a dim light flared, brightening the room so that she could see.

"Reese?" she asked, still feeling disoriented. He was bending over her, a look of worry in his steel-gray eyes. "Reese, where am I?"

"We're back on board my ship, heading for Io, one of Jupiter's moons."

"But how . . . ?" She shook her head. "I thought you were supposed to kill me."

"I was." His eyes darkened. "But I couldn't. I've always hated that part of the job. I've even appealed it in several cases but I always lost. Clones have no rights in our system—even primary clones."

Taylor rubbed the side of her neck which still stung. "So what did you do?"

He looked grim. "There were too many witnesses. I had to give you a near-lethal dose to make it appear that you'd really died. I . . . I wasn't sure you'd be able to come back to me."

"I'm here now." Taylor grimaced. "But I ache all over."

"Being nearly killed will do that to you." Reese's deep voice was light but suddenly he crushed her to him, his hold on her almost smothering. "God, Taylor, I thought I'd lost you . . ."

"But you didn't," she said softly. "Please, Reese, I can hardly breathe."

"Sorry." He loosened his grip but pulled her into his lap to keep her close. Taylor rested her throbbing head against his shoulder.

"What about the other Taylor? The real one, I mean," she asked at last.

"Gone back in the Shifter to 2006," Reese answered.

"Poor girl—back to Miles." Taylor sighed contentedly. Then something occurred to her. "But, Reese, what about the fugues? Unless one of us has a DNA change—"

"I already thought of that." He reached to get something from the other side of the bed platform and then held it up to her face. Taylor realized it was a small holo-mirror that showed her face from all angles.

"What?" she began and then looked more closely.

"I hope you don't mind having blue eyes." Reese sounded apologetic. "It was the smallest change the gene therapy center could make that would effectively break the link."

"Mind? No, I . . . I guess not." Taylor looked at the blond girl in the mirror. She looked familiar except for her startlingly beautiful sapphire eyes. She looked up at Reese. "Couldn't you have gotten them to make me skinny instead, though? I mean, speeded up my metabolism or something?"

"Don't want you skinny." He nuzzled his face into her hair, kissing her gently. "I want you just the way you are."

"Mmmm." Despite her aches and pains, Taylor felt her body responding to his touch as always. "But, Reese, where will we go? I mean, I'm illegal, right?"

"On the lunar and Martian colonies, yes. But the new colonies on the Jovian moons are desperate for people and that's where we're headed. No one will ask any questions—you'll be safe."

"But . . . but what about your job?" Taylor frowned until Reese kissed her lightly on the nose, making her giggle.

"My job is done. Ycaza and his Multiple Men are in jail and scheduled for execution. That was all I ever really cared about." He kissed her again.

"So you quit your job and we're relocating to a new planet . . ." It made Taylor's head spin. "What will we do now?"

"Do?" Reese shrugged. "I don't know. Live together. Love each other. Plan a joining ceremony." He kissed her again. "Who knows, maybe we can even re-invent the formula for that 'I scream' you're always talking about."

She pulled him down for a long, slow, kiss. "Reese, at this point I don't care if I ever see another pint of Ben and Jerry's ever again. I have everything I need right here."

Wildmen and Wormholes

1

"For heaven's sake, Milton, if you don't want to come then just stay home." Ariel Stone-Tarrington jerked the shift-release lever on her space hopper into neutral to give her reluctant fiancé one last chance to abandon ship. His whining was already getting on her nerves and they hadn't even left her family's private space port yet.

"No, no, if you're going of course I don't want to stay here." Every bit of Milton's body language from his hunched shoulders to his obvious reluctance to strap himself in said otherwise. Staring at him in exasperation, Ariel couldn't help thinking that he reminded her one of the Tergals from Petra Six.

Tergals were scrawny little rodentlike mammals that were the main food source for Zors, the large, six-legged carnivorous predators that shared their planet. As a result, the Tergals spent their entire lives scampering for shelter and diving into the holes that pocked the sides of Petra Six's volcanic mountains. Female Tergals were actually born pregnant—a good thing since they had no time for mating—no time for anything but hiding in holes and twitching their whiskers in terror.

With his wispy mustache and watery eyes, Milton looked exactly like a Tergal. And he seemed to have the courage of one of those timid creatures as well. She sighed and pushed a thick sheaf of pinkish blond hair behind one ear as she worked the hopper's gears. The pink in her hair wasn't a fashion statement or the latest trend in mop-tops; it was the remains of an anti-glare coating Ariel had treated her tresses with for her last expedition to Zairn, a desert planet where the atmosphere got murderously hot because of its three suns.

On Zairn, she had been studying the natives of the deep desert, the Amon-kai, because of their shape-shifting abilities. Her research had made a fascinating paper which had been published in *Alien Anthropology Today*, the leading periodical for xenological anthropologists of which Ariel was a card-carrying member.

Since interstellar travel was prohibitively expensive, it was a field only the very wealthy could enter. In fact, most of the major universities in the galaxy wouldn't even accept a student into their xeno-anthro programs unless the student's net worth exceeded ten billion credits. Ariel didn't have to worry about that, though—her family fortune far exceeded the requirements and her academic excellence ensured that she had studied with only the best.

Anthropology was her true love and Milton didn't even run a close second, she thought, staring with distaste at her fumble-fingered fiancé as he attempted to buckle himself in. Still, she had to marry *someone* or the vast Stone-Tarrington fortune her father kept dangling over her head would sit in the trust fund forever. And without funding, her expeditions to foreign planets would be impossible.

"Are you sure you want to come with me?" Ariel asked him, as the hopper entered pre-liftoff mode. "Tordanji Prime is no place to go if you're not absolutely certain you want to be there. It's a jungle planet—that means large, carnivorous predators, poisonous plant life and possibly hostile natives. And it's remote and unsettled—there isn't going to be any nice air-conditioned hotel room to hole up in if you don't like it once we get there."

Milton's narrow face had taken on a distinctly greenish hue but he finished strapping his harness together with a decisive snap. "If you're going, I'm going," he said, crossing his skinny arms over his chest. "But I still think this could wait, Ariel. After all, we only have a month before the wedding. Most girls would be spending this time making sure the seating chart was perfect and the caterers had everything in hand. You know—last minute arrangements."

"Well, Milton, I am not most girls." Ariel gave him a withering look and revved the engine. She flipped the hover lever and the hopper began liftoff. "And besides, worrying about all that last minute crap is the wedding planner's job—that's what my father's paying him that ridiculous amount of credit for, isn't it?"

Milton's thin mouth twisted into a petulant frown. "Look, if you want to neglect your responsibilities to jaunt off to some uncharted wilderness planet right before we get married, we'll go. I just wish we didn't have to go through a wormhole to get there."

"Where's your sense of adventure, Milton?" Ariel tried to make her voice light although she felt like gritting her teeth and growling the words. "After all, what's the worst that could happen?"

"We could go a millimeter off course and be sucked *into* rather than *through* the wormhole and die instantly," Milton said darkly. "Or once we get to Tordanji Prime we could be eaten by the animals, poisoned by the plants, savagely dismembered by the natives . . ." He counted them off on his fingers. "After all, isn't that what happened to the last anthropologists that went to Tordanji?"

"Nobody knows what happened to Professor Trafalgar and

his wife," Ariel snapped. "But that was over twenty-five years ago."

"And you think conditions will have gotten *better* by now?" Milton raised a skinny, sarcastic eyebrow.

"Milton, *darling*," Ariel said with forced cheer. "I've been on over a hundred expeditions and lived to tell about them. We'll probably survive but if you don't want to go, just say so. I'll be happy to turn the hopper around and leave you at home." She tried not to sound too hopeful but it didn't matter because Milton was clueless when it came to reading her emotions.

He sighed hugely and gave her a long-suffering look. "No, sweetheart, if I don't go, who will protect you?"

Who would *protect* her? She'd been on some of the most dangerous uncharted worlds in the galaxy and always managed to protect herself just fine. Ariel bit her tongue hard. The last thing she needed was an argument, even though it irritated her to no end that her fiancé had insisted on accompanying her on her last expedition as a free woman. Milton hated to travel but he had some ridiculous notion that they ought to 'bond' before they began their life together which was, of course, complete and utter crap. Ariel hadn't picked him because she wanted to 'bond' with him, she'd picked him because of all the suitors her father had approved, he seemed like he would be the least trouble.

It sounded cold to pick a husband for such purely practical reasons but it wasn't that she had a heart of stone, she told herself as she piloted the hopper into deep space. And it wasn't like Milton wasn't getting anything out of it—her dowry would be a substantial sum, her father had made certain of that to attract the "right sort of man." It was just that she had never met a man she loved as much as her work.

Oh, she'd had a few flings on her expeditions—usually with explorer types that were good for a one night stand and not much else. One of those might have done for a husband, she mused as the stars streaked past her viewscreen in fiery arcs and Milton fidgeted uncomfortably beside her. At least she would have had more in common with such a man. But none of them would have gotten her father's approval because they all lacked something that her fiancé had in spades—the right family background and breeding.

Milton, for all his faults, had an impeccable pedigree. He came from one of the best families in the galaxy and had the weak chin, slender build, and whiny temperament to prove it. For generations, the four and forty families, the crème de la crème of the galaxy, had been intermarrying, so Milton was most likely her sixth cousin twice removed or something like that, not that Ariel cared. She herself was something of a throwback because her grandmother Stone on her father's side had refused to marry within the families. Instead, her feisty grandma had gone and picked herself what she affectionately called a wildman. Her husband had come from an asteroid mining crew, infusing the Stone-Tarrington family tree with common blood which showed in Ariel's high cheekbones and curvy figure.

It was from her spunky grandma that Ariel had inherited her very improper taste for adventure and she would have been happy never to marry at all. But her father, Lord Stone-Tarrington, had laid down the law. He had always been scandalized by his own roughneck father and free-spirited mother and was determined that Ariel should marry a man more suited to her station—one with bloodlines to overcome the social stigma he himself had always carried. Perhaps, Ariel thought sourly, her children would have the washed-out coloring and insipid temperament that denoted a true blue blood of the four and forty families and her father would at last be satisfied.

Ariel shifted her attention to the controls—they were rapidly approaching the Telgar Three Wormhole and it wouldn't do to get herself killed just because she was irritated about her upcoming nuptials. As she navigated toward the treacherous center of the inverted black hole, she consoled herself with the thought of what awaited her on Tordanji Prime.

The mysterious natives that lived on the planet supposedly weren't even humanoid. And they were said to be touch telepaths—able to read each other's thoughts through physical contact, so they had never developed a spoken or written language. Ariel wasn't sure how she was going to communicate with them because her universal translator wouldn't work without words to translate, but she was eager to find out. Also, her expedition would make one hell of a paper—even better than the one on the shape-shifters of Zairn. Of course, a month wasn't much time in which to do a study, but she could at least make a start. And after the shortest honeymoon on record, she'd come back and finish what she started, even if it took a year.

"Darling, are you *sure* you know what you're doing?" Milton's whining, nasal tone interrupted her pleasant fantasies. He was gripping the armrests so hard his knuckles were white and his thin lips were pinched in fear. Outside the viewscreen, the galaxy had begun to run and stretch like rainbow-colored taffy as the little hopper entered the distortion of the wormhole's immense gravitational field. Then the space time continuum caught them and pulled them along as smoothly as a boat on a river with a fast current. At this point, one wrong twitch of the controls would send them hurtling into the abyss where the ship would be torn apart like wet paper and Milton obviously knew it.

Ariel had to bite her tongue again. She had gotten her pilot's license at fifteen and she'd flown through the wormhole dozens of times but there was no point in reminding Milton of that. For a minute she considered pretending that she *didn't* know what she was doing and that they were going to die—but a look at Milton's pinched face convinced her that it would be too mean a trick to play, even on her irritating fiancé. After all, knowing his timid temperament, he had probably never traveled through a wormhole before, an experience that could be a little frightening the first time you did it.

"We're fine, Milton," she assured him, nodding at the weird corridor of multicolored taffy where time and space stretched and compressed simultaneously. "See, we're right on target—directly in the center of the hole."

"We are *not* fine." Milton's squeaky voice held a fine edge of panic and his watery eyes were as big as dinner plates. "We're going to die!" he yelled as the distortion on the viewscreen got more intense.

"We're *not* going to die." This time Ariel couldn't keep the irritation out of her voice. "Just relax—I know what I'm doing. Look, we're almost through." She motioned to the viewscreen where the end of the twisting corridor was in plain sight. Normal black space dotted with pinprick stars was clearly on the horizon. They would leave the wormhole's sphere of influence in less than a minute. She adjusted the controls to compensate for their immense speed; Tordanji Prime was a straight shot from the end of the hole and she didn't want to overshoot it.

"What are you doing?" Milton nearly screamed as she made the adjustments. "You're going to kill us!" In one motion he unstrapped his harness and leaned over to grab the steering lever.

"Milton, no!" Ariel tried to push him away but she hadn't counted on his panicky strength. Grabbing the lever, he jammed it to one side, skewing the space hopper's course.

The sensation of traveling on a smooth fast current ceased at once to be replaced by an ominous vibration that made her teeth chatter in her head. If they had been in the heart of the wormhole's tunnel, they would have been very dead very fast, but they were almost at the end of it.

"Milton, l-let g-go!" she shouted, fighting for control of the lever. If she could just get them back to center before they drifted too far . . . But she was too late. The leading edge of the hopper clipped the side of the hole, sending them into a deadly spiral Ariel couldn't pull out of despite her years of experience. The ship's engines whined as they attempted to compensate for the crazy course and from somewhere in the control panel Ariel caught a hot whiff of burning as the navigational system breathed its last. The ship was shaking so wildly that everything in the entire cockpit was jouncing up and down.

"L . . . look out!" Milton screamed, pointing at the viewscreen with an arm that wavered wildly due to the vibrations.

Ariel looked up from her desperate fight with the unresponsive controls. The last thing she saw was the huge purple curve of Tordanji Prime growing with suicidal speed in the viewscreen. Then blackness.

2

"Oh, Goddess, my head." Ariel rubbed the part in question. There was a lump the size of an egg forming behind her left ear but at least her hand didn't come away bloody when she looked at it. She looked at the disabled space hopper and sighed. At the last minute the gravity failsafe had kicked in. They had experienced a bumpy landing—very bumpy in her case, as she rubbed her head again—but at least they had gotten to Tordanji Prime's surface in one piece.

Neither she nor Milton had any broken bones and the ship and all the equipment was intact if somewhat battered. Ariel thought they had gotten off lucky. Of course, with the navigational system fried, the ship was nonfunctional but she had already activated the emergency beacon. It would take the signal a while to reach her home planet but they could probably expect a rescue party sent by her father in a few weeks. They would still get back just in time for the wedding, she thought sourly. Not that she was anxious to tie the knot with Captain Commando. What an idiot Milton was, grabbing the controls like that!

The hopper had skidded to a landing in a small clearing in the deep jungle and Ariel was carefully observing the alien life all around her. Everywhere she looked, she saw dense purplish vegetation crowded with brilliant turquoise and red flowers. The colors should have clashed horribly but somehow here on Tordanji Prime, they complemented each other. Far off in the jungle, she could hear muted squeaking and chattering and a kind of long, low whistling sound that might be the native fauna.

Despite her headache and the crash landing, Ariel felt the familiar thrill of being on a brand new, unspoiled world as she always did at the start of an expedition. She took a deep breath of the steamy jungle air, inhaling the wild, mossy, growing scent, drawing this new world into her lungs. She couldn't wait to get started!

"Well, this is just *great.*" Milton, who had also exited the space hopper for a look around, interrupted her attempt to commune with Tordanji nature. He skulked around the side of the ship and kicked a patch of lavender weeds which promptly tried to eat his foot. He pulled back quickly, his watery eyes wide with mistrust.

"I wouldn't do that again if I were you, Milton," Ariel said dryly, feeling her soaring spirits fall with a plop into her practical hiking boots. So much for adventure and high expectations. "I know you haven't spent much time on other planets," she told him, "but it's best to approach everything on an unknown world with caution."

"Caution, hell." Reaching behind his back, Milton pulled out the sonic stunner he'd had tucked into the back of his pants. "If I see anything weird so much as twitch..." He waved the stunner in a wide arc, swaggering toward her. "Let's just say it won't have a chance to twitch twice."

"Put that down," she said sharply. "Or at least have the good sense not to point it in my direction."

"Good sense? You want to talk about sense? How about having some yourself?" Milton crossed his arms over his skinny chest. "*You're* the reason we're in this mess in the first place!"

"Excuse me?" Ariel stared at him blankly. He couldn't really be blaming the wreck on her, could he? "The *reason* we're in this mess is because you grabbed the steering lever and nearly flipped us into the heart of the wormhole," she reminded him. "The only reason we're still alive is that we were almost out of it when you started acting like an idiot."

"You were steering us wrong," Milton said stubbornly. "If I hadn't taken over when I did, we'd be dead right now."

"As opposed to just *wishing* we were dead, which is how I'm beginning to feel," Ariel ground out. There was no point in trying to explain anything to her thickheaded fiancé. Milton would continue to willfully misunderstand her and she would only get a bigger headache than she already had. She suppressed a sigh. What in the world had made her think Milton would be the least troublesome of all her suitors? Well, lesson learned. She was never taking him on another expedition. In the meantime, it was time to get things underway on this one.

"Help me unload the supplies," she told Milton, heading for the dented hopper. "We need to set up camp. I want to gather some preliminary readings and data before it gets dark."

Milton gave her an incredulous look. "You can't mean you're actually going to go ahead with this nonsense—not after everything we've been through?"

Ariel clenched her jaw to keep from screaming. "This *nonsense* is my life's work," she said, trying to keep her voice steady. "And we won't be rescued for another couple of weeks at least, so what else am I supposed to do? Sit around with my thumb up my—"

"All right, already." Milton held up a hand to stop her. "Fine, I'll help you set up c . . ." His voice trailed off into a weak whisper and his pale, no-color eyes suddenly got very wide.

"Milton, what is it?" Ariel asked sharply. He looked like he was having some kind of attack and they were light years from any kind of medical facilities.

"Y . . . Y . . ." He was staring at something over her left shoulder and backing slowly toward the ship. Ariel became aware that there was a low hissing, growling sound coming from the jungle, which was directly behind her. The sensitive hairs at the back of her neck stood on end as Milton continued to make goggle eyes at whatever was making the noise.

The hissing growl was growing louder and Ariel's heart was beating triple time in her chest. She never let herself get in this kind of situation! If only she hadn't let Milton distract her. Slowly, taking care not to make any sudden moves, she turned to face what was stalking her.

A dark green creature covered in scales and nearly as big as her space hopper was creeping up behind her. The noise was coming from its opened mouth where rows and rows of foot-long, saber-length fangs formed perfect circles all the way back to its purple gullet. Its yellow compound eyes glared malevolently, clearly waiting for her to make a move.

Ariel caught her breath. Whatever she did, she must not panic. She knew if she bolted for cover, the huge creature would be on her instantly. There was a coiled tension in its segmented body that told her it was eager to lunge. If only she had some kind of weapon. Wait a minute—Milton had a stunner!

"*Milton,*" she hissed, not daring to move. "*Milton, the stunner! I'll drop to the ground and you stun it—okay?*" She dared to turn her head and look behind her but her useless fiancé was still just standing there, the stunner hanging forgotten at his side. If she hadn't been in mortal danger, Ariel would have rolled her eyes.

"*Milton,*" she whispered again, not wanting to startle the menacing creature into an attack. Milton's no-color eyes rolled toward her at last but she wasn't sure he was really seeing her. "*Ready?*" she hissed, "*On the count of three. One . . . two . . .*"

The Tordanji predator pounced. It seemed to happen in slow motion to Ariel. She could see its weirdly jointed body coil for the attack and then it seemed to roll forward almost as though it was a billow of smoke rather than an animal. Despite the sudden clarity of her vision, it moved with a horrible speed that was unavoidable.

Ariel threw herself to one side and waited for the echoing cough of the stunner—but it never came. Instead, the beast was suddenly on top of her in a mountain of thick, heavy flesh that felt vaguely reptilian to her seeking fingertips. It opened its mouth even wider and Ariel found herself staring down the rows of glistening fangs. Its breath blasted over her like a furnace with a sickening sweet reek like carrion left in the sun to rot and she nearly retched.

"Milton! Milton—stun it! Stun it *now!*" she shouted, but still there was no response. The monster bent its head and bit. Its teeth caught in the front of her practical naird-hide shirt and ripped through the tough fabric like cobwebs, exposing her breasts. Ariel tried to roll out from under it but it was too damn heavy—she was securely pinned to the ground.

"For Goddess's sake, Milton—stun it!" she nearly shrieked. Again there was no shot, no sound but the growling hiss of the monster and her own frantic heartbeat thrumming in her ears. Milton was probably standing rooted to the spot and watching with his mouth hanging open—if he hadn't already locked himself safely in the hopper.

The huge head lowered again and this time she knew it would bite her in half. She was going to die. Going to die because she'd gone against her better judgment and brought a

Goddess-damned idiot along with her instead of leaving him home looking over the wedding cake and the seating chart where he belonged.

Ariel dug her fingers in under the creature's multi-hinged jaw and tried to push it back and away from her but it was like trying to push a huge boulder uphill. She had no leverage and the monster had plenty. Its weight was crushing the breath out of her but at least it looked like it had changed its mind about biting her in half. Instead, it appeared to be aiming to bite off her head.

Gonna die! Ariel thought wildly. She'd been in messes before, but it didn't look like she was going to get out of this one. Her one consolation was that she wouldn't have to marry that idiot, Milton, after all. But just as the foot-long fangs, slimy with reeking saliva, were inches from her face, a tan blur knocked into the side of the beast and toppled it off her.

Ariel rolled on her side, gasping and retching. From the corner of her eye she could see that Milton was still standing slack-jawed, gaping at the monster. The monster who was currently being wrestled into submission by a . . . a naked man? Arial blinked and shook her head. Surely that couldn't be right. She'd bumped her head again when she hit the ground and she was seeing things. Wasn't she? Tordanji Prime was completely un-inhabited by humans so it was impossible that a large, naked, muscular man was wrestling with the predator that had pinned her to the ground and nearly bitten off her head.

Impossible or not, the naked stranger seemed to be winning. He had thick, light brown hair streaked gold by the sun and the muscles in his broad back bunched and flexed as he struggled with the beast. From somewhere he produced a shard of metal and stabbed at the yellow compound eye closest to him. The green scaly creature howled and jerked in agony as the shard punctured the amber globe. But strangely, the naked stranger didn't shout or scream in triumph—he fought in total silence, all his concentration focused on the roiling mass of flesh beneath him.

"Oh, Goddess—look out!" Ariel screamed to her savior. The monster had been thrown to its side by his initial attack but now it managed to right itself with a convulsive effort of its segmented body. As she watched, its long tail swept in behind the naked man for a killing blow. But even though there was no way he could have seen the tail, the muscular stranger leapt straight into the air just as the tail swished toward him and the monster slapped itself in the face instead of its intended victim. It was a vicious blow and the spiked tail landed right on the remaining compound eye, blinding that one as well.

This seemed to be as much as the segmented beast could stand. With a low, hissing howl, it turned and blundered with horrible speed into the jungle, breaking vegetation and flattening bushes with its scaly bulk as it went.

The man she had already begun thinking of as her naked rescuer let the monster go and turned back to Ariel who was still lying on the ground. He came toward her, an expression of concern on his face that centered in his greenish blue eyes. But still he said nothing.

It was then that Ariel saw the motion out of the corner of her eye. Milton had finally unfrozen and he was pointing the stunner directly at the man who had just saved her life.

"Milton, *no!*" Ariel yelled. "Are you crazy? He saved us—you can't shoot him!"

But Milton seemed intent on doing just that. He was still aiming the stunner at the naked rescuer who was staring down its muzzle in uncomprehending puzzlement. Ariel wondered wildly why he didn't move. Why would he just stand there and let Milton the idiot point a stunner at him? The stranger took a step forward and she saw Milton's finger tighten on the firing mechanism. Ariel couldn't believe it. Her asinine fiancé was *actually* going to shoot him.

Without thinking about it, she scrambled to her feet and threw herself between Milton and the stranger. "Milton, I said put that d—" A coughing roar interrupted her and suddenly it felt as though a large rough hand had whacked her in the chest. Ariel felt the tingling numbness of the sonic blast that started at the point of contact and rushed through her body.

The huge invisible hand pushed her backward and something or someone caught her. She felt strong arms wrap around her waist and she was hoisted high in the air over someone's shoulder. Milton was shouting about putting her down and she was staring at the clump of lavender colored weeds that had tried to eat his foot earlier.

Then the full effect of the sonic blast reached her brain and everything went black.

3

Ariel swam back to consciousness slowly. She was having the most interesting dream, all about a man with shaggy golden brown hair and greenish blue eyes. He had his hand on her chest as though he was feeling her heartbeat and he was asking her all kinds of questions. She was doing her best to answer him but some of the things he wanted to know didn't make any sense. He wanted to know why she talked with her mouth instead of her mind. And why did she wear such strange coverings over her skin—what did she call them? Clothes? He himself was naked and seemed to have trouble with the concept of hiding his skin with unnecessary coverings. He also wanted to know why she looked so different—why her body was different from his when it was obvious they were the same species.

She tried to explain that she was from a different planet so she didn't understand everything he was asking, but the man just got more and more confused. Still, his hand on her chest felt warm and good. He was curious about her breasts and she let him touch them, cupping their full curves in his hands and stroking her nipples until they hardened under his touch and she had to bite back a gasp of pleasure. She wondered if he knew what he was doing to her, but he seemed completely ignorant of the way he was making her feel just by touching her with his warm, rough, calloused hand.

Ariel opened her eyes to a dimly lit space that was blurred and out of focus at first to her stunned brain. There was a warm stroking sensation across her bare breasts which reminded her of the strangely erotic dream she'd been having moments before. Then a pair of curious, greenish blue eyes came into view and she realized the naked man from her dream was leaning over her, watching her intently. A moment later, she looked down and realized that the warm pleasurable sensation across her breasts was his hand—he was really touching her and it was no dream. For a moment she was mesmerized by the sight of his tan hand cupping and stroking the pale silky skin of her breasts. Then order returned to her mind and with it, fear.

Oh, Goddess! She was half naked and being fondled by a strange man. *Rape!* She thought with a sudden surge of panic. *He's going to rape me!* Then her paralysis broke. She had to get away from here! Away from this strange man!

"Ahh!" Ariel sat up so suddenly that her head spun and for a moment she saw three of everything. The man who had been touching her—she recognized him as both the man from her dream and the man who had saved her from the Tordanji predator—jumped back from her, a look of confusion on his face.

She took stock of her surroundings rapidly. She was in what looked like some kind of a vehicle, a space hopper very much like her own, but it had clearly been years since this ship had flown anywhere. Patches of rust decorated the walls of the ship and the luminescent glows that marched in parallel lines along the floor and ceiling panels flickered weakly as though they were at the end of their life span. The pilot's and passenger's couches had been removed to make a small but snug living space and their cushions had been used in the construction of a makeshift bed, on which she was currently lying. Large mats woven of purple reeds covered the floor and a blanket made of the hide of some animal was pulled up to her waist.

Ariel dared to lift the blanket and saw to her relief that while she was bare from the waist up, her naird-hide trousers and hiking boots were still intact. She pulled the scratchy animal-hide blanket up to her chin to hide her bare breasts and looked across the room to where the naked man was crouching in a defensive posture, watching warily for another outburst. Now that she had calmed down somewhat, Ariel thought that he didn't look like a rapist at all—more like a curious boy who had been caught with his hand in the cookie jar. Although she didn't know any little boys that were six-feet-three, naked and extremely muscular.

"Hey," she said, attempting to make her voice soothing. "I'm sorry I screamed but you scared me. Who are you, anyway? And how did you get to Tordanji Prime?"

The naked man frowned, a look of incomprehension on his tanned face. So maybe he didn't speak standard dialect. Ariel repeated her question in several of the more common languages around the galaxy, including Esperanto, but still the man looked confused.

"What language do you speak?" Ariel asked him, beginning to feel frustrated. "You must be from somewhere. This makes it obvious you're not from here." She gestured at the space ship that had been turned into a living quarters. "So where are you from?" She didn't really expect any kind of an answer—the man was still looking at her with a frown of concentration, like someone trying very hard to understand. But then he surprised her by touching two fingers to his chest and speaking a single word.

"Kor," he said, indicating himself again. His voice was a deep, rusty rumble and he pronounced the single syllable hesitantly. It was almost as though he had never spoken before, or, hadn't spoken for years and was trying to relearn how.

Ariel was delighted—now they were getting somewhere! She placed to fingers over her own heart as he had done and said, "Ariel." The man shook his head, a look of frustrated confusion on his face again. Ariel beckoned for him to come closer. Though he was so huge and obviously powerful, she found she had no fear of this strange savage, her naked savior.

Hesitantly the man approached her and Ariel was careful to make her motions small and nonthreatening. When he was crouched only two feet away from her, she tapped her chest again lightly and said, "A . . . ri . . . el," very slowly.

"Aaaariall," he repeated, drawing out the vowel sounds and clipping the consonants. Again Ariel got the impression of someone just learning to speak. She reached out to him and tapped his broad, bare chest lightly with two fingertips.

"Kor," she said, repeating what he had told her. He looked delighted and nodded at her. Up close, she couldn't help noticing that his big green-blue eyes were startlingly beautiful and fringed with the longest lashes she had ever seen. The eyes softened his face, which had much stronger features than she was used to, and made him look thoughtful instead of frightening. His eyes weren't the only thing drawing her attention, however. It was hard to ignore his nakedness when he was within touching distance but she tried to keep her gaze focused on the top half of his body instead of allowing herself to look lower.

The only mark on his smooth tan skin was a necklace of tattoos that circled the broad column of his neck. They were thumb-sized ovals of turquoise blue that were connected by silvery lines marching all around his throat. Ariel thought they were the most beautiful and intricate native tattoos she had ever seen. Then Kor grabbed her hand and entwined their fingers and all thoughts of his nakedness or his tattoos were wiped from her mind.

I am Kor. I have lived here in the place of Those Who Share for as long as I have known myself. Who are you and what place do you come from? Are you like me? One of my kind?

The deep melodious voice flooding through her brain was a shock. Ariel yanked her hand away in fright and it stopped at once. Then, seeing the hurt look on Kor's face, she put a hand to her racing heart and shook her head.

"I'm sorry. I just . . . I'm not used to that kind of thing," she said. She had traveled through the galaxy on many anthropological expeditions and had seen the native peoples of many planets. Some of them had even claimed to be able to communicate telepathically. But until now, she had never actually seen any evidence of truth telepathic ability, let alone had it applied to herself.

Kor was still staring at her in incomprehension and she realized he couldn't understand her if they weren't touching. Hesitantly, she lifted her hand to his and let him entwine their fingers once more.

I did not mean to frighten you, the deep voice said, filling her head once more. *This is the way Those Who Share have always spoken—mind to mind. We do not make mouth noises.*

Those Who Share? Ariel asked him, concentrating on pushing her thoughts through the thought connection she felt with him while their fingers were touching.

Kor looked pleased that she had managed to communicate. *Those who raised me when those who bore me died,* he explained. *Look.* He broke their connection for a moment and went to the far end of the ship where the control panel, overgrown with moss and native weeds, was located. He brought back a small holo-cube and handed it carefully to Ariel. She took it from him with the same caution he had showed, feeling that Kor was sharing his greatest treasure with her.

The holo-cube had several burned out facets but there were at least two that still glowed and showed their original images.

In the first one, a toddler of about two with golden brown hair and startling greenish blue eyes stared back at her. Kor as a baby, she realized with delight. The second glowing facet of the holo-cube showed what looked to be a wedding picture. The bride had blond hair and pale green eyes and she was staring with loving devotion up at the groom who had brown hair and eyes the same color as the baby in the other picture.

Ariel handed the cube back to him carefully and entwined her fingers with Kor's again. *Those are your parents,* she said motioning at the cube he held in his other hand. *And the other picture is you as a baby. But do you know how you got here?*

Kor shook his head, looking puzzled. *I cannot remember much of the time before Those Who Share took me in. They who bore me were devoured by a sloarn when I was little older than this image.* He nodded at the cube.

A sloarn? Ariel frowned, wondering if that was some other kind of Tordanji predator.

A sloarn is the same kind of beast that attacked you and the other one. Kor sent her an image of the huge segmented scaly beast he had driven off of her and Ariel shivered involuntarily.

Oh—a sloarn. She nodded, then looked at him a little shyly. *I would like to thank you for saving my life. The, uh, sloarn was both vicious and dangerous and you risked your life to save mine. I am in your debt.*

Kor shrugged. *I have a grudge against all sloarns. And I could not let the first one of my kind I had seen since those who bore me died be devoured.*

How can I repay you? Ariel asked him. She had studied enough primitive cultures to know that they often took the ideas of debt and gratitude very seriously. She wanted Kor to know that she acknowledged her debt to him and was willing to pay it.

Kor leaned forward and looked into her eyes eagerly. *Teach me,* he said. Yearning tinged his mental voice. *Teach me about Those Who Come from the Sky—the people I am descended from.*

Ariel smiled at him. *I would be delighted to teach you anything I can, Kor. And I hope I can learn of you and those who raised you—Those Who Share.* Those Who Share had to be the natives that inhabited Tordanji Prime, she reasoned. What incredibly good luck to find herself in the company of a man who knew them intimately!

I will take you to meet those who raised me. He smiled at her hesitantly. *They always said that I would meet another of my kind some day. For years I have dreamed of it and yet . . . you are so different from me.*

Well, Ariel hedged, biting her lip, *how exactly do you mean?*

Kor looked her up and down with a critical eye. *You are smaller than me for one thing—more delicate. And this is a different shade than mine.* He touched her hair hesitantly, running his fingers through it in a way that made Ariel shiver for some reason.

Hair, she told him. *We call that hair. Mine is blond—yellow, like the sun. Among my . . . our people, there are many different colors of hair. Eyes, too.* She indicated her eyes with her free hand.

Eyes. Kor seemed to be trying out the word. *Our eyes are different too. Yours are blue, like the sky.* Kor stroked her cheek, looking into her eyes wonderingly. *And on your chest you have . . .* He looked at her, a frown of puzzlement on his face.

Ariel bit her lip, uncertain of how to reply. On one hand, she owed him her life and she was hoping to get Kor to introduce her to the natives. On the other, it was completely unprofessional to start playing doctor with the wildman, no matter how gorgeous he was. She decided to try for a detached tone. After all, Kor wasn't ashamed of his naked body, so why should she be?

Reluctantly, she dropped the hide blanket, revealing her bare breasts. *They're called breasts, Kor. Only the females of our species have them. Do, um, Those Who Share have two sexes—male and female?*

Of course. He nodded. *But the females do not have these . . . breasts as you do.*

Ariel made a mental note—the natives of Tordanji apparently had no secondary sexual characteristics. *Then how do you tell male and female apart?* she asked Kor.

Males are the color of the dendow plant and females are the color of the tendar when it comes to first bloom, Kor answered. *Just as I am a different color from you.*

Your skin is tan from being in the sun with no clothing—no hides to cover it, Ariel said. She was trying to get used to have him looking at her bare breasts. It was only curiosity, not lust, she told herself. But having those piercing eyes directed at her body was making her feel flushed and warm all over.

Kor lifted a hand and cupped one of her breasts rubbing his thumb over the nipple. Ariel bit her lip to suppress a gasp. She knew it was innocent curiosity on his part but his hand was so large and warm and she could feel her nipple hardening at his touch.

Abruptly, Kor pulled his hand away. *I was hurting you?* The deep mental voice sounded anxious.

Ariel didn't know whether to be relieved or disappointed. *No, Kor. But among our kind, female breasts are very sensitive. They are used for pleasure and reproduction.*

Reproduction? He raised an eyebrow in confusion and Ariel cursed herself inwardly. Now she'd done it. The last thing she needed was to have to start explaining the birds and the bees to Kor.

Um, producing young. Making more humans, which is what you and I both are, she said, trying to change the subject.

Those Who Come from the Sky are humans?

Yes. Ariel nodded. *We are all descended from the people who once lived on a planet called Old Earth in a solar system many light years from here. You and I, and your parents too.* She looked at him closely. *Do you know your parents' names, Kor?*

He shrugged, frowning. Apparently he was trying to digest the large amount of information she'd just given him. Gently, Ariel unlaced their fingers and climbed out of the bed made of cushions. She debated on taking the hide blanket with her and decided not too. Her shirt was gone—it had been ripped to shreds by the sloarn and had probably fallen off her when Kor brought her to his home. She didn't like going topless, but it wasn't like Tordanji Prime was cold enough to really require clothing, and she knew that Kor's interest in her was purely innocent and in no way sexual.

She needed to get over her own feelings of embarrassment and modesty and learn to live as he did, she lectured herself as she made her way around the ship, looking at various things. Acting otherwise might significantly hurt her chances of establishing a good rapport with the natives tomorrow. *So why not take off your trousers and panties, too?* she asked herself practically. But . . . she wasn't quite up to explaining the other differences between male and female to Kor just yet. She had neatly sidestepped the birds and the bees question and she didn't need to open it for discussion again.

She made her way to the control panel and began working the switches and levers, trying to see if the machine had any juice left in it. To her excitement, she found that the ship's log was mostly uncorrupted. She listened intently to several entries and Kor ambled over to stand beside her, a look of incomprehension on his face. Ariel grabbed his hand in delight.

Listen, Kor, those are the voices of your parents! They're telling what happened to you and how you got here. She looked up at him, her eyes shining. *Your true name is Corrin Trafalger. Your parents were the last people to come and study this planet and your mother was pregnant with you when they came.*

He raised an eyebrow at her. *Pregnant?*

Uh . . . she was carrying you. She brought you with her, Ariel explained hurriedly. *Their ship crashed just the way mine did but their emergency beacon was burned out in the fall. They were trapped here but they started to make friends with the natives—with Those Who Share.*

Kor looked at her with amazement. *You understand all of this just from listening to mouth noises?*

It's called a spoken language, Kor, and almost every species and subspecies of human has one. She tapped the tan column of his throat, right above the necklace of blue and silver tattoos. *Don't you ever use your voice?*

He shrugged. *Those Who Share have no voices—they speak with their minds with the help of the thought keepers. But I would learn this spoken language from you, if you would teach it to me. I would like to understand the voices of those that bore me.*

Ariel smiled. *I would be pleased to teach you. Come, let's sit on the bed and we'll begin.*

4

I know a few things, Kor told her, when they were settled facing each other on the cushions. *I know eyes,* he touched her eyelids lightly and said the word out loud, *and hair.* He ran a hand through her tangled blond tresses, repeating the single syllable. *I remember mouth from a long time ago,* he said thoughtfully, *but these . . .* He cupped her cheek and brushed the pad of his thumb across her full pink lips.

"Lips," Ariel told him, feeling herself tremble under his gentle touch. It was ridiculous but she found she couldn't help it. Kor's touch excited her in a way she had never been excited before. Then she pushed the thought out of her mind and concentrated on their language lesson.

She taught him "ears" and "eyebrows," "nose" and "throat," "chest" and "skin" and then his large warm hand wandered down to cup her breasts again.

"Breasts," he said softly in his deep voice. His thumb brushed over one of her nipples, making her gasp. *What are these?* he asked through their link

"Nipples," Ariel said softly. She bit her lip as he repeated the word and teased the other nipple to hardness with his thumb as well.

You said they were for pleasure? How do they make pleasure?

They . . . it feels good to me—to a woman when a man touches them as you are touching them now, Ariel confessed. *And many men find it pleasurable to touch a woman there because they know it gives her pleasure.*

So they receive pleasure from giving pleasure. Kor's mental voice was thoughtful. He looked at her directly. *Am I pleasuring you now, Ariel?*

Unable to lie about something so obvious, Ariel nodded. She knew she shouldn't be deriving sexual pleasure from letting him gratify his curiosity, but there was just something about Kor. He was so big, so primal, and yet so gentle. She had never believed in love at first sight and she still didn't. But *lust* at first sight was an entirely different thing.

What else do men do to pleasure women? he asked softly, still touching her breasts.

They suck . . . put their mouths on a woman's breasts, her nipples . . . Ariel broke off, uncertain why she was telling him this. She needed to stop before every bit of her scientific objectivity went straight out the window but she couldn't seem to help herself. And she didn't resist when Kor laid her back gently on the cushions and began sucking and licking her breasts. He pulled one of her nipples completely into his mouth experimentally and sucked hard, making her moan out loud.

Ariel buried her fingers in his thick mane of hair and arched her back shamelessly, giving in to the pleasure of his hot wet mouth on her bare breasts. She could feel the heat gathering between her thighs and she was thankful she'd had the good sense to keep her trousers on.

Ariel, Kor's mental voice whispered in her ear. They were no longer holding hands but apparently his touch on her bare skin was enough to retain the connection.

Yes, Kor? She was too busy moaning to answer him out loud. He looked up for a moment from her nipples, red and swollen from his attentions.

I find it very pleasurable to pleasure you. I like the touch and taste of your skin and the way you move under me when I put my mouth on you. I feel good but strange, he gestured between his legs, *here.*

Ariel dared to look down and saw his thick shaft, which she had been trying so hard not to notice since she'd awoken, fully erect and pulsing between his muscular thighs. *Oh my Goddess!* she thought to herself in dismay. There was no longer any doubt that Kor's interest in her wasn't simple childlike curiosity. No, it was definitely sexual.

Kor looked at her, frowning. *What does it mean when this happens?* he asked through their link.

It means . . . Ariel fumbled for the right way to phrase it. *It means your body is ready to mate—to join with a female.* She touched his heated shaft lightly with her fingertips and Kor hissed as though she had burned him.

It feels . . . different when you touch me than when I touch myself, he said. *Why?*

That's just . . . part of being human, Ariel told him. She knew she ought to stop touching him, ought to leave him alone, but somehow she just couldn't. Maybe it was the intimacy of mind-to-mind contact that made her feel she had known him much longer than she had. Or maybe it was the warmth of his skin against hers, the musky, wild, entirely masculine scent of his desire that filled her senses like a drug. For whatever reason, she could not stop herself from touching him again, grasping his thick shaft greedily in her hand and stroking its silky length until Kor groaned through their mind link.

Ariel, he growled, *will you show me how humans, how our people mate?*

Ariel drew back in dismay. *Kor, I can't,* she said. Not that she didn't want to, but she'd only known the big wildman for a few hours, not counting however long she had been unconscious. There was no way she was ready to do *that* with him. It was completely unprofessional and besides, as much as she hated it, she was promised to marry Milton in less than a month. No, she couldn't do it—it wouldn't be right or fair. However, she reasoned, looking at the desire burning in Kor's green-blue eyes, it wasn't fair to leave her rescuer in this state either. Maybe there was something she could do—some way to help him out and repay him for saving her life.

Kor, she said, taking his thick shaft in her palm again and stroking him gently, *I can't show you . . . how to mate. But there are other things that we can do, things I can show you, that are very pleasurable. Would you like that?*

Yes, show me. Kor lay down on the cushions and pulled her down on top of him. He nuzzled under the shelf of her chin, his hot breath sending shivers down her spine. Goddess help her, but she wanted him badly. There was something so primal about the man—an animal instinct that made her body respond to his helplessly. Ariel pushed her thoughts away and tried to concentrate on doing what she could to ease Kor's discomfort without going too far.

She took his cock in her hand again, marveling at its thickness and length. It was like handling a bar of hot iron sheathed in silk and she couldn't even wrap her fingers all the way around it. Without thinking about it, she found herself on her knees bending over him so that her blond hair trailed across his muscular abdomen. She rubbed the rose-petal soft head of his cock experimentally across her cheek, inhaling his scent, giving herself up to the pleasure of hearing him gasp through their link.

Kor, she sent him, still stroking his thick shaft with one hand while she fondled the lightly furred sac between his legs with the other. *It's all right to make noises out loud when you're feeling good. I like to hear the sounds that you make when I touch you.*

He responded with a low groan as she placed a soft, experimental kiss on the broad head of his cock. Encouraged by his sounds of pleasure, Ariel dared to do more than kiss. She licked a long, slow trail from the base of his shaft to the head, tracing the pulsing blue vein that ran the length of his hardness with her tongue. He tasted salty and warm and utterly delicious.

Ariel had never been very eager to perform this particular act before because she was afraid of getting it wrong and wondered how she measured up to other lovers who had done the same thing for the man she was with. But Kor hadn't had any other lovers so she felt free to experiment and try to give him pleasure any way she could.

She licked a warm wet circle across the sensitive spot just below the head and blew a stream of cool air on the same place, just to tease him. Kor groaned out loud again and then she heard him through their link.

Ariel! Ah! That feels so . . . He didn't seem to have a word that fit the situation but his actions made up for his lack of eloquence. Large warm hands threaded through her hair and urged her gently downward, mutely begging her to stop teasing.

Taking the hint, Ariel bent her head and took as much of the thick shaft as she could into her mouth. She felt the broad head hitting the back of her throat and still well over half of his cock was free. She used one hand on him, stoking in time with the motions of her mouth as she sucked his thick shaft.

Kor gasped at the double stimulation of her mouth and her hand and began to pump his hips, very carefully, in rhythm with her movements. Ariel had been with a few men who seemed to think it was their Goddess-given right to shove as much down her throat as was humanly possible, but it wasn't like that with Kor. He seemed to realize that he could hurt her if he wasn't careful and he never pushed too far or too hard.

Ariel's jaw was getting tired but she was still enjoying this more than any sexual experience she'd ever had—and she wasn't even the one getting the attention. She could feel the hot wetness between her thighs growing with every sensuous stroke of Kor's cock in and out of her mouth. It felt good to be in charge of a sexual encounter like this—good to show a man so receptive to her teaching, exactly how pleasurable sex could be. And that was all it was, Ariel promised herself—just sex. She was just showing Kor what he had been missing all these years, introducing him to a few key facts like a teacher with a willing student. A *very* willing student.

Kor was groaning and gasping and at last she felt the big muscles of his thighs tense and turn to iron under her hand. "Ariel!" he moaned out loud, his big hands reaching to touch her face, her neck, her shoulders, trying to stroke her everywhere at once.

At the sound of her name on his lips, Ariel almost felt that she could almost orgasm herself. Here was a man who hadn't spoken aloud in over twenty-five years and he was shouting her name at the top of his lungs. It made her feel powerful and hot. She had been planning to pull off at the last minute because she didn't much care for the taste of cum, but now she pressed closer, swirling her tongue over his shaft as she sucked and licked him to the point of no return.

"*Ariel!*" Kor gasped again, both out loud and through their link, and then she felt the thick, hot jets hitting the back of her throat as he came. To her surprise, his cum wasn't bitter or sour but sweet. In fact, it had an almost chocolaty flavor. She swallowed eagerly and wondered if it could have something to do with his diet here on Tordanji Prime. She waited until his fierce erection had begun to go down and gave his cock one final kiss. Then she slid up the length of his body to press her naked breasts against his broad, muscular chest. They were both sweating lightly but a cool breeze filtered through the cracks in the sides of the ship and cooled them off.

"Ariel," Kor whispered hesitantly, his deep voice still sounding hoarse and unused. Then he continued through their link. *That was . . . there are no words. No mind words and no mouth words for what you have showed me. It was pleasure beyond anything I ever dreamed.*

Ariel couldn't help blushing at his extravagant praise. She knew it was probably wrong to have sucked Kor's cock until he came, but somehow she couldn't make herself be upset about it. Sure it was unprofessional, but it had been a hell of a lot of fun too. And besides, she promised herself, this was the first and last time anything like that would ever happen between her and the wildman. Tomorrow she would go to meet the natives and become the impartial observer she always tried to be when she interacted with a new people. But in the meantime, she could enjoy snuggling close to Kor and feeling his big body close to hers and his strong arms wrapped possessively around her.

She could see through the cracks in the sides of the ship that it was fully dark outside now. It occurred to her that Milton was probably wondering where the hell she was but she didn't feel any particular guilt over it. Let him worry for a while. After acting like such a profound know-it-all idiot, he deserved it. She would spend one day with Kor, getting to know the natives, and then return to her base camp to let Milton know she was all right.

5

A single day turned into several weeks almost without Ariel noticing it. The next morning when she had woken up, Kor had already gone out and gathered some food for their breakfast. When she sat up in bed and rubbed her eyes sleepily, he filled her lap with bright blue pods and round bright pink fruit like nothing she had ever seen before.

Kor touched her knee as she examined one of the round pink fruits that just filled her palm. *Like this,* he told her, punching a hole in the fruit near the top by the stem. Then he took a small sip from the hole and passed it to her.

Ariel looked at the fruit doubtfully, which appeared to be filled with liquid instead of pulp, but one experimental sip later she was hooked. The juice of the bright pink fruit had a tart-sweet flavor unlike anything she had ever tasted before. It wasn't quite like the citrus fruits she'd had that were imported from Old Earth, or the flame flower juice from the Nandar system, but it was a little bit like both and absolutely delicious.

When she had finished two of the pink fruits, Kor broke open one of the blue pods to reveal a rich brown cream that oozed over her hand when she took it from him. Ariel was only reluctant to taste this until she got a whiff of it. There was no mistaking that smell, she thought, when she brought the pod to her nose—chocolate, or the Tordanji equivalent. She lapped at the brown cream experimentally and found that it tasted as good as it smelled. The flavor of the darkest, richest chocolate she had ever tasted exploded across her tongue with just a hint of some exotic spice mixed in.

Kor was watching her reaction eagerly. *You like it?* he asked, touching her knee again to make the link.

Ariel nodded and smiled at him. *It reminds me of a sweet treat we like to eat back on my home planet—only better.* She remembered the faintly sweet and chocolaty flavor of his cum from the night before and raised an eyebrow at him. *Do you eat a lot of these?*

Kor nodded. *Yes, they are what the males of Those Who Share bring to the females at mating time as a gift. But I like their flavor as well.* Then he said aloud, "They are . . . good."

Ariel nodded encouragement and smiled at him. It was obvious that he was anxious to learn to speak out loud, to communicate verbally as well as mentally. She wondered how he had gained telepathic abilities in the first place. Were they another by-product of a Tordanji diet, or some latent ability the natives had somehow awakened within his brain?

As she finished off the pulp of several more of the blue pods, Kor shaved, scraping at his face with the sharp piece of metal that served as his knife. It looked as though it had come from part of the ship that had been twisted in the crash and he stored it in a sheath made of animal hide. The sheath was tied around his waist with a belt made of thin, tough purple vine.

He looked at her after he had finished shaving. "You are ready?" he asked, haltingly. Ariel looked down at herself. She was still topless and had none of her equipment. And yet, Kor had less than she did—just the makeshift knife in its hide sheath tied around his waist, and he was ready to venture out into the jungle. For a moment she considered asking him if she could go back to the site of her own crash to at least get a recorder to take notes on. But then she would have to explain to Milton where she had been and why she was half naked and . . . no, it was just too much trouble. So she simply nodded.

"Yes, I'm ready. Let's go."

Kor smiled at her, a big warm grin that made her tingle all the way down to her toes. Goddess, if he had any idea how gorgeous he was . . . but he didn't. As they tramped through the jungle, Ariel reflected that it was so refreshing to be with a good-looking man who didn't know he was good-looking. Among the four and forty families, Milton was considered quite a catch and he never let Ariel forget it. She had often wondered if there was something wrong with her, not liking her fiancé's tall, skinny build and receding chin which were the hallmark of good breeding among her social set.

But then again, her Granny Stone hadn't liked the cave-chested, weak-chinned look of a true aristocrat either. Holo pictures of her husband, Grandpa Turrington showed a big, robust man with broad shoulders and a chin like the front of a cargo freighter. Maybe, Ariel speculated, she had inherited her love of big, strapping men from her grandmother along with her unfashionably curvy figure and taste for adventure. To the day she died, Granny Stone had believed in living life to the fullest, and she had encouraged Ariel to do the same.

Ariel put aside the fond memories of her wild grandmother and concentrated on following Kor. But she wasn't just following—she was observing him closely, as she would with any native of a new planet she had come to study. He moved like a wild animal through the dense jungle vegetation—there was a spring in his step and a coiled tension in his large body that said he was ready for anything. There was an unconscious grace about him, a silent nobility that appealed to Ariel on many levels. And then there was his body.

The rippling muscles in his back and ass worked under his smooth tan skin as they walked and his shoulder-length hair was tied off with a twist of grass. Goddess, the man was a walking porno-vid, she thought, trying not to drool. *But he's not for me,* she reminded herself sternly. *And last night was a one-time only deal.* Now if only she could get her hormones to agree with her mind . . .

The only thing that ruined her enjoyment of the trip and her wonderful view, was the constant buzz of insects around her ears. About an hour into their journey through the deep purple jungles of Tordanji, a particularly large and ugly looking bright orange insect as long as her hand landed on Ariel's shoulder. Being an experienced anthropologist, she made it a point to try and remain calm no matter what strange thing she saw on a new planet but she did have a weakness—her fear of bugs, especially *big* bugs.

She shrieked and slapped at the orange insect, revolted at the feel of its spiny multiple legs crawling on her skin. Kor turned around at once, concern written over his face. The huge insect buzzed away when he put out a hand to touch her shoulder and Ariel shivered reflexively.

"Ariel?" he asked aloud, then continued through the link, *Are you all right? Is there something troubling you?*

The bug! The . . . that thing that landed on me. Ariel took a deep breath, trying to get a grip. Her fear of insects was one she was always trying to overcome. It was so unprofessional to be screaming like a little girl just because some of the native fauna happened to be creepy-crawlies.

Those who fly? Kor looked around and seemed to notice for the first time that insects were swarming them. But no, Ariel realized, not *them,* just *her.* For some reason the same insects that thought she was a new taste sensation were leaving Kor strictly alone.

"Here. I will make it better. I will show you," Kor said haltingly. He was busy gathering the flowers of a dark blue climbing vine that snaked its way up the side of a thick purple trunk beside them. When he crushed them between his palms, they released a liquid that had a thin, astringent odor that burned Ariel's nose. But before she could protest, he was rubbing the thick, slippery sap all over her upper body.

Ariel had always had fair, sensitive skin and she waited to feel a burning sensation where the flower juice touched her, but there was only a blessedly cool sensation as the liquid soothed her multiple insect bites. Kor's large warm hands seemed to linger longest on her breasts and nipples and Ariel squeezed her thighs together tightly, trying to fight the desire that threatened to overcome her as he massaged the anti-insect serum into her skin. A quick glance downward let her know that this was affecting him as well. Ariel had a quick mental image of herself bending over to suck his hard shaft in her mouth and when Kor growled approvingly, she knew she had inadvertently sent the thought to him through their link.

"Is better?" he asked at last, his deep voice rough with desire.

"Yes." Ariel pulled away reluctantly from his hands, blushing deeply. "It's much better, Kor. I . . . thank you."

He seemed about to say something more but maybe he sensed her embarrassment and the confusion she was feeling. She was relieved when he simply nodded his head and turned to lead the way farther into the jungle to his adopted people.

6

The native village was completely invisible, at least to Ariel, until they were almost standing inside its borders. The conical huts the natives of Tordanji Prime lived in were constructed completely of the leaves and vines of the surrounding plants, which meant that they faded neatly into the jungle when seen from any distance at all.

Even more surprising, to Ariel at least, were the natives themselves. They weren't exactly humanoid in shape, but they were at least bipedal and they walked upright, although their knees bent backward instead of forward like human knees. Instead of arms, they each had multiple sets of flowing tentacles and thinner vinelike tentacles sprouted from their heads instead of hair. This might have been horribly alien to look at, at least to the eyes of someone not used to them, but the whole effect was lightened by the fact that all of the natives had a deep, rich coat of silky fur covering almost their entire bodies. Ariel noticed that the only bare spot in their rich fur was a thin shaved band around the neck where each native had a blue and silver necklace of tattoos exactly like Kor's.

The natives had wide oval eyes that were shaded in vivid jewellike tones. The eyes looked almost human until she noticed the double pupils in each one. They also had long, beaky noses and wide mouths that seemed to smile and frown to indicate moods very like humans. The males, Kor told her silently, were the slightly larger natives whose fur was a deep purple-blue and the females were slightly smaller and had a pale lavender tinge. Neither sex made any noise and Ariel was soon to find out through careful observation, that this was because they had no larynxes. Nor did they need them—everywhere around her the silent telepathic communication was in evidence.

The first native they met when entering the village was a large male, although he wasn't nearly as tall as Kor. He bowed with what Ariel could only describe as a graceful awkwardness, and waved his arm tentacles in the air in slow, underwater motions. His fur was so long and silky that it seemed to float in the jungle's faint breeze like translucent blue feathers.

Kor nodded and appeared to be communicating with the native, although they weren't touching in any way. Despite her contact with Kor, Ariel couldn't hear the exchange. Then, although the native hadn't called to anyone or made any kind of announcement, at least one that Ariel could hear, the other members of the village began arriving in twos and threes. There were about fifty in all and they all seemed to be very excited about her presence in their village. Ariel wished earnestly to communicate with them, but Kor explained that she had not been adopted into the tribe, so their minds were closed to hers. He was good about translating between her and the natives, however, for which she was grateful.

This is Zatzoo, the male of Those Who Share that raised me, he said, indicating a male whose fur was so dark it was almost black. *His name means Fast Water and he was very kind to me when those who bore me passed over.* Behind Zatzoo was a female native with pale lilac fur who came forward eagerly and wrapped her fluffy tentacles around Kor. He returned the embrace gently, with great affection. *This is Dorzala, she who raised me,* he told Ariel. *Her name means Wind Through The Leaves at Night. She is very pleased that I have met one of my own kind at last.*

Many silent hugs and embraces followed and Kor told her that he hadn't been home to his village for a while. *I grew too large for their lodgings,* he told Ariel, nodding at the small conical huts all of which were a good foot lower than his head. *And . . . I was lonely,* he admitted hesitantly. *The people of Those Who Share mate early and stay mated for life. It was hard to see that everyone had a mate, someone to care for, but me.*

I understand, Ariel told him, squeezing his hand. How difficult it must have been for Kor growing up among people so very different from him physically. But though their outward appearance was strange, at least to her eyes, their manners were gentle and deferential. She lost count of the many warm fuzzy embraces she received and the joy shining from the jewel-toned eyes of the people who loved Kor was easy to read.

They're happy for him, she thought, being careful that she wasn't touching him when she thought it. *They think he's found someone—someone to mate with him. Goddess, if only they knew.* She felt a deep well of sadness for some reason, even though she knew it was ridiculous. She wished she was free to have a relationship with Kor, but she wasn't. She didn't really want to marry Milton, but it was necessary to continue her work. And her work was the most important, fulfilling part of her life—wasn't it?

They want to have a great feast tonight, Kor told her when she took his hand again. *They wish to celebrate our meeting.*

That sounds . . . wonderful, Ariel said, trying to mean it. The natives were really taking to her—she would be able to learn everything about them. It was always so much easier when they were friendly instead of hostile. What an amazing paper she was going to write for *Alien Anthropology Today* when she got back home. But somehow the paper seemed like the least important part of all this. Instead, she kept thinking how disappointed Kor's native family would be if they knew she wasn't the answer to all his hopes and dreams. That instead, she was promised to another.

The feast was a huge, if silent, success. The Tordanji natives were a basic hunter-gatherer society and they built a bonfire in the middle of the village square and roasted their finest meats and produce, including some more of the blue chocolate pods. When roasted, the creamy brown goo inside the pods took on a thicker consistency, almost like the moist cakelike treats Ariel remembered eating at a bakery on Old Earth once. Brownies, that was what they had been called, she remembered, eagerly licking the inside of one blue shell to get the last crumbs.

When everything had been eaten down to the last morsel and the fire had died down, the natives sat around in obvious pairs, leaning against one another. Ariel noticed that the furry tentacles on their heads tangled together in a kind of slow-motion dance and wondered if it was some kind of a mating ritual or a simple display of affection. Then, one of the males stood and waved his arm tentacles, obviously calling for everyone's attention.

That's Kawfan, Kor told her through their link. *His name means He Who Shows The Way. He is the leader of the village. He says he wishes to tell a story now.*

Mmm, Ariel sent sleepily. By now touching Kor to keep the mental link had become almost second nature and she was snuggled comfortably against his side staring thoughtfully into the fire. On the other side, Kor was balancing one of his younger adopted brothers on his knee, a pale blue male child called something like Fbt or Ptb, Ariel wasn't quite sure which. She did notice, however, that Kor had a gentle touch with the child who had been playing energetically earlier, and was now nearly about to drop with exhaustion. Ptb's mouth opened wide with a silent yawn and his bright eyes were glassy with fatigue. Kor tucked the sleepy child under his other arm, just as he was cradling Ariel, and began to translate the story the chief's tribe was telling them.

Ariel sat up a little straighter and struggled to shake off the sleep that wanted to claim her. Fighting her way through the jungle for most of the day and the heavy feast she had just eaten were conspiring against her to close her eyes, but she was afraid to miss something important, some part of the Tordanji native's mythology that she might be able to use in her paper.

But instead of a myth or legend, Kawfan was telling the story, obviously often repeated and cherished, of Those Who Come from the Sky—Kor's parents, Ariel realized after a while.

They were strange to look on and at first we feared them, Kor translated for her as Kawfan waved his tentacles in a slow, hypnotic rhythm presumably in time with his telepathic delivery. *But Those Who Share are not hasty by nature and most of us felt we should try to live with them in peace. Then Those Who Come from the Sky came to us and said they wished to learn our ways and we saw that they were good and we agreed that they might. Then she who came from the sky brought forth a child and he was strange to see on the outside, but on the inside, we knew he belonged to Those Who Share. We knew this because the thought keepers accepted him at once as one of their own when he was adopted into our tribe. His name is Kor, which means Strength In the Shadows and he grew tall and strong in the ways of his own people and of ours.*

But Kor had a sadness, Kawfan continued, *one which none of Those Who Share could help him with. He had no mate and he was too different outwardly to take one of us for his mate. Instead, he was doomed to wander through the jungle, lonely and alone, although we of this tribe of Those Who Share all cared for him dearly.* Kor blushed briefly when he translated this and Ariel hid a smile behind her hand.

But there was a prophesy, Kawfan continued again. *A wise female saw it in the pattern of starlight in the moving waters of Steam Falls. She said that someday a female of Those Who Come from the Sky would fall to earth once more and Kor would find her. She told us he would have to do battle to win her, but once won, her heart would ever belong to him and his to her until the time when the stars burn out and the cold evernight covers us all.*

Ariel looked up at this last part and saw the hope shining in Kor's eyes and it nearly broke her heart. She sat up abruptly, severing their connection, and put a hand over her eyes. She could feel hot tears pricking behind her eyelids and as much as she tried to tell herself she was just overtired, she couldn't quite make herself believe it.

I'm sorry, Kor, she thought, wrapping her arms around herself to keep her thoughts to herself. *Oh, Goddess, so sorry.*

7

The next two weeks passed in a blur. Ariel slept in a small hut with other unmated females and Kor slept in a similar hut meant for males. She might have been upset about the sleeping arrangements, except it gave her such a good opportunity to study the Tordanji natives' culture. Also, it was considerably easier to ignore her growing attraction and avoid temptation when she wasn't sleeping with Kor at night.

They spent plenty of time together during the day and she learned how to hunt using cunning little traps woven of vines and sticks and to gather edible crops and plants, especially the blue chocolate pods, which continued to be her favorite Tordanji food. But everywhere they went, the people of the village congratulated Kor on finally finding his mate, which made Ariel terribly uncomfortable. It was clear the members of the village were curious and surprised that she and Kor didn't sleep together, but they were much too polite to ask. Or if they did ask, Kor never told her.

From the night of the feast, Ariel waited on tenterhooks for him to bring up the subject of her becoming his mate, but he never did although she caught him casting an occasional yearning glance her way. She didn't know whether to be relieved or annoyed that he didn't seem to want to broach the subject. Having already told him once that she couldn't mate with him, although she hadn't told him why, she wasn't about to bring it up again. She kept wondering when he would decide to talk to her about it, but it wasn't until near the end of her second week at the Tordanji village that he did.

Ariel was trying to get comfortable on the slippery leaf mat placed on the floor of the unmated females' hut and not succeeding very well. She had a lot on her mind tonight, and not all of it was about Kor. She knew that her time in the Tordanji village was coming to an end. By now a search-and-rescue party sent by her father would probably be on the way, if they weren't already here. While she didn't care about worrying Milton, she didn't want her father to suffer any distress thinking she was dead or kidnapped. So she needed to go back, and soon, but she found herself reluctant to leave. It wasn't just her fascinating experience studying the first genuine telepathic society she had ever seen, it was the fact that Kor was here, she admitted to herself. She didn't like the idea of leaving him behind.

"Ariel." The low whisper jolted her out of what was turning into a really good worrying session. Ariel poked her head out of the leaf and vine flap that served as a door for the hut and saw that Kor was crouched in the darkness, waiting for her.

"I'm so glad you called," she whispered, coming out to join him. "I couldn't sleep at all."

"I also could not sleep," he said. His deep voice was much stronger and less hesitant than it had been two weeks before. He was mastering spoken language with a speed that astonished Ariel, although he still had trouble with contractions. She had been practicing with him every day and it delighted the children of the village to sit and watch them make the mouth noises at each other.

Kor reached out a hand for her and she took it, staring up at him in the Tordanji moonlight. Tordanji Prime had a large moon and it was full that night. In its pale blue light Kor's muscular body looked like it had been carved out of pure silver.

"I want to show you something. It is an important place for Those Who Share," he told her.

So they were going on a field trip. Ariel was willing, although she wouldn't have dared to venture out into the dark and dangerous jungle at night with anyone less able to protect her. Kor led her out of the village and down a twisting trail that ended by a round glassy lake with a waterfall at the far end. The water was silver in the moonlight and steam was rising gently from its surface.

"This place is called Steam Falls," Kor explained. "The water is warm and so no predators can live in it. We bathe here at special times of the year for purification." He looked at her. "Would you like to bathe?"

It had been almost two weeks since she'd had anything approaching a hot bath or shower so the question was a no-brainer for Ariel. She nodded eagerly and Kor took her hand and began leading her into the water.

"Wait a minute." Ariel had gotten used to going topless but she didn't want to get her hiking boots or trousers wet. Keeping a hand on Kor's bicep for balance, she kicked off the boots, then hopped on one leg awkwardly, removing the trousers. When she finished and looked up, Kor was studying her with astonishment.

"You . . . you have no . . ." He gestured between his own legs and then gestured between hers.

"Oh, right. I never told you the other differences between human males and females," Ariel muttered, blushing. She had gotten so used to going topless that it was strange to suddenly feel so nude and vulnerable. "Um, let's get in the water first and we can discuss it later. Okay?"

Kor shrugged but he was still plainly curious about what she had, or rather, what she didn't have, between her legs. Feeling suddenly shy, Ariel dove into the steaming water and swam for the far end of the pool where the miniature waterfall was flowing. There was a smooth rocky ledge just under it and she stood and let the heated water pound down on her head, trying to clear her brain.

"Ariel." Kor was suddenly beside her, drawing her into his arms. He pulled her backward until they were sitting on the ledge behind the falls, watching the curtain of water jet down in front of them.

"Kor." Without thinking about it, she turned her head and kissed him on the lips. He didn't respond at first, but then he seemed to get the hang of it and kissed her back eagerly.

Ariel, he sent through their mental link since his mouth was too busy to talk, *I like this . . . this lips on lips.*

Kissing, she sent back, opening her mouth slightly and inviting his tongue inside. *It's called kissing. Humans do it to show affection.*

Is it part of mating? Kor had slowed the pace down now and he was kissing her like a pro—making a long, leisurely exploration of her mouth as though he owned her. He tasted slightly salty with just a hint of the blue chocolate pods they'd been eating at dinner.

It . . . can be, Ariel sent carefully.

Tell me more about mating. Kor's large fingers explored her wet skin, sliding over the sensitive curve of her breast to cup the damp mound of her sex in one sensuous motion. *Tell me about this,* he said. *Why are you different from me here? I thought that male and female humans were the same except for size and coloring.*

Well, he would think that, Ariel reasoned, trying not to shiver as his warm hand pressed against her mound. The Tordanji natives who had raised him had no discernable sexual differences. She had learned that the twining of their head tentacles, which she had observed that first night at the feast, was the way they mated. So since Kor had never seen her with her naird-hide trousers off, naturally he would assume that she was the same as he, as a Tordanji female was the same as a male. It was time to give him the birds and the bees lecture she had been dreading.

Hesitantly, feeling foolish, she explained the difference in male and female biology, as it related to humans and gave Kor the relevant names of their different parts. She spoke out loud, trying to make her voice dry and scholarly despite his hands on her naked body.

"So a male would place himself here?" He traced the slit of her cunt lips with one careful finger and Ariel nodded, biting her lip to keep back a gasp. She didn't know the last time she had been so aroused or so embarrassed. Kor looked at her, obviously puzzled. "But how?" he asked. "There is not room. It would not . . . fit."

"It, um, slides into a woman's body. If she's aroused it usually fits with no problem." Ariel scooted back on the rock ledge, her legs dangling down into the water, and spread her thighs a little to let him see. She told herself that she was just trying to educate him, because she had promised herself that nothing sexual would happen between them after that first night in his ship. But she couldn't help the way her heart raced when Kor spread her gently to stroke the tender pink inside of her cunt with one careful finger.

"How can I know when she is aroused?" he asked, his deep voice quiet and intense.

"You can tell because my, I mean, *her* nipples, are hard," Ariel gasped as his finger slid over his clit. "And because she will become wet."

"But you're already wet," he said softly, meaning that her skin was still damp from swimming in the warm pool.

"No, I meant wet there . . . where you're touching. The wetness is a natural . . . ah! . . . lubrication that makes touching m-more pleasurable and the entry of the m-male easier," she stuttered, trying to think past the pleasure he was giving her simply by his gentle exploration.

"Am I pleasuring you now?" Kor asked, searching her eyes with his own.

"Yes," Ariel gasped, unable to deny it. To her surprise, he dropped to his knees before her so that he was chest deep in the water again.

"And now?" he asked, licking a long, hot trail from the inside of her knee to her inner thigh.

"Yes," Ariel moaned again. She could see where this was headed and it wasn't exactly scientific or professional but she couldn't seem to stop herself. Before she knew it, Kor was kissing and licking avidly between her legs. He parted her cunt lips carefully once more and pressed forward, eager to taste her. Ariel felt powerless to stop him. She lay back on the smooth, cool rock ledge and gave herself up to the pleasure of being eaten.

Kor started by lapping at her clit, finding the small bundle of nerves as if by instinct. He sucked it into his mouth and made love to it with his tongue, drawing circles around it in a way that seemed designed to drive her wild. Ariel groaned and buried her hands in his thick wet hair. He had never done this before but he was a genius at it—maybe he was picking up her needs through the mental link they maintained whenever they touched. But Ariel didn't care how he was doing it—she just didn't ever want him to stop. She could feel herself getting close to coming almost immediately, but she needed something else . . . something more . . .

As though reading her mind, which he probably was, Kor

bent lower and his tongue found its was to the entrance to her body. *Here!* she heard him think, and then he was pressing forward, lifting her thighs to get better access in his attempt to put his tongue all the way inside her. Ariel nearly shrieked with pleasure and tightened her grip on his damp hair. She had never been eaten with such enthusiasm, such utter abandon. Kor wanted to give her pleasure and he would stop at nothing to do it. She moaned as he worked his way up to her clit again and then she felt his fingers once more.

Here, Kor told her as two long, strong fingers entered her pussy and began to stroke in and out. *I want to be here, inside you, Ariel. What is the word?* She felt him searching her mind. *Fuck—I want to fuck you, Ariel. I want to claim you, fill you, make you mine forever!*

The deep, growling voice inside her head along with the swirl of his tongue over her clit and the insistent thrusting of his fingers inside her cunt were too much. Ariel moaned out loud and arched her back as she came, pressing her pussy up to meet his eager mouth. Kor lapped at her juices hungrily, still pressing deep inside her with two long, strong fingers. Through their mental link she could feel his desire for her and his pleasure in making her feel so good.

At last when her quivering stopped, Kor climbed out of the water and lay beside her on the flat shelf of rock. He pulled her into his arms and kissed her mouth, sharing her own salty sweet flavor with her.

"Mmm," Ariel murmured aloud. She didn't think she'd ever had such an intense orgasm before. Kor was better at oral sex than any man she'd ever been with, even if he was a novice.

"You taste good. Sweet. Hot." Kor's voice in her ear brought her back to reality.

"You're very good at that," she told him, stroking his cheek. The moonlight filtering in through the waterfall made a dappled pattern on the strong planes of his face.

"I gave you pleasure?" he asked, nuzzling against her neck.

"Very much pleasure," Ariel told him breathlessly.

"I want to pleasure you again. I want to be inside you." He pulled her close to him, raising her top leg to gain access to her wet pussy. "Like this," he murmured, thrusting forward, and Ariel felt the broad, plum-shaped head of his cock part her cunt lips and press against the entrance to her body. She felt just the head enter her, sliding easily into her wet heat and for a moment she wanted him as she had never wanted anything in her life. It would have been so easy to spread her legs a little wider and just let him in. She wanted to feel him filling her, owning her, fucking her. His fingers had been wonderful but she needed *more*. She wanted to feel his weight pressing down on her as he spread her wide and thrust his cock deep inside her until he bottomed out. She wanted to feel him thrusting into her and filling her with his hot cum, spurting inside her, claiming her for now and forever . . . but she couldn't.

With a little cry, Ariel pulled away and scooted back from him. Kor made no move to follow her, only watched with concern as she sat up and put her face in her hands.

"I'm sorry, Kor," she whispered, her voice choked with sobs. "But . . . I can't do that with you."

"Of course you cannot." His voice was reasonable and level. She looked up at him with surprise. "I have not asked you properly yet," Kor amended. He sat up and scooted closer to her, not making any attempt to touch her. Instead, he tapped with one finger at the necklace of tattoos around his neck, using a slow, soft rhythm.

"I don't . . ." Ariel began but then something strange began to happen—the necklace of turquoise blue thumb-sized tattoos came to life. The flat images suddenly became 3-D, and Ariel realized she was staring at a chain of living creatures, their round blue bodies linked by long silver legs. They swayed lightly, as though in some wind she could not feel, making a live necklace instead of a flat one.

Kor tapped again and one of the creatures disentangled itself from the chain and stalked down to perch on his shoulder, waving silver feelers in the air inquiringly.

"What . . . what is that?" Ariel swallowed hard. It looked very much like a blue and silver spider to her—too much for comfort, in fact.

"These are the thought keepers," Kor told her, indicating the chain of living creatures around his neck. "They live within our skin and share our warmth. In return, they let Those Who Share share their thoughts with each other."

"Really?" Ariel leaned forward to examine the small creature sitting on Kor's shoulder, her revulsion overcome by scientific curiosity. Could it really be? A creature who had a symbiotic relationship with its host and allowed the people that gave it shelter and warmth to communicate telepathically?

Kor nodded. "Yes, when I was adopted into the tribe, each person gave me one of their thought keepers and so I was able to talk to everyone in the village." He ducked his head to look into her eyes. "It is the same custom when a new female is brought to the village to mate with a male. He gives her one of his thought keepers and she gives him one of hers so their minds are one." He tapped his shoulder and the little turquoise creature skittered down his arm on its spindly silver legs and balanced on the tip of his index finger.

"Oh." Ariel put a hand to her chest, trying to still the beating of her heart.

"Ariel," Kor said softly, gazing intently into her eyes, "I want to mate with you. I want us to be together always. As a token of my love I offer you one of my thought keepers. Will you take it?"

Ariel felt hot tears begin to gather behind her eyelids. Kor wasn't just offering her the Tordanji equivalent of an engagement ring; he was offering her a piece of himself and the ability to communicate with him telepathically always, even without touching. It was the single most beautiful gesture anyone had ever made to her and she couldn't accept it.

"Kor," she said softly, trying to hold back the tears. "I am so sorry but I can't take your thought keeper. And . . . and I can't mate with you." She looked up at him, reading the hurt and confusion on his strong features.

"But why?" Kor seized her by the shoulders and the little thought keeper skittered back up his arm to join the living necklace around his neck. "I love you, Ariel. I need you as I have never needed another before. We are meant to be together. Can you not feel that to the very center of your bones?"

Ariel shook her head and pulled away from him. "I should have told you this in the beginning but . . . but I have promised to mate with someone else."

"Who?" Kor demanded. "Not the one who pointed a weapon at you and wounded you?"

Ariel nodded grimly, not meeting his eyes. "Unfortunately, yes. Milton isn't very big in the brain department—or any department, for that matter—but he's the man my father wants me to marry. And if I don't, I won't be able to work any more."

"Work?" Kor frowned at the alien concept.

"*This* is my work." Ariel waved her hand vaguely. "I go to different planets to meet the people that live there. Then I write about it. That's putting your words down on paper so other people can see them and you won't ever forget them," she added, seeing his puzzled look.

"I would like to visit other worlds." Kor sounded wistful now. "And I would like to meet others of my kind. But more than any of those things, I want to mate with you."

"I'm sorry," Ariel said again, feeling miserable. "But . . . but maybe you just think you want to mate with me because I'm the first human female you've ever seen." She had a sudden inspiration. "You should come with me when I leave. Maybe . . ." she could barely get the words out, "maybe you'll meet someone else on my planet. Someone who isn't already spoken for."

"Ariel." Kor tilted her chin up so that their eyes met. "I will come with you when you leave. But not to find another. You are the only female I want to mate with. I love you and my love cannot be contained simply because you are promised to another." He bent his head and kissed her, a feather-light brush of his lips over hers that made the tears rise in her eyes again.

"Oh, Kor," she whispered brokenly. She wanted to tell him she loved him, too—that he was right and they should be together. But she had only known him for two weeks. How could she give up her entire life as she knew it for a man she had only known two weeks? *Kor is ready to give up everything he knows for you,* an accusing little voice whispered inside her brain. But Ariel pushed the thought away resolutely. Anthropology was her entire life—wasn't it?

Kor tried to kiss her again but she slid away from him and dove back into the water. Tomorrow it was time to go home and she would take her wildman with her, even if she could never have him. The thought made her heart clench in her chest and she dived deep into the steaming waters, trying to forget her grief, trying to forget everything at least for a moment.

8

"Ariel? Is that really you?" Milton certainly didn't look over-joyed to see her.

"It's me, all right," she said, thinking that the feeling was entirely mutual.

"But . . . but . . . I mean, I thought you were dead," he stammered, his watery eyes wide.

"I can see how you would think that after stunning me and letting me be carried off into the jungle," Ariel snapped. "Oh, shut your mouth before you catch an insect, Milton. I'm not a ghost. It's really me—in the flesh." She pushed aside the large flappy purple leaves of what Kor had told her was a phoon plant to step out into the clearing where they had first crashed.

"And in the nude, I see." Milton's surprise rapidly changed to disapproval. "What happened to your clothes?"

"Torn off by wild jungle creatures," Ariel said flippantly. "Speaking of which, Milton, meet Kor." She stepped aside and Kor strode out of the jungle, huge, naked, and more than a little imposing.

Milton cringed. "For heaven's sake, Ariel, what is *he* doing here?"

"He happens to live here. His parents were Professor and Mrs. Trafalger. After they died, he was raised by the natives," Ariel said. "And he's coming home with us." She surveyed the extra ship parked beside the dented hopper. "I see the rescue team is here."

"Yes, they just arrived." Milton frowned. "Your father even came—they're out scouring the jungle for your remains . . . uh, for you, I mean."

"Better call them and let them know I'm fine. Thanks to Kor." Ariel entwined her fingers with Kor's out of habit and saw her fiancé frown when he noticed the familiar contact.

"For heaven's sake, Ariel," he blustered, getting red in the face. "You can't seriously mean to take that . . . that big idiot back with us."

Kor took a step forward, his face like a thundercloud. "If you think I cannot understand your words, you are mistaken," he said clearly. His deep voice was little more than a growl.

Milton shrank back even more. "You . . . you taught him to talk?" he asked, in the same tone he might use to ask her if she had taught a large and unpredictable predator to speak.

"I think he already knew," Ariel said thoughtfully. "He just needed to be reminded. Now you boys make nice while I go find some clothes and call off Father's hunt for my body. Milton, do you think you have anything that might fit Kor in your luggage?" She compared her skinny fiancé with Kor's large muscular frame and shook her head. "Well, probably not," she answered her own question. "But I guess it can't hurt to look."

She left Kor glowering at Milton and went to dig around in her pack in the disabled space hopper. Her stomach was in knots, seeing her fiancé again, but she didn't want to show it. It was best to play it cool, she decided, and try to pretend that nothing out of the ordinary had happened in the past two weeks. Of course, being attacked by a vicious sloarn and rescued by the naked wildman of her dreams, then introduced to the first truly telepathic society in the known galaxy *was* out of the ordinary. But all of it was nothing compared to losing her heart. *That* was what Ariel was going to be trying to hide, from herself as much as from Milton.

She had just finished pulling on her clothes and had found a pair of Milton's stretchy exercise trousers that she thought might do for Kor in a pinch, when she heard a familiar voice right behind her.

"Ariel, is that you?"

Ariel turned to see her father. There were dark circles beneath his blue eyes, which she had inherited, and his salt and pepper hair was mussed as though he'd been running his hands through it.

"Hello, Father." Ariel nodded at him coolly. "I'm surprised to see you here," she added, wondering why he had come himself instead of just sending a herd of flunkies as was his usual practice.

"I thought you were dead. Milton said as much in his transmission." Her father had apparently already gotten over it. Now that he was sure she was alive, his voice was as cold as her own. He and Ariel had never quite seen eye to eye since the day he had called her into his study and told her in no uncertain terms that she was going to marry and produce an heir for him or he would cut off her funding for further anthropological expeditions.

"I'm alive and well as you can see," Ariel said. "I've still got all my reproductive organs intact too—isn't that what you were worried about? That if I was dead you'd have no one to carry on the family line?"

"Ariel, please, enough melodrama. Of course I'm glad you're all right and not just because I want grandchildren." Her father glanced at the blue exercise trousers dangling limply from her hand. "What are those for?"

"My new friend." Ariel gestured him around the side of the ship where Kor and Milton were still locked in a silent standoff. "Come meet Kor."

9

***

"Tell us again about the wild animals on Tordanji," Amanda Bedafellow gushed, hanging on Kor's muscular arm.

"Oh—and the natives. I heard they have feelers instead of arms—like great big *spiders*." Tanya Peckabit shivered theatrically as she caressed his other bicep. But Claudia Limefitter was the worst.

"Is it true you were actually *raised* by them?" she asked, batting her long green lashes at Kor as she stroked his chest meaningfully. Her fashionably stick-thin boyish figure was wrapped in a bright red creation that could only be one of the more expensive designers and her tiny, perky breasts were fully visible through the slinky fabric.

Ariel watched from the other end of the ballroom, taking in the flirting going on with deep disgust. So much for thin and scrawny being the ultimate in male perfection, even if it was considered the ideal body type among the four and forty families. The girls she had grown up with had taken one look at Kor's broad chest and muscular arms and had fallen all over themselves to ditch their dates and hang on his every word.

Not that he was saying much, Ariel noticed. Her one consolation was that Kor didn't seem to be flirting back at all, despite
the bevy of slender and pretty girls that were currently throwing themselves at him.

She eyed the red sheath dress that Claudia Limefitter was
wearing with a mixture of scorn and envy. There was no way
she would ever be able to fit her too-large breasts into something so skimpy. Not that she had ever cared about that kind of
thing before. She had always shunned her father's superficial
and snobbish social set in favor of her work. But now, seeing all
the fashionable and elegant girls gathered around Kor she suddenly cared—cared very damn much, in fact.

". . . party," someone said in her ear.

"Hmm?" Ariel turned to see Christy Smitherson smiling at
her elbow, a glass of blue fire flower juice held loosely in one el-
egantly manicured hand.

"I said it's quite the most exciting pre-wedding party I've
ever been to." Christy smiled at her. "And it's all because of
your friend there."

"Who, Kor?" Ariel frowned at her, trying to fight down the
green jealousy that was eating away at her gut. "Yes, he's, uh,
something isn't he?" Damn, she had never been much for small
talk. She was an anthropologist but the social customs of her
own society continued to confound her. Maybe that was why
she had gone looking for something better outside her own
planet.

Christy didn't seem to mind her terse answer. "Oh, he's
something all right," she practically purred, batting her lashes
in Kor's direction. "In fact, I was thinking I might make a run
at him myself as soon as he gets tired of Claudia's idiocy. That
shouldn't take long, do you think?" She laughed and nudged
Ariel lightly in the ribs, making her spill her nearly untouched
drink on the black marble floor.

"I guess not," Ariel said, through gritted teeth. She looked at

Kor again. He looked stiff and uncomfortable in the formal dining clothes but he was still listening politely to everything the laughing, chattering girls were saying to him. She wished that she had accepted his offer of a thought keeper so that she could know what he was thinking right now. But no, she couldn't have accepted such a personal and permanent link to one man when she was about to marry another.

Speaking of the man she was about to marry, Milton was sulking unattractively in the corner with the other jilted dates. No doubt he felt that Kor had usurped his rightful place as the center of attention and he was prepared to pout all night if necessary.

"So is the wedding gown a fabulous creation?" Christy asked, pulling her back to their one-sided conversation. "I heard it was an Eliah original. Do you think it'll top Millicent Wainwright's?"

"I really don't know," Ariel said, biting her tongue to keep from saying what she really thought, which was that she didn't give a good goddamn if her dress was as foofy as Millicent Wainwright's.

"Well, we'll find out soon enough won't we?" Christy nudged her again. "Tomorrow Milton's taking you off the market for good. What priestess did you get to do the ceremony again?"

"I . . . can't remember." Ariel's eyes kept straying back to the girls surrounding Kor like insects flocking to some sweet treat. *He's not mine,* she told herself, *I don't have any right to feel jealous. I brought him back with me specifically so that he could find someone else. Someone unattached.* But the knot of acidic envy aching in her stomach wasn't buying a word of it. All the knot knew was that she wanted Kor and she couldn't have him. What a fool she had been to think she could give him up so easily.

"Now, about the flowers. Is it really true that your father is flying in five hundred thousand rare orchids from Old Earth?"

Ariel looked at the girl beside her in disbelief. Christy was still talking. Would the idiot never shut up? She thought with longing of the silent natives of Tordanji Prime. Of the long quiet nights in front of the communal fire before going to sleep when Kor had translated chief Kawfan's lengthy tales. She had leaned against her wildman's side and breathed his musky, masculine scent, feeling utterly content and at peace with herself. There had been nothing to listen to but the popping of the fire and the soft noises of the jungle. That was where she had really felt at home—not in this glittering ballroom filled with pretentious snobs in designer clothes prattling on and on about the latest fashions and the hottest gossip.

"And the cake," Christy was saying. "I hear your father brought in a team of pastry chefs all the way from—"

"Excuse me," Ariel interrupted her. "I really have to go." If she stayed and listened to another word of this complete crap, she was sure her head would explode. With a last glance at Kor, she strode past the offended Christy Smitherson and left the ballroom.

10

"Damn, damn, *damn,*" Ariel raged, as soon as the door to her bedroom was safely shut behind her. "Shit!" she added, kicking one of the solid Telgar wood posts that supported her plush dreamsleep bed. Since the age of fifteen, she'd spent more nights bedded down on the ground of uncharted planets than she'd spent on the hundred thousand credit airfoam mattress. Her grandmother had taken her camping and encouraged her interest in anthropology. And until a month ago, that was all she'd been interested in.

When her father had told her she had to marry, Ariel thought, *why not?* She'd had a plan—to pick the least troublesome suitor, marry him, and leave him at home with her father while she continued life as usual. But she *hadn't* planned on falling in love.

She looked at the holo-picture that hung suspended over the head of her bed. Granny Stone looked back at her, a little smile on her lips, her blue eyes faded but bright. If only Granny was here now to advise her, Ariel thought. She had been the most unconventional, outrageous, and all around fun person Ariel had ever known. Granny Stone hadn't wanted to get married to the man her father picked and so she hadn't. Why couldn't Ariel be as brave?

She stared at herself in the viewer, taking in the ridiculous yards of stiff blue fabric that made up her formal gown and the tight twisted updo that forced her plain blond hair into a fountain of glittering strands. She looked like a perfect bride-to-be but she felt like crap.

In the corner of her room, the mountainous wedding dress floated inside a stasis bubble, every flounce and sequin kept in a perfect state of suspended animation until tomorrow at nine when she was scheduled to put it on. Looking at the dress, which had cost her father as much as a small space ship, was like looking at a set of prison bars. Was it really worth getting into that get-up and saying "I do" to Milton just to keep her father's funding? Did she really want to spend her life with a man she didn't love—a man she actively *loathed*? While she was contemplating the answer, a brisk rapping sounded at her door.

"Ariel?" Her father opened her door without waiting and walked into her room. He looked at her flushed face sternly, a frown hovering around his thin lips. "Is everything all right? People are wondering why you left the party so abruptly."

"Father . . ." Ariel took a deep breath and decided she might as well just come out with it. "I'm having serious second thoughts about marrying Milton. You see, I don't love him. In fact, I think he's an idiot and I just don't know if I can tie myself to a man like that for the rest of my life."

"Ariel, listen to me." Her father strode forward and took both her shoulders in his hands. "You're just getting a case of cold feet. You need to take a deep breath and get over it. I gave you a choice and you chose Milton."

"No," Ariel said, pulling away from his grip. "You *didn't* give me a choice. You told me I was going to marry and you gave me a list of eligible candidates. Isn't that how you put it?"

She crossed her arms over her chest. "And that was fine with me at the time because I wasn't in love. But now I am. I love someone else and I can't marry Milton—I just *can't.*"

Her father's expression softened somewhat. "Well, I do know a little bit about young love. Who is it you want, Ariel? Nathanial Silverton? Byron Benders?"

"No." Ariel bit her lip and decided to just say it. "I want Kor. That is if it isn't too late. I . . . I told him to find someone else but I just can't—"

"You want to marry the wildman?" Her father's voice was incredulous. "Ariel, have you gone insane? Do you know *anything* about his background? His bloodlines?"

"His parents were professors of anthropology," Ariel said defensively. "And I don't give a damn about his bloodlines."

"Well, I *do,*" her father snapped. His usually cold face had turned red with anger. "And I'm not about to let you pollute my grandchildren with inferior blood. Do you have any idea what that would do to our family's social standing? We'd be sunk—ruined!"

"What's wrong with you?" Ariel stormed. She could feel tears of rage rising to her eyes and tried to hold them back. "Is your precious social standing more important than your only daughter's happiness?"

Her father took a step forward and pointed a finger in her face. "Listen to me, young lady. I have put out over ten million credits to make sure you have the wedding of the season and a good part of that money was to insure that you got a groom with proper bloodlines. Now, I don't care *who* is standing beside you tomorrow when you say 'I do' as long as he's on the list of acceptable candidates that I gave you. And that . . . that *foundling* you brought home from the jungle is most certainly not on the list."

"I don't give a damn about your list," Ariel said, her voice low and intense. "What if I just decide to do what I want—the same way Granny Stone did?"

"You leave my mother *out* of this." Her father's voice dripped venom. "I spent my entire life paying for her mistakes and I don't intend to pay for yours, too. You will walk down the aisle tomorrow morning with Milton or someone who is his social equivalent or I will *cut you off*. I mean it, Ariel, you'll never see another credit of my money for your ridiculous 'expeditions.' Just think about that when you decide if you want to follow in your grandmother's footsteps."

He turned on his heel and marched out of the room, slamming the door behind him, vibrating the entire room with the force of his exit.

Before Ariel could scream or throw a conveniently placed vase at the door, it opened again and a new face appeared.

"Ariel?" Kor stepped into her room hesitantly, a frown on his strong features. "I would like to speak to you," he said. "I heard . . . all that you said."

"Oh, did you?" Ariel felt her face grow red and she hastily wiped at her eyes. After all, she didn't even know if Kor still felt the same way for her. They had been back on her home planet for the better part of two weeks and he hadn't reopened the subject in any way. Then again, he'd been busy with the deportment and social skills classes her father had put him in so that he wouldn't embarrass himself or his hosts in front of the upper crust of the four and forty families. All of Ariel's time had been taken up with wedding plans and arrangements and she had been equally busy. Tonight was the first time they'd been alone together since their last night on Tordanji Prime.

"I heard," Kor said again, shutting the door and taking another step toward her. There was a look of yearning on his face, a look that twisted Ariel's heart. "And I wish you to understand that I know why you must be mated to another."

"What?" Ariel shook her head, feeling like she must have misheard him. "I don't understand."

"I know . . ." Kor seemed to be struggling with the words. "How important your . . . work is to you. And—"

"It's not as important to me as . . . as other things." Ariel looked up at him. "Kor, I don't want my father's money. I don't care any more if he cuts me off." As she said the words, she knew they were true. She had made her decision, the only decision that was possible.

Kor pulled her close and cupped her cheek, looking deeply into her eyes. *Your work,* he said, through the mind link. *You cannot hide how important it is to you.*

It is important, Ariel told him. *But so is living my life the way I want to live it and being with the man I love.*

Ariel . . . Kor stroked her cheek. *I still feel as I did our last night on my home planet.*

Really? She searched his eyes hopefully. *I thought maybe, with all the other girls . . . and all of them wanted you . . .*

You are the only one that I want. And I will never stop wanting you. Kor bent his head and slanted his mouth over hers, stealing her breath with a passionate kiss. Ariel wrapped her arms around him and returned it wholeheartedly. It felt so good to be held in his arms again—so completely right. Well, maybe not completely, she admitted to herself. There was something in the way.

"Clothes," she said, pulling away from him.

"What?" Kor tried to pull her back but she resisted and started tugging at the formal dinner jacket he was wearing.

"There're too many clothes in the way," Ariel said. Kor got the picture and began pulling off his evening wear and she started on the row of tiny pearl and platinum buttons that marched down the front of her blue dress. "I've always hated wearing this kind of crap," she complained, fighting with the buttons. "It's too tight, too stiff . . ."

"Here." Seeing her difficulty, Kor grabbed the front of her dress and ripped it open, sending the priceless buttons skittering to the far corners of her room. He was already half naked himself and there was a heat in his eyes that made Ariel warm all over.

Ariel . . . He reached up to cup and knead her breasts, bending at the same time to nuzzle her neck. Ariel groaned and began stripping away the bottom of her dress as well as she could. It seemed like an eternity since she'd had skin-to-skin contact with her wildman and she couldn't get naked fast enough.

Kor, she told him through their link, *I want to mate with you right here, right now. I can't wait any longer.*

His only answer was a low, needful growl and before she knew it, both of them were naked on the bed, kissing and stroking each other, their hands hungry for flesh. She felt Kor's hard cock branding her belly and knew she wanted it inside her, as deep and as hard and as fast as possible. Later, there would be time for a long, leisurely lovemaking session but for now she just wanted to *fuck*.

Ariel, he sent through the link, *I want you, want to be inside you. But I am not sure . . . I do not want to hurt you.*

With a shock she remembered that this was actually going to be Kor's first time. Maybe it would be better for her to take the lead. *I'll show you,* she sent, reaching down to stroke his cock. *Lie on your back and relax.*

Kor rolled over on to his back but it was clear there was no way he could relax. Every muscle in his body was tense and Ariel sensed it was a real effort for him to lie still when he wanted to reach for her with everything that was in him. His long, thick cock pulsed in the air above his belly, begging for her attention.

Like this, she whispered, taking the thick shaft in one hand. Kor groaned deep in his throat as she straddled him and lowered herself to slide the broad mushroom-shaped head against her open pussy. Ariel rubbed his cock against her clit, shivering with the erotic sensation of his hot smooth skin against her slippery cunt. Then she couldn't wait any longer.

Carefully, she slid Kor's shaft lower, pressing the thick head against the entrance to her body. Then she lowered herself, inch by inch, into his cock, sliding down slowly as she tried to accommodate his girth. Kor was bigger than any man she'd ever been with, not that she'd been with that many, and it had been a long time for her. Ariel moaned out loud as she took him inside, arching her back and biting her lip as she gave in to the painful ecstasy of being so completely filled. She could feel Kor's large hands on her hips, but he was resisting the urge to thrust. Ariel could feel through their link his fear of hurting her warring with his urgent desire to fill her over and over with himself. She loved him even more for holding still and letting her take him at her own speed.

At last he was all the way into her and Ariel knew he could go no farther. She felt the head of his cock kissing the mouth of her womb and she was stretched to the limit with his thickness. Kor's hands caressed her hips restlessly and she felt the wordless, urgent question he sent through their mental link.

Yes, she sent him. *Now.* Never had their connection seemed deeper or more intense. Ariel lifted herself an inch and lowered herself back down, fucking herself on the thick shaft that strained inside her. Kor took a firmer grip on her hips and the next time she lifted and lowered herself, he thrust up, pumping into her with a fierce passion he was still struggling to contain. Ariel threw back her head and moaned, giving him control of the situation, letting him do what they both needed so very badly.

Yes, Kor, she sent through their link. *Yes, fuck me! Fuck me!* He didn't need to be told twice. With a low growl, he pulled out and slammed back up into her, filling her pussy to the limit and setting up a rhythm as primitive and ancient as the jungle of Tordanji Prime.

Yes, oh, Goddess. Yes, yes! Ariel told him. She pushed down to meet each fierce thrust, opening herself for him, giving in completely to the domination of her body. Goddess, but he was good! Kor pulled her forward to suck her nipples into his mouth as he continued to fill her, thrusting over and over into her wet, open cunt. Then he grasped her hips and with a sudden motion he flipped her, rolling her under his big body so that he was lying on top of her, still buried to the hilt in her wetness.

Now, she heard him growl through their link and she understood that she was in for a ride like nothing she'd ever had before. Kor was no longer trying to control himself in any way. The animal part of him, the wild feral part that had dominated his life on Tordanji Prime, had taken over. His only instinct was to thrust, to *breed*. To fuck into her as deeply as possible and fill her cunt with his cum, claiming her completely and without reservation as his own.

He grasped her thighs and repositioned her so that her legs were over his shoulders, spreading her wide and ready for his assault. Ariel felt herself open, felt her pussy spread for him in a way she had never experienced before. She had never felt so helpless or so hot and she loved it, loved the sensation of being completely helpless beneath the man she loved. *Yes, Kor! Oh, Goddess, fuck me! Need you to fuck me so hard . . .*

With a low roar he pulled out almost to the head and thrust in again, burying himself balls deep in her open, unprotected sex, battering the mouth of her womb as though seeking entrance there. Ariel had to bite her lip hard to keep from screaming. It was the most intense physical pleasure she had ever experienced—being opened, used, fucked in this way. It went beyond wild and into primitive. She felt like a sexual sacrifice to some pagan god, like an offering in some primal ritual, spread open upon the stone altar of lust, helpless to do anything but submit to his fucking.

Kor seemed to catch the image from her, or at least the essence of it. He strained against her, pouring himself into her, pounding into her willing cunt as though he understood her need to be utterly helpless beneath him. He wasn't just fucking her, Ariel realized, he was claiming her, marking her and making her his forever.

The thought was too much. To be owned by him, to be his always, to give herself body and soul to the huge man thrusting into her, pounding her into willing submission . . . With a low cry, Ariel began to come.

Goddess, Kor! she moaned through the link. *In me . . . in me so deep!*

Ariel . . . so sweet . . . so soft. Your body under me, open, hot . . . I need you . . . need to . . .

Suddenly Kor pulled her close, pressing into her so deeply it felt like he was reaching for her heart. Ariel felt him pulsing into her, filling her with his cum, claiming her forever as his and her own orgasm crested as well. She threw back her head and cried, unable to hold her need and pleasure inside any longer and Kor gasped her name, his deep voice trembling with emotion.

It felt so good . . . so right. And as she began to come down from the intense sensation, Ariel knew she had made the right decision.

11

"Kor, that was . . . amazing." Ariel cuddled close to him, enjoying the warmth of his strong arms wrapped around her. How could she have ever, even for a minute, believed she could give him up? How could she have thought she could just get married to Milton and live according to the plan her father had set for her life?

"Ariel . . ." His deep voice was a rumble of contentment that vibrated her entire body. Ariel smiled and snuggled closer. This was the voice she wanted to wake up to for the rest of her life. Then she frowned—the only question was where. It was a given that if she was going to go against her father's wishes and refuse to marry Milton, he would not only disinherit her but also kick her off the family estate.

Ariel, Kor said again, this time through their mental link. *You are concerned about something. Tell me what it is.*

Ariel sighed. *It's just that my father isn't going to be too happy about this—about us, I mean. He really wanted me to marry Milton so he could have a grandchild with the proper bloodlines to carry on our family name.*

I am so sorry, Ariel. Kor sounded stricken. *Not only have I taken your work from you, but also your home.*

She propped herself up on one elbow and looked at him. His green-blue eyes were filled with regret. "Don't worry," she said aloud, stroking his cheek. "This was never my home, not really. It was just a place I stopped to refuel between expeditions." She tried to smile. "Anyway, it doesn't matter because I have a new home now."

He looked confused. "You do?"

"Mm-hmm." She grinned at him. "Wherever you are is my home, from now on."

"Then . . . it does not matter where we stay, as long as we are together?"

"Exactly." She snuggled close to him again, breathing in his spicy, masculine scent and enjoying the comfort of his big body pressed close to hers. The space hopper parked in the family space port was legally hers and it was fueled up and ready to go. They could pick a planet and settle down. They could go anywhere. They could . . .

We could go back to Tordanji—back to my home planet. There was a longing in his mental voice that touched her heart. Ariel knew, suddenly, that Kor had just been going through the motions here on her planet. He hadn't come here because he wanted to see others of his kind or learn about his people. He had come here for her and only her. Now that they were together, he was longing to return. In fact, there were waves of homesickness rolling off him and filling her mind.

Through his eyes she could see the lush purple jungles of Tordanji, vibrant with color and full of life. She could taste the wind, heavy with the threat of rain, and hear the hooting and chattering of the wild animals that lived in the jungle world. And most of all, she could feel the warm embrace of the members of his village and the simple affection and love that had sustained an orphaned boy from another planet who had lived among them for years. Kor wanted to go home.

Well, why shouldn't he go home? Suddenly, it all made sense to Ariel. Xenological anthropology had been the love of her life—that was, until she'd met Kor of course, and she'd been under the impression that she had to give it up in order to be with him. But that wasn't true at all!

"Kor," she said excitedly, turning to take his face in her hands. "We *can* go back to Tordanji, and live there if you want to. Just think about it," she said. "There's enough native culture in your home tribe alone to give me a lifelong study. I've always wanted to do that, you know, find an especially fascinating culture and settle down there and live with them for years and years—to make it my life's work. And I'll have a unique perspective—I'll actually be *adopted* into the tribe, just as you were."

She was getting more and more excited now as the hope grew in Kor's eyes. "I can transmit my papers to *Alien Anthropology Today* and all the universities electronically and we won't need my father's money to live," she finished triumphantly. "Don't you see, Kor? It's perfect!"

"Perfect except for one thing—it's never going to happen." The new voice in the room made them both turn their heads and Ariel gasped when she saw whose it was.

12

"Milton!" she exclaimed. "What the hell are you doing here?"

"I might ask you the same thing—if it wasn't already so obvious." Her fiancé stood in the door, a grim expression on his rodent-thin face. His cheeks had flushed an ugly, dull red and his no-color eyes were narrowed to slits.

In his hand was a weapon far more deadly than the stunner he'd been carrying on Tordanji Prime. Ariel swallowed hard as she saw the sleek silver muzzle of the sifter pointed directly at her and Kor. One twitch of the trigger would turn both of them into hundreds of unrelated molecules, effectively dismembering them down to their most basic components in a split second.

"Milton," she began, sitting up and trying to cover herself with her hands. "How . . . ah, how long have you been outside the door?"

"Long enough to know this is exactly what it looks like," Milton sneered. "Now both of you get up. And put some clothes on, Ariel." He made a curt gesture with the muzzle of the sifter and they slowly climbed to their feet.

Ariel could feel Kor tensing beside her, maybe getting ready to try and jump Milton. Quickly she took his hand and sent, *Do exactly what he says. That weapon in his hand is powerful enough to turn both of us into two little piles of dust. Understand?*

Yes, Kor had time to send back before Milton growled,

"Stop holding hands and hurry the hell up, *darling.* We don't have much time before the party ends."

"Why do you care about the party?" Ariel asked, pulling on a thin silk robe that happened to be hanging over the end of her bed. There was nothing else at hand and the blue dress she'd been wearing earlier was in tatters and missing all its buttons besides. Beside her, Kor pulled on his dress pants.

"I don't care so much about the party as the alibi it's going to provide for me."

Ariel felt her heart rise in her throat but she tried to look unconcerned. "If you think you can get away with killing me, you can think again, Milton. There's no way—"

"Who said anything about me killing *you,* my dear?" Milton cut her off. "Why, if I did that, I'd miss out on all that lovely credit your father is going to pay me to take you off his hands. Did you know that your dowry is going to be the largest ever paid? So you see, I'd be a fool if I killed you now."

"If you think I'm actually going to marry you, *you're* the fool," Ariel spat. She stepped in front of Kor. "And if you think you can kill Kor without going through me, you can forget about that too."

"*Me,* kill your primitive paramour?" Milton laughed, an ugly sneering chuckle that grated on her nerves. "Oh, no—I'm not a murderer. You see, *you* are going to kill him yourself." He stepped forward swiftly and slapped something sticky against her forehead. Before Ariel could move to peel it off her skin, she felt it begin to melt, forming a seal with her flesh that she knew would be impossible to break. She and Kor both tried anyway, tearing at the alien patch on her skin but it was hopeless and Milton only laughed.

"It's a Kidor mind patch," he said as she tugged uselessly at the sticky substance. "And I trust you've been around the galaxy enough to know its purpose."

Ariel felt cold—of course she knew the purpose. The Kidor mind patch was the most insidious form of mind control in the known galaxy. It adhered to the victim's skin and formed an unbreakable bond of control for the person who had applied it. Basically it meant she would be trapped inside her own body, forced to do everything Milton ordered whether she wanted to or not. And because the patch blended seamlessly with the skin tones of its victim's epidermis, no one would ever know. Even now she could feel the coldness inside her brain as the patch went to work, forming a barrier of ice between her and her natural impulses.

"Milton," she said, trying to keep her voice from trembling. "You'll never get away with this. The Kidor mind patch has been outlawed on every civilized planet in the galaxy. I don't even know how you got your grubby little hands on one in the first place."

Milton smirked. "By going to an *uncivilized* planet, of course, darling. Did you really think you were the only one who went on expeditions?" He laughed. "Now, I think I've had enough back talk from you. From now on, nothing comes out of your mouth unless you have something nice to say to me. In fact, you can start by telling me how much you love me."

Ariel's mouth opened and though she wanted in the worst way to curse her idiot fiancé at the top of her lungs what came out instead was, "I love you, Milton." She clapped a hand over her mouth as soon as it was out and Milton laughed delightedly.

"Excellent. Really, much better than your sarcastic little barbs. I was getting so tired of those, you know."

Ariel turned and saw that Kor was staring at her with a look of disbelief on his face. She shrugged helplessly, wanting to make some kind of explanation but she couldn't say a thing. Milton had ordered her not to say anything unless it was something nice about him and the Kidor mind patch had already established a neural link to the motor cortex of her brain, making it impossible to disobey his command. The slab of ice inside her mind grew thicker and more impenetrable by the second.

More than anything, she was afraid that Kor would lunge for Milton and get himself disintegrated. She could see the muscles tensing under his smooth tan skin and there was murder in his green-blue eyes. Apparently the look made Milton nervous as well, because he waved the sifter at them again, motioning them out the bedroom door.

"Come on, we're going down to the space port," he said, when they were all safely out and into the deserted hallway. "Ariel, tell your wildman not to try anything because I'm more than willing to use this." He motioned with the weapon again.

Freed for a moment to talk to Kor, Ariel turned to him at once. "Kor, don't try anything because I don't want you to die and I love you so much," she blurted quickly before Milton could stop her.

"Ariel . . ." Kor reached out a hand to touch her cheek but Milton knocked it aside with the sifter's muzzle.

"No more touchy-feely stuff," he said sharply. "I think you've had enough of that. And shut up," he added, when Ariel was about to say something else.

Ariel's jaw clamped shut as though an invisible hand had jammed it closed and she felt misery and anger welling up inside her until she thought she would burst. Was this what the rest of her life would be like? Taking orders from that spineless, brainless . . .

"All right, now everybody down to the space port. March!" Milton commanded, interrupting her thoughts. He led them the back way, taking the old staircase that no one ever used any more since the insta-porter had been installed decades ago. Ariel kept hoping they might run into someone from the party. The sounds of music and laughter were clearly audible from the ballroom on the other end of the house but apparently, no one was leaving it.

Her heart sank when they reached the lowest outside level and Milton herded them toward her little space hopper. "Now, stand here," he said, arranging them in front of the ship. Kor was still giving him murderous looks but Ariel knew there was nothing either one of them could do with the sifter pointed right at them. She just hoped Kor knew it too.

"Now," Milton said, when he had them arranged to his satisfaction. "Here's the story, Ariel. This big animal kidnapped you and forced you to come down here so you could take him back to his home planet where he planned to keep you as a slave forever. Fortunately, you happened to have a destructor-class sifter stashed in your hopper for just such an emergency." He hefted the weapon in his hand and laughed. "You shot him and then screamed, overcome by the horror of what you had done. I happened to be looking for you and I found you with the sifter in your hand and the little pile of dust that used to be Kor." He mimed wiping a tear from his eye. "Oh, so *sad*. Of course, I'm going to ask if you want to postpone our wedding tomorrow but you're going to say no, that you love me too much to wait even one more day." He grinned nastily. "Now, won't that be sweet?"

Ariel glared at him, wishing that looks could kill. If so, Milton would have been eviscerated by now. She recognized too late that she had seriously underestimated her fiancé. He had probably had something like this planned from the very beginning—from the moment he asked her to marry him and she grudgingly accepted. She wanted to deny that she would ever shoot Kor, to shout at the top of her lungs that she hated Milton and wanted to kill him, but she was completely unable to do it. Instead, she just stared dumbly ahead, face to face with the man she loved. The man she was about to kill.

"Now, before we do this, let's just make certain nothing goes wrong, shall we?" Milton drew something else from his pocket and aimed it at Kor. Before either of them could move, a sticky web of blue and purple fibers shot out and wrapped around Kor's body from neck to ankles. Kor struggled but couldn't break free of the containment net. It was all he could do to wriggle his fingers, which were trapped against his thighs.

Milton laughed in delight. "There, now we're all set." He turned to Ariel. "Darling, I'm going to give you the sifter now and you're going to point it at Kor and only at Kor." He raised Ariel's hand and placed the sifter in it. She wanted in the worst way to turn it on Milton and squeeze the trigger, but her arm was pulled immediately around to point the weapon at Kor, like a piece of iron drawn to a magnet. The ugly snout of the sifter was barely a foot from his chest. At this range there was no way she could hope to miss.

"Very good." Milton nodded in satisfaction. "Now, I guess there's no time like the present so let's get it over with." He looked Ariel in the eye and she glared back at him, feeling hatred and despair well up in her. He couldn't make her do this— he wouldn't! But apparently he would. She felt the ice of his hatred in her brain, the neural link the mind patch had used to establish control over her.

"I'm going to count to three," Milton told her. "As I count, your finger will be tightening on the trigger. When I reach three, you'll pull it and kill this big idiot you were stupid enough to drag home with us. All right? Nod if you understand."

Ariel felt her chin jerked up and down like a puppet's and she hated Milton so much she could barely see. Tears of rage were clouding her vision but no matter how hard she tried, she was unable to release the sifter or point it anywhere else but at Kor. The ice in her brain wouldn't let her.

"One," Milton said in a gleeful voice. Obviously he was relishing the situation. Helplessly, Ariel felt her forefinger begin to tighten on the cool, slick tongue of metal that was the sifter's trigger. She stared at Kor, tears running down her face, wishing they were touching so she could tell him through the link how much she loved him—how much she didn't want to do this. She would rather shoot herself than him, but Milton and the ice in her mind were giving her no choice.

"One and a half," Milton said playfully. "We might as well drag this out a little while—the look on your face when you can't say anything is simply priceless, darling."

Ariel felt her finger tighten a fraction more on the trigger. But her fingers weren't the only ones that were moving, she saw. Still trapped in the blue and purple web of fibers, Kor's fingers were tapping a slow rhythm against his thigh. As she watched, the necklace of turquoise and silver tattoos around his neck went from flat to 3-D as the thought keepers came to life at his call. They were almost invisible behind the vividly colored netting but she could see them swaying, getting ready for some action. But what good could they do her now?

"Two," Milton said. He was too busy looking at her face to notice the tiny spider-like creatures that had sprung to life on Kor's neck. Ariel felt her finger tighten on the trigger some more. Was there going to be time? What was Kor planning to do? She looked deep into his green-blue eyes, which were calm and filled with love for her.

"I wonder if we're drawing this out a little too long," Milton mused as he paced behind her. "I wonder how much you can take before it breaks your mind. After all, I don't want a lunatic for a wife. Not that anyone will be able to tell, my dear." He laughed. "Even if you're raving on the inside you'll be perfectly calm and collected on the outside. Just imagine—the perfect wife."

Ariel struggled not to let his words rattle her. He was such a complete bastard! She wanted to rip his throat out with her bare hands but she was stuck pointing the sifter at Kor, hoping whatever he was planning he would do it quickly.

One of the thought keepers had managed to wriggle through the netting that held him in place and as she watched, the tiny turquoise and silver creature gathered itself and leaped from Kor's chest to the muzzle of the sifter. It scampered forward, along the ugly silver barrel and suddenly Ariel felt a light ticklish sensation right in the hollow of her throat, followed by warmth that spread out to encompass her entire body, almost like a mini orgasm. The thought keeper had taken her as a host, she knew. Soon she would have a permanent mental link with Kor. But what good could that do her now? If only the warmth would reach higher, above her neck, but she could still feel the ice in her brain where the mind patch held absolute control.

"Two and a half," Milton said and she felt her finger squeeze even tighter on the trigger. At the same time she heard Kor's voice inside her head with a richness and vitality she'd never heard before, even when they were making love.

Ariel, resist, he was telling her. *You must resist—give the thought keeper time to work.*

I'll try, she sent frantically. *I'll try. But Kor, I'm completely out of control. My body won't do anything Milton doesn't want it to.*

"Two and three quarters," Milton said, laughing. Despite everything she could do to stop it, Ariel's finger tightened again. Another hairsbreadth and it would be all over. Then she felt something, a tickle of warmth at the base of her brain that seemed to fill her entire head.

Ariel, whispered a voice in her head. *Resist—you can do it. Resist.* It was joined by another voice and then another and another, all of them telling her the same thing. It wasn't Kor's voice, or not just his voice, she realized as the chorus of encouragement and strength filled her mind. She was hearing the voices of his tribe—the natives of the village on Tordanji Prime that were literally millions of light years away. She was connected to all of them now, as well as to Kor, through the tiny creature in the hollow of her throat.

As the voices grew, she felt the ice inside her brain begin to melt. Her arm, which had been holding the sifter straight and solid as a rock, began to tremble and the muscles began to ache from holding the same pose for so long. But still she couldn't lower it or release any of the pressure from the trigger.

Please! she begged the voices, *Help me!*

Resist, resist, resist, they urged, the warmth growing until it filled her entire head, melting the ice, returning control of her body. But slowly . . . so *slowly*.

"I think it's time." Milton's voice interrupted her concentration to Ariel's despair. *No,* she wanted to scream. *Just a minute longer. One more minute is all I need!* But it was a minute she wasn't going to get.

"Three," Milton said—giving the word to kill with a calm deliberation that made her sick at her stomach. As the single syllable left his lips, she felt the last of the ice begin to thaw. But it was too late—her finger was already tightening on the trigger. She couldn't control the small muscles of her hand, but the larger muscles, the ones controlling her arm were hers again.

Kor, she thought, *I love you!* In one motion, she swung her arm around to point the deadly sifter at Milton and squeezed the trigger that last fraction of an inch. She had just enough time to see the look of surprised horror on her fiancé's face and then the space port was filled with a silent, icy pale blue glow and Milton disappeared completely.

The next moment she had control of her entire body and she dropped the sifter to the metal plated floor with a clatter. A strangled cry left her throat. There was nothing left of Milton but a small heap of ashes, smoking faintly.

13

Ariel wasn't the type of girl to let herself become completely hysterical but she had never killed anyone before. And she had come so close to killing the man she loved—the only man she would ever love. Kor, was still immobilized by the fibers of the control net but he touched her mind gently, calming her as well as he could while Ariel knelt on the cold metal floor and cried.

Ariel, he sent, *we are together now and we will never be parted.* In the back of her brain, she felt the comforting weight of the rest of the tribe saying the same things. *You're one of us now and we protect our own. Come home, come home, come home.*

Yes, she thought, lifting her head as the hot, frightened tears dried on her cheeks. *I want to go home.* She stood on legs that shook and walked across to the hopper. She kept a blade in her kit, more for chopping and eating while on an expedition than for fighting. She had it out in an instant and was sawing away at the sticky fibers that covered Kor from neck to ankles. She had trouble getting it to let go of his pants, but Kor solved that problem by slipping them off and standing before her nude, as he had been when they first met.

The moment he was free, he drew her to him, hugging her hard and tight and kissing her hair over and over. *Ariel,* he sent. *Love you so much. So very, very much!*

I love you, too, Kor. She leaned up on tiptoes to kiss him, feeling the thrill of heat all the way down to her toes. She couldn't wait to make love to him again, but now wasn't the time. *Help me,* she told him, climbing into the hopper and priming it for lift off. *We have to gather Milton's ashes and the sifter and your pants and the net and everything that might give them a link to us. We've got to get out of here and not leave a trace. Once we get to Tordanji Prime we'll be safe—they'll never be able to track us in the jungle.*

Are you certain you do not want to say good-bye to your father? Kor raised an eyebrow at her.

Ariel shook her head. *No. No, I want to leave everything behind. There's nothing for me here now.*

All right. He kissed her gently and they gathered everything into a pile. Ariel even used the handheld suck-u-vac Milton had given her for her last birthday to clean up his ashes.

In a matter of ten minutes, they were both strapped in and lifting off. Ariel piloted the hopper into deep space, watching her home world turn into a blue and green speck behind them, knowing she might never see it again and not caring a bit.

"Come on, Kor," she said, reaching out to take her wild-man's hand as the Telgar Three Wormhole came into sight. "We're going home."

Don't miss this scorchingly sensual peek at
Lucinda Bett's MOON SHADOW,
available now from Aphrodisia . . .

"I specialize in love potions," E. H. Sokaris said to me while I sat alone, spell-free, on her settee made for two. She sat across from me in a stark black-lacquered chair. Its high back towered above her head, making her look like a queen. Her regal bearing added to that impression.

I thought about a number of smart things to say, smart-assed comments about her and me and love and potions. But for once, I said the smartest of all things: nothing.

"Please," she said, handing me a gilt mirror. "Look into this."

"A *Wabizi* mirror," I said.

"Yes." Did she look surprised that I knew this?

"I've never seen one," I said, taking it. "But I've heard of them." I examined myself. "Is it keyed just to you somehow?"

"Yes," she said. She enunciated perfectly, as if each sound were carefully crafted and controlled. "The particular mirror shows me what I most need to know about the person holding it."

No wonder she didn't ask for references. Like lightning, fear forked through me. I had nothing good at all to show this woman. There was nothing in my life that made me proud.

"Do we have to do this?" I asked.

The Gold Wizard gave me a steady look. She wasn't like Uriah at all. There was nothing oily or smarmy about her. "I need to know the state of your heart."

The state of my heart . . . Empty. Forsaken. Drunk. I had nothing more to lose. Silently I held out my hand for the mirror and looked into its depths.

A different kind of man might've seen lank hair in need of a wash and cut, round dark eyes with even darker circles under them, a wan, sickly pallor seen in street-living drunks.

But I wasn't the man to see myself that way. Instead, I brushed my hair from my eyes and saw finely chiseled cheekbones, twinkling eyes, and a strong chin—in short, a handsome devil that E. H. Sokaris would have a hard time resisting.

"You're missing the point entirely," Sokaris said, with more than a hint of exasperation. "Setting the mirror in your lap may help."

I obediently put the mirror on my thighs and spent some time trying to find my nose hairs appealing. No luck. I was about to give up when something flashed, like a fish deep beneath the surface of a pond.

"Yes," she breathed, her voice huskier now. "You've got it."

A delicate toenail came into focus in the mirror's depths, the palest pink and breathtakingly feminine. Apricot-colored sheets, which may have been satin, provided a fitting backdrop. The nail belonged to a narrow foot with a lovely arch.

The foot couldn't belong to Sokaris. Her skin was the same shade as the midnight sky, so black it approached purple. The foot in the mirror was the shade of barely toasted bread, lighter than honey but just as sweet.

Something about that foot . . .

"Keep looking, please, while you answer my questions."

"Okay," I said. Watching wasn't difficult. The foot was beautiful in its proportions. Delicate and strong at the same time.

But the pink-toenailed foot wasn't alone in those satiny sheets. A thick, manly one had just come into view, too. A few black hairs crinkled along its toes. I blinked. Her foot was easier to look at.

"What's your name, Brown?"

So she could see my level, somehow. "Gage," I answered. "Gage Feldspar." The calf of the mirror girl was coming into focus. The play of muscle beneath her tight skin tantalized me. What a perfectly shaped calf. I wanted to run my hand over it, feel its warm smoothness under my palm.

Mirror Boy apparently had the same thought. His hand traced the length of her leg, obviously enjoying the texture like I would have. The same scant dark hairs that decorated his toes covered his hands. His skin was darker than hers.

For no good reason, I hated him.

"Gage," Sokaris said to me, grabbing only some of my attention.

"Hmm?" I answered. I'd heard of this sort of magic, of course, but never seen it in action. I was Gage Feldspar, proud Brown magician and proud owner of an attractive face and fine physique. I'd never needed a love potion. Ha!

"Gage!"

Until this moment, I'd never appreciated the voyeur's pleasures, never thought that watching a couple enjoying each other's bodies would turn me on. But watching these two people make love . . . I realized I could get to like this. My cock was throbbing, and if Sokaris hadn't been sitting right next to me, I might have grabbed it while I watched.

I shot a look at the Love Wizard. Her erect nipples stuck straight out through her purple kirtle. Maybe there was something more to this interview than I thought. Maybe it included . . . But I couldn't. Lyric was still my wife.

"Watch the mirror, please," Sokaris said with her perfectly formed words.

I swiped my hand across the stubble on my chin as I watched. Mirror Boy worshipped the woman's legs, and her legs were worthy of worship. His palms snaked behind her knees. His lips traveled up her thighs.

Watching his fingertips slide over her skin, I could imagine the silky smoothness of that vulnerable area, so often ignored in lovemaking but worth the effort nonetheless. Mirror Boy took his time, caressing every bit of her long legs.

My cock pulsed watching him savor her. I moved my free hand so that my wrist masked my tented trousers.

Mirror Boy's head was between her thighs now. I watched the woman pull him around, leaving his mouth exquisitely latched to her clit. I could easily imagine his groan of pleasure, muffled to be sure, as she pulled his cock into her mouth.

The sight of the lithe naked woman sucking Mirror Boy's cock while he sucked her clit made me clench my teeth. Despite the beautiful Wizard woman sitting next to me, I pressed my hand against the bulge in my pants.

I suppressed a groan. You had to really like a woman to enjoy this position, and she had to like you, too, since both partners had to give up a little of their own pleasure to give some away. The incessant throb of my cock had long ago become painful.

Mirror Boy was lucky to have this woman, luckier than he deserved . . . but I bet he wasn't properly appreciating the silky spot behind her knees.

"Gage," Sokaris said so softly that I had to strain to hear. The mirror's focus shifted perversely to his hands, which firmly grasped her peach-shaped ass as he suckled like a newborn calf on her clit.

But my mind saw Mirror Boy's cock in her mouth. I knew her lips would be as pink and delicate as her toenail, and pouty to boot. Her eyes would be rolled back in ecstasy as she inhaled his thick cock. I knew she loved to suck and suck hard.

"Gage, I make love potions," Sokaris said.

But I waved her words away with my hand. Watching the pair in the mirror, I felt like a wild animal, trapped. Frustration and tension mounted, and I wanted to be freed. I'd become mad, a little insane.

In the mirror, they'd switched positions. The girl's hand came into view. Long graceful fingers with neatly tapered nails. That pink. Again. Could I really detect boldness and shyness through this magic? She grasped Mirror Boy's hand and tentatively led his fingers to her breast, to her nipples. Did Mirror Boy know what that cost her, that act of courage?

"If you're to be my assistant, do you realize what that entails?" Her voice barely penetrated my concentration. The woman was heart-achingly pretty, like someone I'd love to protect and keep safe.

I was aware of myself enough to know I really wanted a Brown Worm. Or three or four. But even if I had them I knew I could get completely shit faced and the heat between my legs wouldn't go away. Neither would the guilt in my heart.

"Do you know what Love Wizards do?" Sokaris asked again.